Praise for the novels of LJ Cohen

DERELICT

"Cohen has real talent with character development and interaction, and prickly, defensive Ro is a sympathetic and interesting heroine."
—*Publishers Weekly*

"LJ Cohen deftly weaves together realistic teenage characters, futuristic technology, and big stakes for a real page turner."
—*Wen Spencer, Award winning SF&F novelist, author of the* Ukiah Oregon *and* Elfhome *series*

"Get on board Derelict, and you'll take an edgy, nonstop flight into an audacious SF future with unremitting danger as your pilot—and thrilling adventure your destination."
—*Lynn Viehl, NYT best selling author of the* Stardoc *and* Darkyn *series*

"Intricate plotting melded seamlessly with delightful characterizations kept me turning pages as fast as I could go in an attempt to keep up with the unfolding story. A cracking yarn set in a lush future I'm hoping we'll hear more of."
—*Nathan Lowell, Creator of the* Golden Age of the Solar Clipper *and the* Tanyth Fairport Adventures

ITHAKA RISING

"As the story unfolds and the pieces come together, the inexorable pressure of fine story telling, smooth characters, and compelling action rocket the reader into jump space where anything can—and probably will—happen."

 —*Nathan Lowell, Creator of the* Golden Age of the Solar Clipper *and the* Tanyth Fairport Adventures

DREADNOUGHT AND SHUTTLE

"...engaging characters and a believable universe. ...The admirably brave and übercompetent Dev shines as a stellar addition to the genre..."

 —*Publishers Weekly*

"If you love the kind of space story where ordinary people with flaws and fears are the heroes, and good people need to make choices in a messy and uncertain world, then DREADNOUGHT AND SHUTTLE is the kind of book you'll want to clear your evening for."

 —*Audrey Faye, author of* The KarmaCorp Novels

"A fitting third installment to the Halcyone Space series...brings together again the team we learned to love in DERELICT and ITHAKA RISING, for a rollicking adventure of rescue and justice."

 —*Lou J Berger, author of* "Leaving Bordeaux" *and other short fiction*

PARALLAX

"Parallax is an adrenaline rush, ripping you across the galaxy at the speed of light. LJ Cohen's seemingly effortless narrative about a galaxy drowning in corruption and rebellion features a group of teens struggling to protect not only themselves but those they love. It will take hold of you at page one and never let go. ..."
—*KB Wagers, author of* The Indranan War *and* NeoG *series*

THE BETWEEN

"...a moving tale of heroism and compassion. ... Lydia is a young woman utterly unprepared for the world she's about to enter—but she learns fast. She's a character you'll want to meet again, from a writer you'll want to read again. Take good note: LJ Cohen is a new voice to follow."
—*Jeffrey A. Carver, author of* The Chaos Chronicles

Litany for a Broken World

Also by LJ Cohen

Halcyone Space
Derelict (book 1)
Ithaka Rising (book 2)
Dreadnought and Shuttle (book 3)
Parallax (book 4)
A Star in the Void (book 5)

Changeling's Choice
The Between (book 1)
Time and Tithe (book 2)

Future Tense

Short Stories
Stranger Worlds than These

Litany for a Broken World

Entangled Realities, book 1

LJ Cohen

Interrobang Books
Massachusetts

Published by Interrobang Books
Massachusetts, USA

www.interrobangbooks.com

First print edition: February 2025

ISBN-13: 978-1-942851-08-0

Original cover art by Chris Howard, copyright 2025
www.saltwaterwitch.com

*Epigraph from William Sloane Coffin's Memorial Day: A Prayer
used with permission*

To the ones who do the work.
Without fanfare.
Because it's the right thing to do.

And to my father of blessed memory, who taught me this.

Epigraph

You are not obligated to complete the work of perfecting the world, but neither are you free to abandon it.

—*Rabbi Tarfon, Pirkei Avot*

"...give us the vision to see that the world is now too dangerous for anything but truth, too small for anything but love."

—*William Sloane Coffin, from Memorial Day: A Prayer*

Chapter 1

Jace Vettel

AT FIRST JACE THOUGHT he'd chosen well. No one had paid him any attention when he first arrived—a lone man wandering the streets of a small, post-industrial, pre-spacefaring city. He'd found a sweet spot: a world technologically advanced enough to have a diverse and mobile population but not so advanced that there were ruthlessly efficient means of tracking the populace. It made it easy for a Traveler to blend in.

And most critical: This world didn't have an ongoing Network presence. Of course that also meant Jace had little actual intel to go on before his transit. A risk, but with the stakes this high, he had no choice.

He wasn't prepared for the cold, but then again, Jace hadn't counted on being here more than a few hours. Just long enough to lay a trail for Wellerman to follow into a dead end and maybe even get mired there. It was an extra bit of insurance he hadn't risked sharing with Corinne. Now he regretted that, but he'd made his choice, and you couldn't Travel into the past.

It was a good plan. Up until it wasn't. Until he discovered he was the one trapped, unable to rejoin his wife and child. Jace wrenched his mind from the long, miserable night and his failed attempts to open a portal from this side.

Without access to Network tech, he had no idea what the time differential was. How long had it been for Corinne? And how long would she wait before doing something that would bring the Network down on all of them?

"You still don't get it," Jace had said in their last conversation before he'd left. "After all this time, you still believe they let us retire, just like that."

Corinne sighed. "We've been over this. Pregnant agents are prohibited from Travel assignments."

It had taken Jace over a decade and dozens and dozens of risky, secret trips to Network-controlled realities to finally amass the evidence. He twisted the ring on his thumb, struggling to find a way to keep Corinne listening, willing to accept the truth, to even examine what he'd discovered.

"Of course that's what they told you." He struggled to keep his voice down. Under control. Rational. Across the hall, Reina was asleep. She deserved to have the childhood Jace didn't. But he had waited too long and to protect her, he had to act. Now. Even if Corinne refused to believe him.

"There have only ever been a few other pregnant agents. And none who carried to term. Only you."

"Of course most agents don't have children. We do dangerous work."

"Corinne..."

"Let's be logical. You're the son of a Network agent."

She was still holding on to the mission. Still looking for reasons to justify the Network's actions. Jace clenched his teeth until his jaw ached. "Trust me, that's something they are very interested in."

"Even if what you say is true, we were close to our limit, anyway. If we hadn't retired, they would have pulled us from active duty soon enough."

"Reina has the potential to be the first-ever third-generation Traveler. They want her, and we can't let them have her."

"You're scaring me."

"Good. You need to be scared. We're not safe here. But she isn't ready yet." He forced himself not to pace their small bedroom. Not to raise his voice and wake Reina. Corinne was already worried enough about his state of mind.

"Jace, that's..." She shook her head.

"Crazy?"

A gust of cold wind penetrated his thin jacket, reminding Jace he needed to focus on surviving here and now. The past was already set. The choices both he and Corinne had made narrowed down their possibilities to this reality in this moment.

Jace had no regrets, save one: He should have told her everything years ago. About Wellerman. About his father and how the Multiverse Travelers Network had destroyed his mind. How they pushed Jace into risking his own sanity on too many missions. That Reina would always be a target. But he was afraid of breaking their already strained marriage without absolute proof. And by the time he had it, it was too late. Reina was already starting to manifest her abilities. It was only a matter of time before the Network tracked her down and took her from them.

The MTN had been Corinne's whole life until she reluctantly walked away from it with him. The work had given her purpose and community. Had given that to both of them. Even with everything that had happened, he was still perversely grateful for it: Without the Network, they would never have met, never would have had Reina. Their daughter had been worth losing everything else. Even if he were trapped here forever, apart from them.

A thin layer of dirty slush coated the slippery sidewalk, and he picked his way carefully in his inadequate shoes. Men and women wearing sturdy overcoats passed by, their gazes skipping right over him. Most had listening devices in their ears. Some were in deep conversations with an invisible other. They wandered through their world blissfully unaware that each choice they made could splinter reality and change the timeline in thousands of ways. Some subtle, some profound.

Jace could see the potentials like a film of haze in the air. If that woman stepped off the curb into this deep puddle, she would get to work late, miss a call that would have been an opportunity to work on an interdepartmental project which led to dozens of other branching nodes into new futures. But the light turned just as she reached the corner, and instead of crossing the street there, she walked along another block. No puddle. No delay. The call would come and so would all those options. Choices layered thickly one upon another and not just with her. Everywhere he looked, multiple realities shimmered in and out of view.

He had never seen a world this chaotic.

It was so hard to focus. Pain, sharp and rhythmic, beat through his mind. It had been little more than a day in local reckoning, but he missed his wife and child with an ache stronger than the burning in his exposed hands. Worse than that, Jace couldn't stop glancing over his shoulder, studying each face in the crowd. Wellerman was the biggest threat, but the Network could have sent any number of agents after him.

He needed shelter. From the brutal weather, from the pull of so many possibilities, from Harnett Wellerman. He shook his head. No, his former handler couldn't have known Jace would come here. Even with all of the resources of the Network behind him, Wellerman would only have seen this world as one alternative among a near infinity of choices.

But the longer Jace languished here, the greater the chance he would be discovered.

He shuddered, but not from the cold. It was as if invoking the agent's name could give Wellerman power over him. He knew he was being irrational; yet, it was impossible to shed the fear. He needed to believe his actions weren't a sign of the illness that had splintered the minds of so many good agents. The illness Wellerman had insisted claimed Jace's father.

He finally had proof. Enough to convince Corinne of the danger Reina faced. Maybe even enough to bring down the Network and ensure his family's safety forever. The files he'd painstakingly gathered were safeguarded in a private pocket universe accessible through the ring he wore as his focus, but unless he could get free of this reality, it would all be for nothing.

It had been over twelve years since he'd escaped the MTN, but he still could harness the skills that had once made him so very valuable to them. Ahead of him loomed a large stone building. Across disparate worlds and timelines, people made libraries more than places to house knowledge: They were sanctuaries. And as fraught as this reality seemed to be, the existence of this library was a good sign.

The building occupied an entire city block. Words carved in its stone facade were initially incomprehensible lines, but as Jace relaxed and let his training take over, they resolved into clarity.

THE PUBLIC LIBRARY OF THE CITY OF BOSTON
BUILT BY THE PEOPLE AND DEDICATED TO
THE ADVANCEMENT OF LEARNING.

Inside, he should be able to find warmth and information—the two commodities he needed most of all right now.

He waited in a shadowed doorway, watching as a few people ascended the broad stairs and entered the building. If he were an agent looking for a rogue, this was one of the places he'd go. Wellerman would know that. The man had trained not only him, but his father before him. Jace gasped as a well-muscled man paused nearby. The seconds moved with excruciating slowness as the man finally turned. It wasn't Wellerman. Of course it wasn't. The Network didn't know Jace was here. But if he didn't escape, they would find him. They had near-unlimited resources. And once they found a trace of him, it would only be a matter of time.

The cold air seared his lungs, and it took a long time for his breathing to return to normal. No one had noticed him. No one was following him. Yet.

He was certainly noticed as he walked through the front doors and into the library proper. But the gazes that followed him had everything to do with his current appearance. Jace didn't make eye contact with anyone, and he wasn't going to challenge their assumptions that he was just another of this city's desperate. Still, the expressions of some who watched him held pity rather than disdain. Perhaps there was some hope for this unstable world.

Jace found an isolated desk in the midst of the stacks. It was warm. The scent of old paper comforted him, reminding him of his childhood home. Before the contents of his father's treasured personal library had been destroyed.

Certainly his father's disintegrated sense of reality was real, even if Jace was sure Wellerman had lied about the cause of his death. And despite all the classified Network documents he'd uncovered, there was still the chance that Jace's genetic code did hold the seeds of the disorder all agents lived in fear of.

No. Those memories only led to dark places. He forced himself to think of Corinne and Reina and the home they'd finally made for themselves, by the seaside and away from the looming threat of the Network.

Turning the chair around to face the aisle in case anyone wandered his way, Jace focused on his connection to his family. It shouldn't matter where in the multiverse he had landed. He twirled the simple silver band on his thumb. Time and distance made no difference to the link they shared. Or it shouldn't. It hadn't ever before.

A few beams of light shone though the high windows. The air around him was thick with dust motes. A hum, too low to hear, vibrated in his ears and through his chest. It was the echo of the Moment which had deposited him in this reality. That meant the way should still be open and Jace should have been able to follow it home. But resonating with that Moment were an infinity of Moments, all leading to other alternatives. He searched for the thread that tied him to his unique instance in the multiverse, to his version of Corinne and Reina, but he was linked to all of them and none of them.

A discordant symphony of possibilities filled his head to bursting. The more he struggled to trace his way back, the louder the cacophony became.

There was no way home. Or rather there were too many ways, each of which splintered off into more, like a crack spreading through glass. In all his years of training and Traveling, he'd never experienced a world like this one.

Jace stifled a sob. Corinne and Reina were waiting for him. Counting on him.

He rubbed tired eyes and refocused on the light dancing in the air between the library's shelves. So many Moments, and no way to find the right one.

He had to keep trying. What choice did he have?

A muffled voice came through the building startling him: "The library will be closing in thirty minutes." Jace didn't relish another night wandering Boston's cold streets. And if he didn't act soon, there was no telling what Corinne would do. Everything he'd been working and sacrificing for would be undone if she turned to the Network for help.

How could he have been so stupid?

"The library will be closing in twenty minutes. Please make your selections and bring them to the circulation desk."

Footsteps echoed from across the stacks. Another day wasted. Jace's stomach grumbled. His feet were still damp. If trying to force his way into another alternative didn't kill him, the Boston weather might.

"Sir?"

He glanced up at the uniformed guard and narrowed his eyes. Could he be from the Network? The man looked like every other person on this world. But Jace didn't look particularly out of place, either. "You need to leave now. We're closing in a few minutes."

Jace clenched his jaw and nodded. An agent would have confronted him. Or more likely, just opened a random doorway and pushed him through. It's what he had planned to do with Wellerman.

He walked slowly through the stately building and toward the ornate front doors. Three choices: force open a portal at random and risk getting lost further away from his family. Raid the Network cache he knew was somewhere nearby and risk tipping them off to his presence. Spend another night in the cold and risk freezing to death.

None of the options were appealing. None were safe.

Last night he'd been lucky—in the predawn hours, after walking most of the night, he'd stumbled upon a few desperate men huddled around a fire burning in a metal can in an empty lot near an abandoned brick building. When the day broke, so did the small group. No one said a word to him. Jace wasn't even sure he'd be able to find his way back, and even if he did, there was no guarantee the men would be there again.

At the library's door, he paused, readying himself for the cold night to come.

"Hey, mister."

The guard's voice, deep and hesitant, startled him. Had he been wrong? Was the man working with Wellerman? Jace turned around slowly, preparing himself to run or fight.

The man's expression held no malice or special interest. Just concern. Jace exhaled and let his body relax. Maybe he'd violated some local rule.

"A nonprofit runs an overnight shelter not far from here. It's nothing fancy. Cots and basic meals. But it's warm and dry. And mostly safe."

Safe. What would this man know about safe? His life was simple. He moved through his days blissfully ignorant of the complexities swirling around his every choice. And the workings of those who had the power to manipulate the outcomes when it suited them.

"Gonna snow tonight."

Jace didn't understand. Why was he concerned? No one in the Network would care about one lone man in one particular reality. Guiding the greatest good. It was the Multiverse Travelers Network motto. For most of his life, Jace had believed it. Then he discovered his father's hidden journals. Even after he'd read them, he'd been ready to dismiss them as the ravings of a fractured mind. Until Wellerman had his father institutionalized.

And, he was certain, ordered his father's home burned, turning the journals to ash.

"It's a mile away. On Bedford street."

Before he could figure out how to ask for directions, the man glanced down at Jace's still-damp shoes.

"Aw, hell, you can't walk out there like that." He pointed to a bench. "Stay right there. I got you."

The guard pulled out his communication device and mumbled something in the speaker.

Jace's glance stuttered between the guard and the door. His heart raced, and again, he struggled to gather his panicked thoughts. No one was following him. No one here knew who he was.

The guard approached and rifled through his pocket for a scrap of paper and a pen. Wrote something down. Handed it to him with a second piece of paper. This one, rectangular and embossed with a moss green ink. Likely local currency.

"Time to lock up now, so you got to wait outside. Sorry, man. But the cab will be here in a few minutes. That'll cover the fare."

Jace met the guard's deep brown eyes for a brief second, but the man winced and looked away. As if he had done something wrong. Or had been embarrassed by his inability to do more.

"Thank you." Jace nodded and stepped out into the night. There was at least kindness here.

A biting wind stole all the warmth he'd garnered inside the library. He paced a small area in front of the building, waiting for the promised ride. The guard was right—after only a few minutes, a vehicle glided to a stop and a horn sounded.

Still, Jace hesitated. In his experience, kindness wasn't as common as it should have been.

"You call a cab? The mission, right?"

He startled. Fear hammered at him to flee. To open up any possible doorway. They couldn't follow him if even he didn't know where he was going.

The driver sounded the horn again. Jace took a deep breath. Corinne and Reina were counting on him.

"Listen, man, meter's running. You want a bed for the night or not?"

That must be another name for the shelter. Mission. The breath he'd been holding emerged as a half-strangled laugh. As he got closer to the cab, he categorized it as an internal combustion engine, based on the rumbling sound as it idled and the sharp scent of the exhaust. Pretty common on worlds of this tech level. Effective, if terribly inefficient. He reached for the door latch, but it was locked. The driver looked annoyed and pointed to the door behind him.

Jace climbed in. The heat was roaring and welcome. His shoes made damp prints on the soft material of the floor. He sneezed at the sweet, tangy perfume filling the car. It was as unlike a pine tree as the green saw-toothed cutout that hung from the mirror by the driver.

"Library guard said you'd pay in advance."

Jace glanced at the papers gripped in his hand. He smoothed out the foreign sheet of currency and handed it across the seats.

"At least you don't smell. Last time I did a shelter run, I had to fumigate the cab."

It would be impossible to smell anything over the artificial tree's scent.

The man kept up a one-sided commentary during the short trip. Jace stared out the window at bundled-up passersby hurrying toward their destinations. Blocks of buildings lined both sides of the street. It was a small city. The structures were mostly under eight stories tall and a mixture of commerce and residences. No evidence of industrial production here, though it had to be somewhere. Well lit, both by illumination inside the buildings and by streetlights.

He wondered about this world. Nothing on the surface seemed to be particularly remarkable. Yes, the haze of nascent futures was disturbing, but the overall tech here was far below the level of the Network's. They only sealed off worlds they considered a threat to their hegemony. In most cases, they simply recruited anyone with even the hint of talent, convincing them that the Network could help them reach their true potential and be of service to the multiverse.

If they couldn't be recruited, their timelines would be snuffed out.

All for the greater good. How could he have been so naive?

Jace watched the patterns of light and shadow outside as the vehicle drove. If only he could figure out what was preventing him from Traveling back the way he'd come, he might be able to use it against the Network. There had to be a cause—some intrinsic property or technology in this reality he had yet to discover. But he had to ensure his family's safety first.

They moved slowly in a swarm of other cars. Jace imagined warm, well-lit homes and waiting family. Corinne and Reina weren't anywhere this cab could reach. They were separated by his mistake. And if he didn't find his way to them, they might pay the price for it, too.

The vehicle pulled to a stop in front of a large boxy building. "Here you are."

Jace exited the cab and stepped into a puddle of slush. The driver raced off, leaving him shivering again. He looked up at the building. *Safe Harbor Mission* was spelled out on a large banner across the entrance. Everything would be better after a meal and some real rest.

He had to believe that.

Chapter 2

Reina Vettel

REINA SAT AT THE EDGE of her parents' bed and picked at a loose thread on the heavy quilt. The bedding had been smoothed and tucked in, the pillows neatly stacked. All of their clutter—her father's half-folded clothes, her mother's piles of papers and books—had been carefully put away. The silence in the house was more than just the absence of sound; it was a vast and terrible emptiness.

How could they have both abandoned her?

She folded and unfolded the handwritten letter her mother had left until the creases were as deep as the lines on her father's forehead. The words trailed off as if she had been interrupted in the midst of writing and might return any moment to finish her thoughts. But as Reina looked around the too-neat room, she knew that was just a story she was trying to believe.

Her mother was gone. Swallowed up by the same looming danger that had taken her father half a week before.

A danger neither of them would talk to her about.

Dearest Reina,

I'm sorry. I don't expect you to understand, but leaving you is the hardest decision I have ever made. Know that if there were any other way, I would have risked everything to stay here with you. It's not just your father's safety at stake, but yours and mine and beyond that to realities we haven't even dreamed of. It may be too late for your father, but there is no world in this tangled universe where I don't at least try.

The words burned a pathway in her mind. Reina tossed the letter aside and hugged her mother's pillow. Her light scent filled the room with a hint of flowers and spice. "You should have told me the truth. You should have trusted me."

Too many nights she had retreated to her room to the echoes of their angry voices. No matter their assurances, she was sure they were fighting about her. The past few years had taught her there were some questions that couldn't be asked, but not why. Now she wished she had asked all the questions that burned inside her.

I've sent word to your grandparents. If I don't return, they will come for you. Be strong, Reina. I love you.

How much time did she have? A day? A week? She had never met them. All she had ever known of her mother's family was that they had disowned her a long time ago. Was that even the truth? And no one had ever talked about her father's family. Anything

Reina knew about her grandfather she learned from her parents' late-night shouting matches. He had been sick. And her mother thought her father had the same sickness.

But he didn't seem sick to her. Only sad.

In her earliest memories, it was just the three of them, in this town several stops beyond the back of nowhere. They had no connections, no history here. When Reina had asked about it, her mother only said they'd moved to the seaside for her father's health.

Their neighbors were friendly, but her parents had kept to themselves. Had educated Reina at home. Hadn't kept her from making friends, but hadn't encouraged it, either. They never even had to teach her about keeping secrets. That had come naturally.

Promise me you won't try to follow us. It's far too dangerous. Your very sensitivity is what puts you at risk.

She could practically see the tremor in her mother's hand as she had written that. "You said everything was going to be okay. That Papa would be home soon."

When Reina was very young, her mother would tell her stories about their grand adventures Traveling from here to there, fixing the broken places. Tales of other worlds. Other skies beneath other stars. Places so familiar they seemed like home, and others so strange, it was like being in a dream.

Until she refused to talk about any of it, insisting they were just stories for children and Reina wasn't a child anymore.

Not long after that, around her twelfth birthday, Reina began to see the way potentials hazed the air and knew the stories were all true. When her parents found out, Papa became almost feverish with purpose. He worked with her every day, teaching her how to identify and slip through the thin places without tearing a rent. How to let the critical Moment guide her to where she would find the right anchor or pivot. How to weave a thread of energy and intent to follow back home. But it was only theory. He made her promise not to try any of the techniques on her own. Over and over again, he insisted she wasn't ready, but would be when the time came.

As he trained her, her father seemed to get stronger and more focused even as her mother became distant and unsettled. Neither of them would tell her what they were training her for or why. And now there was no one she could ask.

She stood and paced the room. If her mother's family took her away from here, she would never be able to find her parents. The longer she waited, the harder it would be to trace their path.

She wasn't a Traveler. Her father had told her of all the things that could go wrong if she wasn't prepared. But if she did nothing, everything would be wrong. Reina knew with a certainty she couldn't shake that her parents were in danger.

The last conversation she'd had with her father had been about the critical importance of a Traveler's focus. He'd been standing in her doorway, silhouetted by the hallway light.

"What means home to you?" he had asked.

She knew he didn't mean the physical place. Her room was full of the things she'd collected—smooth stones and shells from the shore, iridescent bird feathers, her animal pillows. In her closets were other treasures, once hoarded, now outgrown. "I'm not sure."

He tightened his left hand around the ring on his thumb. Her mother wore its mate on her right. "Trust yourself. You'll know."

But he was gone.

And she still didn't know what to take.

She could feel the layering of potentials in her parents' room. Right now, they represented a near infinity of choices. When they narrowed down to only a few, she would have to act. And for that, she would need a focus.

Reina ran down the hallway. Her stomach churned and she was glad she hadn't risked eating anything. Glancing through her room, she desperately hoped some particular thing would call to her. But the problem was, she had changed this past year. Her room seemed to belong to someone else.

"Trust yourself. You'll know." Her father's voice echoed in her mind.

Her heart thudded and her breathing quickened. She glanced at her bed and the quilted creatures she still slept with. There was the crow her father had made for her, with shiny beads for eyes. Or the little dog that had been her mother's from her childhood, and loved well, its fabric thin and worn. No. Something small. Something she could slip into a pocket. Her father had told her even seasoned Travelers didn't fully understand why some things passed easily between worlds and others didn't.

A bowl on her desk held her beach stones. She found them soothing to hold and had rubbed many of them smooth. Her favorite had shimmers of blue and black through the white. It was right on top, as if waiting for her to choose it.

Grasping it in her hand, she returned to her parents' room. This is where they had each left from. It was where the right Moment would be strongest.

It was now or never. Reina took a deep breath and hummed softly, finding the right resonance that would open the way for her. Sunbeams streamed through the bedroom window, illuminating dust motes in the air and something more: a gauzy curtain of light and shadow. And through it, the silhouette of a willowy figure. "Mother!"

Golden light wavered in the air. It thickened into an opaque curtain.

As the Moment solidified, the bedroom faded into a hazy outline of vague rectangular shapes. Reina counted her heartbeats as they raced by. Dancing lights surrounded her.

Reina took a single step into the shimmer. The light embraced her body in a gilded second skin.

Time stopped.

Her home vanished behind her.

"Mama!" Reina cried out, but there was no sound in the emptiness. She tried to hold on to her father's voice, the memory of him teaching her. His very first lesson was that all Travelers journeyed alone. This was fine. This was normal.

But still, she felt—nothing. No heartbeat, no breath, no warmth or coolness or pressure. All connection to her body had vanished.

And all sense of time. How long had she been here? Her thoughts were a storm of urgency and panic, even as part of her mind watched as if from a great distance. It was like drowning.

Then memory broke across her like the wave that had pulled her under when she'd been just a few years old, collecting stones and shells at the beach.

Her father had yanked her sputtering and choking from the water. Through the day and night that followed, Reina wouldn't open her hand. The small stone she had grasped left a geometric scar on her right palm.

The stone.

Reina forced herself to recall everything about the unusual stone, the focus she had chosen to take with her on this journey.

Her panic receded, like the wave had. Her father's voice whispered in her mind and she remembered. This was the void between worlds. Her parents had warned her about it, but learning about it and being suspended in it were very different things.

Reina concentrated on the stone, a dull lump of white shot through with blue and black streaks. Slowly, she built a sense of self from the hand around its uneven shape, to the arm connected to that hand until she had reclaimed her body from the emptiness.

"Thank you, Papa," she whispered. This time, she imagined she heard the sound of her own voice and felt her father's warm approval beaming over her like sunshine.

Now there was a sense of directionality in the void. As if she were a feather caught in a wind current. Or a kite on a string. And finally she felt it—the thinnest of threads that joined her to her parents. Reina stopped fighting and let them tug her. The stone warmed in her hand. It had been the right choice.

Now that the panic faded, a fierce joy sang through her. She was a Traveler. When the Moment collapsed, she would be in a different reality.

Her father would be there, too, waiting for her. The anger and the secrets could stop. Their family would be whole again.

A shadow fell across her mind.

Something cold and sharp abruptly severed her from her mother and father. From the connection she had reclaimed to her own body. The pain of it bored through her, driving out everything except an icy dread as she tumbled out of control.

Reina tried to scream. The void swirled around her, tightening down like a caul, cutting off her breath. She clawed at her throat, but her hands felt nothing. Her hands didn't exist. The stone she'd once held in her palm, gone as if it never was.

Painful memories tortured her: her mother storming out of the house and vanishing for days at a time, only to return without explanation. Her father's long and uncomfortable silences. Her guilt over the panic attack her father had the first time she told him about seeing invisible doorways. The strained quiet after her parents' arguments, when Reina was afraid to say or do anything that would start the shouting all over again.

And still, she kept falling. Could feel the shriek of air as she tore through the emptiness faster and faster. Knew she would die when she hit the bottom of the endless plummet. There was nothing she could do except desperately long for the end to stop the terror.

"Mama, Papa, help me!" The words reverberated in her mind, trapped in nothingness.

As fast as she could form them, her panicked thoughts were torn away by the wind.

"Papa, Papa," she whispered. But he had been beyond her reach for far too long.

Light and shadow flickered past as if a thousand days and nights each lasted an eyeblink. A roar of sound blasted by her, the pitch wailing, then fading. Voices shouted in an alien tongue, the anger far too familiar. Her senses burned raw with fresh pain.

"Please," she cried, knowing no one could hear her.

The echo of a dog's sharp bark filled her awareness and chased away the barrage for a bright instant. Before she could take a breath, the sound cut off abruptly—leaving her bereft in an unnatural stillness that was even worse than the endless plunge.

She hung, suspended in emptiness, waiting for the next horror.

Below her, rectangles sketched themselves out of the darkness, getting larger and larger, rushing toward Reina as she watched. Dizziness overwhelmed her senses. One by one, the shapes vanished into the periphery until only one remained. A crumbling brick building, its windows broken and covered with splintered wood, grew to fill the black void of an unfamiliar sky.

Without warning, she slammed into it, her mind disintegrating into dust and agony. Time stopped. How could nothingness hurt so much? Slowly, slowly, the world coalesced around her once again. Reina gasped for breath from rigid lungs that refused to inflate. A terrible pressure slammed against her chest over and over again.

A strange voice rang in her ears, the words running together in a string of nonsense, the urgency needing no translation. And then a bolt of lightning struck her chest. She was sure her heart would explode.

Pain burned in every muscle in her body. Her head throbbed. Her hands felt clumsy and distant. She struggled to conjure up her stone, but it was gone. It was so dark, she couldn't even tell if her eyes were open or closed. Cold seeped up from the hard ground until she felt as stiff and frozen as something long dead.

Chapter 3

Thorne Truthscryer

AS THORNE LIMPED ALONG the cobbled street, the narrow alleys of the market rang with the calls of merchants. Women balancing intricately woven baskets on jutted hips swayed from stall to stall. Knots of men sat together on short stools, tossing dice and sipping thick sweetened coffee. It should have been no different from any other market day, but everywhere Thorne looked, a creeping gray that was not simply the coming dusk dulled his second sight. He blinked and rubbed his tired eyes. A damp breeze stirred the limp awnings and pennants. For a welcome moment, the bright colors returned before the pall strengthened, fading the garish fabric, the cobblestones, the wares heaped on rickety counters, even the shoppers' faces to a lifeless hue.

None would meet Thorne's gaze. Not that he could blame them. No one wanted a truthscryer in their midst, especially one who prophesied difficult times.

The dog at his feet looked up and sighed. ::should've held your tongue::

::You know I can't do that.::

::why not? at least you could've waited till after supper::

Thorne laughed aloud, startling several women who had been studiously ignoring him. ::And how would that have helped, Poplar?:: It wasn't the first time Thorne had used his sight to warn. It wouldn't be the last. He sighed. The towns may have changed, but the people never seemed to. Nor did the futures he foresaw.

::would help me:: The scrappy animal yawned, baring a mouth full of tiny sharp teeth and a delicate pink tongue. ::more treats::

She was a remarkably selfish creature, but Thorne loved her more than he would ever admit. ::You are not starving.:: He fished in his pocket for a piece of jerky and held it out to her. She bonked it with her black nose before carefully lipping it from his hand. It vanished in a single gulp.

As the two moved through the market, crowds parted and flowed around them. Thorne might have believed himself invisible but for the furtive glances and interrupted conversations as he passed. One small child toddled toward him, a big, toothless grin on a dirt-streaked face, and reached for Poplar.

With a remarkably human expression of longsuffering patience, the dog lowered her head for the child's hand.

Something eased in Thorne's old and tired heart when the child smiled up at him.

A woman's voice called out, full of anger, full of fear, and the moment of joy shriveled and died. The child's mother pushed through the crowd, wide-eyed, and yanked her now crying babe away from Poplar. There was a moment of stillness—and then, as if nothing had happened, merchants returned to hawking their wares as people swirled around them once more.

Poplar glared up at him. ::they used to like me::

That was before they knew Thorne could see the end of things. He rubbed his dry eyes again with rough-skinned, age-spotted hands. The colors didn't return. Perhaps it would be better to stay away from the market and its death song. And from the people who would never welcome one such as him in their midst. He should have known better. Without looking back, he took the way that led out of town. He knew Poplar would follow.

::where are you going? they need you:: The dog's voice was a whine in his mind.

She was lagging behind, stopping every few steps and calling to him with a sharp bark.

::That may be true, but they don't want me.::

Poplar fell silent, and this time Thorne paused to look back. She was staring at him, her head cocked to the side. ::when did that ever stop you?::

He shook his head and laughed bitterly. ::Never.::

Poplar trotted to his side and they walked together for a time.

::It's not like I haven't tried. What more do you expect me to do?::

She huffed and refused to answer.

He hobbled down the path, ignoring his aching joints, not caring where his steps took him.

::where are we going?::

Thorne kept walking toward the setting sun.

::are we going home?::

One of the possibilities that opened up before him showed his small cabin, burned to ash and memory, the skeletal remains of a man and a small dog scattered in a rising wind. ::No.::

::back to the market?:: Poplar's mind filled with the smells of people and food.

::No.:: Thorne stopped abruptly, noticing for the first time the tall trees shrouding them in deep shadows. An eerie howl split the silence. Another joined it, and another until the thicket echoed with the chorus of wolves. He turned toward the sound of the hunting pack with a terrible eagerness. It would be simple to lose themselves in the woods. It wouldn't take a truthscryer to see how that path ended.

Thorne bent down to scoop Poplar up in his arms. Her little legs would only slow them down, and he had a long way to walk. Cringing, she backed away until she stood shivering at the edge of the animal trail, her wide eyes shifting from him to the darkness between the trees.

She was afraid. Of him.

He collapsed onto his knees and hid his face in his hands. Tears of frustration, of anger, and of shame tracked down his cheeks. None of this was her fault and he had no right to drag her into his misery. ::I'm sorry.::

The darkness deepened as Thorne wept. He had no idea how long it had been when a warm tongue licked the salt from his hands. When he came back to himself, Poplar was nuzzling her face in his beard.

::home. we go home. the den is warm. the den is safe:: She repeated this over and over, like a mantra or a spell.

Slowly, Thorne's breathing eased. He cupped her wiry muzzle in his hands and lifted her head to look into her small brown eyes. "Yes. Home." His voice was nearly swallowed up in the dense night.

Potential futures branched from every step Thorne took: Turn right, and a tree branch weakened by last week's storm might break and crush him. Pause in this clearing for more than a few moments, and the wolves would catch his scent. He heard the howling, but knew it was only in his mind. In some futures,

Poplar gets away. In others she tries to fight off the pack and is killed.

The wolf-song continued to echo from a myriad of paths. Thorne gritted his teeth and kept walking.

Most seers lost their way and fell into madness. Thorne had been one of the lucky ones. Not in the seeing. No, he had been well and truly cursed with that. Lucky in that he'd been found by a teacher while he was still young, before becoming trapped in endless possibility.

While Sharrah—the old woman who took him in as a child after his own family had cast him out—was ragged and desperate, she taught him enough to carry the burdens of foresight. Even though she had not borne them well herself.

Thorne was already older than Sharrah had lived to be. Perhaps he should have joined his teacher and drowned himself when he'd had the chance. There were thousands of ways he had already seen death in visions; it no longer held any fear for him. All things died. Truly, it would be a relief when his life finally ended, but Poplar deserved to be cared for, so he wrenched his mind away from those well-worn paths.

He knew he owed her the security of a good home for when he was gone, but the thought of being apart from her made his heart ache. It was possible that the end waited for them both in the little cabin they shared, but Thorne could never be certain, especially when it came to his own life.

It was never any definite future he saw, only possibilities. And some sense—either innate, or something Sharrah had taught him—let him see which ones were more likely than others. Or at least that was how it had been until recently.

There were elders in town whose sight had dimmed with age, leaving them in a perpetual twilight. That's what Thorne saw now when he looked down the endlessly branching paths. He had thought it was simply the years dulling his other vision, but the colors in the surface world were just as vibrant as they had been in his youth. It was only the deeper sight that had dimmed. And with Sharrah long in the grave, there was no one Thorne could ask.

A squeak from Poplar broke into his morose thoughts. ::home::

The small dog raced on ahead and Thorne followed through the darkness of tangled trees and a moonless sky. Her nose was sure. If only she could sniff out what he needed to know, but other than her ability to hear his thoughts, Poplar had no particular talent. No other creature he had encountered could talk with him like she did. It was another thing he had never had the chance to ask his teacher about.

Her bright barking welcomed him home and Thorne smiled, despite his inner turmoil. Under her nose, the rude cabin was transformed into a rich and wondrous refuge. Something eased in his heart as he opened the door and stoked the still-warm embers in the stove. He didn't bother to light any lamps. The flickering flames and his familiarity with the one-room structure was enough.

Poplar's hunger gnawed at him.

::Cut that out, you beast.::

The sensations faded. Her pleading eyes glinted in the firelight.

::Shameless beggar. Fine.::

She twirled in circles, dancing as he crumbled some jerky and oats into a dish. He ladled soup broth cooled with fresh water over the mixture and set it down beside the stove. Poplar stilled. Her nose quivered, but she waited, shifting her glance between the food and Thorne.

He couldn't help himself. He laughed. ::Go on. It's yours.:: At least he could bring joy to this one small creature. While the dog ate, Thorne forced himself to have some leftover soup. It didn't do to neglect the body, no matter how sparse his appetite. He lay across the small bed, and Poplar curled into a ball beside him. Her warmth was a welcome comfort, even more than the stove's.

The vision of the cabin consumed by fire rose about him, stronger than before, but he forced it from his mind. A true future or not, it wouldn't do to disturb Poplar with his unease. She made small sighing noises and her body relaxed into his. Thorne had always envied her ability to let all but the present go. Perhaps there was a future where he learned her secret. For now, he let his mind drift in her contentment.

For years, he had moved from town to town, alone. The story was always the same. At first, folks would shun him as the outsider he was. Then one brave soul—almost always a young mother—would seek him out to tell their child's fortune. If he could find a way to weave a happy tale from the threads of possible disasters, others would follow. For a time, he would have enough to eat and a warm place to sleep.

But it never lasted. There would be a vicar or a mayor or a wealthy merchant who approached him in the dead of night. They always had dreams full of avarice and sought more. Demanded more. And all their possible futures would collapse into a haze of pain and loss and greed.

It would have been simpler if Thorne could lie. Tell them the futures they wanted. But the gift required truth, and that was its most brutal curse.

He glanced at Poplar's slumbering body. Her needs were simple. She demanded nothing of him that he could not easily grant: a gentle hand, a full belly, a warm bed. And in return, she gave him her trust and her love. He wouldn't have survived these past few years without her. He finally fell asleep, his hand on her soft fur.

Still, in his dreams, he was stalked by unseen predators through a strange landscape of tall boxy buildings and wide streets where lights blinked red and green in a pattern he could almost understand.

A terrified cry and an answering bark interrupted his fitful slumber. Thorne bolted upright, his heart pounding. The embers of the fire glowed a deep, angry crimson.

It's only some animal in the dark, he thought. Wolves, or their prey. His hands shook and an icy cold chilled him to the bone. A familiar cold: the same cold that had crept into his soul the day he'd found Sharrah's body tangled with a fallen tree in the creek that ran near their home. That memory was never far from his thoughts these days, no matter how hard he tried to bury it.

The future was terrible enough. He didn't need the past haunting him, too.

As he reached for the covers, the cry from his dream pierced his heart again. Thorne whimpered, and for a moment he was there, kneeling at the muddy bank, his hands clutching Sharrah's slight body in the swift winter-melt current.

The fire had guttered and the moon had set, leaving the cabin in darkness. There was no sound now, except for the wind through the trees outside the cabin.

He reached out for Poplar, but the dog wasn't there.

A chill that was more than cold moved through him. ::Poplar?::

He felt her whimpering response as if from far away.

A murmur of voices broke the silence of the cabin. The crack of a stick breaking was followed by muffled curses. Thorne's heart raced. Who would be traveling through these woods at this time of night? And walking in stealth?

As vivid as a new memory, the image of his cabin destroyed by flames rose in his mind.

He stood by the small window, peering out into the darkness.

Three pinpricks of light bobbed through the woods at a man's height.

Gooseflesh prickled his arms.

An angry barking came from the woods outside.

The indistinct torches became three men standing several strides apart in front of his cabin.

"Thorne Truthscryer, you are no longer welcome here." Thorne had no need of foresight to recognize the voice of the local pastor. His future, tangled with the death of another man's wife in childbirth.

"What have you done with my dog?" His voice was choked with fear for her. She had no idea how tiny she was. How her small teeth were no match for men armed with hatred.

There was no answer. The two men beside the pastor were silent shadows in the night. They were not important. They would follow the cleric's lead.

Thorne raised his voice to be heard through the window. "Is this the town's will?" Of course it wasn't. No one would have said "Burn him out," but then again, no one would mourn him when his voice was silenced. This wasn't the first time he was forced from a place.

"Come outside and talk. You won't be harmed."

Possibilities fanned out in front of him. A hundred alternate worlds where alternate Thornes and pastors faced off against one another in the night. In none of them did the man speak the truth. Thorne called to Poplar again. There was no reason she should die with him tonight. But if she went for the pastor or either of the men beside him, he was certain her life would end in violence. Thorne wouldn't let that happen.

"Don't be an idiot, Truthscryer. We're giving you a chance."

As the men's patience shortened, possibilities collapsed, nearly all of the remaining ones exploding in heat and flame. Smoke rose around him. Thorne shoved the phantom scent away, struggling to find any path that didn't end here. But this gift, this curse, couldn't overcome the images his fear created. He threw his coat around himself and reached for the door. Poplar could vanish into the woods. They wouldn't be able to find her.

The torches came closer. The pastor's eyes gleamed in the harsh light. There was eagerness in his gaze. He nodded to his companions. The three men stepped forward to lay their torches down before retreating into the shadows.

Smoke rose in lazy spirals and mingled with the smoke in Thorne's mind. He retreated from the door. As the memory of his earlier vision rushed toward him, his despair turned to fury. He gave voice to a shout that pierced through him. From outside, Poplar's voice rose in an answering howl.

The stranger's anguished call that had woken him in the night filled his soul and reverberated through the thickening air.

"No!"

It was Thorne's voice, mingled with another's. Braided with Poplar's fear. In some other reality, across all the possibilities that danced in Thorne's hazy vision, someone whose need was just as great as theirs called and rent the night.

An unnatural darkness blocked the way between Thorne and the now dancing flames. Cold air poured through. Free from smoke. Free from fire. A door to the place with the winking lights and the dark buildings from his dream.

Chapter 4

Melissa Klein

RETREATING TO THE SHELTER of the ambulance, Melissa wondered again what she was doing here. As a volunteer with the mayor's annual homeless census, her job was to assess unmet medical and psychiatric needs among the unhoused—though to Melissa's mind, they all needed services. Choosing to spend winter nights on Boston streets qualified anyone for psychiatric evaluation. Unfortunately, the guidelines they operated under said otherwise. None of the folks they'd encountered tonight had met criteria to be transported to the hospital. Just being cold, desperate, and hungry apparently wasn't enough to merit care and shelter.

She crammed her fleece-lined mittens into her coat pocket and grabbed the thermal mug she'd left on the gurney at the start of the night's shift. The coffee was lukewarm now, but it was better than nothing.

A fresh blast of cold air stole the scant warmth from the emergency vehicle. It rocked as Stirling Hughes, the EMT she was partnered with for the count, stepped inside and slammed the doors.

"Sorry, Doctor Klein."

"Melissa, please." It was at least the fifth time tonight she tried to get him to call her by her first name. "Look, you're the one who knows what they're doing."

"How about just Doc?"

She shrugged. It was better than the stiff formality.

"Don't sell yourself short, Doc. I think you have a gift for this work."

His smile seemed genuine. As did everything else about him. "How do you manage it?"

"It was a lot worse last year," he said. "At least it's not snowing, and there's not a lot of wind tonight."

That wasn't exactly what she had asked him. But she was grateful he didn't understand the real question. Her own selfish needs had no place here. And leaning on Stirling to ease her guilt only sharpened her shame. This wasn't about her. How did the people out there survive? She sighed. Not all of them did. That was part of why she was here now.

"You okay, Doc? Let me see your fingers."

She took another gulp before setting the mug down.

Stirling took her small pale hands in his large brown ones and studied her the way she'd seen him examine the city's unhoused. "First count?" For a big man, he was surprisingly gentle, and his dark eyes were kinder than she deserved.

Still, she stiffened as if he'd accused her of something. "How could you tell?"

"They always give me the rookies." Stirling handed her a small pack of disposable glove warmers. "Slip these in your mittens." He glanced down at her boots. "Feet doing okay?"

"I'm fine." It came out a lot harsher than she'd intended. "I don't..." Melissa shook her head. All she had to do was get through this one night. Then she could turn in her report, and get back to her research and her cushy practice.

Eleanor had urged her to put her name in to volunteer with the mayor's office. It seemed her old college friend had been right: The grief that had haunted Melissa since she'd buried both her parents last year had eased. A little.

"It's when the world feels the most broken that we must heed the call to repair," Eleanor said.

Melissa rolled her eyes. It was a good thing Ellie was on the other end of a long distance phone call.

"I heard that," Ellie said, laughing.

"Look, I don't need a rabbi. I need a friend."

"Lucky with me you get two for the price of one."

Melissa sighed, not knowing what to say. She had abandoned any faith in religion a long time ago. And yet, she'd been the one who called Ellie.

"This isn't something you can logic your way through. Loss is a process, not a diagnostic code."

She could have argued. Her profession's diagnostic manual had specific criteria for Persistent Grief Disorder. Over the past year, Melissa had experienced most of them. Disrupted identity, check. A feeling of disbelief about the loss, check. Avoiding reminders of the individual, check. Intense emotional pain directly related to the loss, check. Trouble getting back to normal life, check. Numbness, check. Feeling that life is meaningless, check. Loneliness and detachment from others, oh yes, check.

It wasn't only about her parents. But that's when it had started, when the long-buried memories had surfaced with a vengeance. "I'm sorry, Ellie. I shouldn't have bothered you."

"Oh, Mel." She could hear her friend's caring across the long miles. "Promise me you'll think about it. It would do you good to get outside yourself."

"Tikkun fucking olam," Melissa muttered in the back of the ambulance.

"I'm sorry?" Stirling said.

"Nothing." She zipped her coat back up. The Hebrew words *tikkun olam* translated into "repair of the world," but everything felt broken to her these days. "I'm ready."

Even through all her layers and her warmest winter coat, the heat and weight of his hand on her shoulder brought comfort. She forced herself not to flinch and shake off his undeserved kindness.

"I know. It sucks. No one should be on the streets in the cold."

"I thought there were shelters."

"There are, but even if there were enough beds, some folks won't go and we can't force them."

That was a quandary in psychiatry, too. The line between danger to self or others and self-determination was a difficult one to define. And one she had contended with even in her own life. She glanced at the folded blankets and the toiletry kits piled on the gurney. "So that's it? We give them some supplies and hope it doesn't get too frigid overnight?"

He shrugged. "Pretty much."

"That's not good enough."

"No, it's not." The hand slid from her shoulder. A chilly silence filled the ambulance.

"I'm sorry. That wasn't fair."

Stirling zipped up his jacket and jammed his hands into bulky ski mittens. "You don't get used to it, but you learn to leave it in the ambulance when you go home."

Melissa nodded. Clinical distance and emotional detachment were part of her world, too. She needed to remember that.

It was time to focus.

She activated the warmers, slipping them into her coat pockets rather than her mittens. That way she could warm her hands between filling out the surveillance forms. "Okay. I'm set."

"This is the last grid square on our list, Doc." Stirling hefted a box with supplies and headed back out into the night.

She envied his ability to stay on task. "Get a grip, Doctor Klein," she muttered to herself before following him. She was the psychiatrist. Hell, she lectured the medical students and interns on professional boundaries when they started their psych rotations.

Wind whipped around her, nearly snatching the ski hat from her head. The momentary warmth from the coffee and the ambulance evaporated. Shivering, Melissa followed Stirling across the street. She flicked on the headlamp he had given her, unable to shake the sense that its feeble light would only paint them as targets. She knew that wasn't fair. The people who squatted here had more to fear from them than the other way around.

They picked their way to the lone brick structure remaining on a block otherwise reduced to rubble. A chain link fence surrounded the property. Inside its boundary, a pile of abandoned shopping carts and metal trash cans cast misshapen shadows across the uneven ground. She wondered why this last building had been left standing. Given real estate prices all around Boston, it was no surprise the block had been slated for revitalization.

As she looked over the rusty and pitted scaffolding, her lamp shone on boarded-up windows covered in overlapping graffiti. "How long has it been like this?"

"A couple of years." He shrugged. "Police clear everyone out and the fire department boards the place up every so often, but the folks just come back. Nowhere else for them to go."

Great. Add fire trap to the general hazard of abandoned building.

" ...majority overseas investor. The local partners got jailed for some big money laundering scheme. Project is in permanent limbo while they try to figure out who owns what and who gets left paying the fines."

Her mind had wandered and she'd missed the beginning of what he'd been saying. She wanted to ask Stirling if the mayor's office knew they were going inside, but one look at his set jaw and narrowed dark eyes and she followed silently.

As she studied the building, shadows pulsed over the structure, synchronized with her heartbeat. Her mouth dried. The taste of stale coffee suddenly made her queasy.

"Is it safe?"

"Define safe."

Even through the cold and her body's unwelcome fight or flight reaction, she felt her face burn. Safe was her condo in Belmont. Safe was her university appointment and tenure, an office with a waiting room, and patients who paid out of pocket. A sabbatical and research enough to keep her busy for the year. The money from selling her parents' house earning interest in her investment accounts.

Safe was the privilege of not seeing panhandlers on her street and the ease of automatic monthly donations to her favorite charities.

It wasn't enough. The memory of Ellie's voice chided her.

Tikkun olam.

As empathic and as sensitive as her friend was, Ellie didn't understand. One night volunteering in the cold could never repair the harm Melissa had done so many years ago. Or even her more recent guilt for failing her parents during their long, slow decline.

Stirling balanced the carton of supplies in one hand and reached up to turn on his own headlamp.

Melissa blinked in the sudden flare, drowning in afterimages. When she could focus again, Stirling was a silhouette, etched in brilliant light. A rhythmic pounding thudded across the back of her head. She swore under her breath. It had been years since she'd had an episode.

"Doc?" He paused, his hand on the large steel front door.

"Sorry. Coming." She just had to get through this and be home before the visual aura's full force made it impossible to see.

The shifting shadows were gone for now, but there were still odd flickers in her field of view. There was little she could do to stop it or the headache that would follow. Not here and not without the meds she had stockpiled.

Melissa looked up. Stirling's lamp swept over her face and she winced in the sudden blinding brightness. He didn't have to say a word for her to hear his unspoken question.

"I'm okay," she said. But she was lying.

He swung the door open. The darkness inside seemed to move and heave. It saw her. But that wasn't what filled her with dread.

This was absurd. Only children were afraid of shadows. She was a grown woman. A well-respected doctor. Paired with an EMT partner who she knew had her back. Nothing here could hurt her.

Stirling's light moved away from hers and Melissa shuddered, suddenly more terrified of being lost and alone than of walking into the building's open maw.

"We're here from the mayor's office. We got blankets and supplies for anyone who wants 'em. Sandwiches, too." Stirling's rich, resonant voice got swallowed up by the heavy silence.

Acrid smoke burned the back of her throat. Beneath it, the cloying scent of trash. Melissa stepped close to Stirling and whispered, "Where is everyone?"

"Deciding if what's in this box is worth risking us not being who we say we are."

Her face warmed again in the darkness. She knew what he probably thought about her. Why was she so concerned about his opinion? It didn't matter. After tonight, she'd never see him again.

Stirling set the box on the floor and opened it. The light from his headlamp bobbed erratically around the room, illuminating nothing. The rustle of cloth and paper bags seemed oppressively loud. Melissa looked down. Her light showed several piles of goods unloaded from the box—blankets, toiletry kits, bottles of water, and food—but she was having a hard time focusing her eyes. Everything had edges sharper than they should have been.

"Gonna leave this stuff here and wait by the door. Take what you need."

Melissa was glad Stirling did all the talking. It was getting harder to anchor her thoughts.

"If anyone wants to talk to me or the doc, just speak up."

She turned to follow the EMT, hoping she could get back to the ambulance before her symptoms got any worse. It had been a long time since she'd had one this bad. Her stomach lurched. She broke out in a cold sweat.

"Stirling? I think...I need help."

The wan light from his headlamp vanished.

Hers winked out. "Shit."

Nothing happened when she jiggled the switch. Her hands were invisible even directly in front of her eyes, but something sparkled in the periphery of her vision. She swore again as her eyes refused to obey her. Shimmering geometric forms hovered just out of sight, moving as her gaze searched back and forth. "Stirling?" There was no answer in the suffocating darkness of the building's empty floor. No sound at all except for the roaring in her ears and her own harsh breathing.

Melissa reached out hoping for something, anything to connect her to the here and now.

The hairs on the back of her neck stood up and she knew something was there. Watching her. Waiting. Judging.

Her mind fragmented. The distortions dancing in the air became the memory of pulsing red and blue emergency lights. The sound of her childhood friend crying as the social workers took him away broke through the walls she'd carefully constructed to hold back the past. She struggled to regain control, letting the part of her who was the rational physician run through the differential diagnosis of her symptoms: migraine, seizure disorder, stroke, brain tumor.

Melissa turned to where she thought the door back to the cold Boston night should have been. There was nothing there.

The scent of burning wood stung her nose, completely different from the heavy smoke from the building's lobby. She heard the rustle of wind through trees. In the distance, a dog barked sharply. A warning.

An unnatural silence fell.

Then the darkness receded from a circle directly in front of her. A crystalline brightness nibbled away at the encroaching shadows until it formed a space large enough to walk through. "Aura. Hallucination. Visual field cut." She muttered the medical terms as if they were a talisman that could protect her.

Then something small and vaguely body-shaped fell through the shimmering hole in the dark and merged with the shadows at her feet.

Chapter 5

Corinne Vettel

CORINNE SHUDDERED AND FORCED her hands not to claw at her face and the imaginary spider silk that seemed to cling to every bit of her exposed skin. One moment she had been in the liminal space between worlds, the next standing at the still point around which this new reality seemed to seethe and move.

A wave of dizziness swept through her. The transit had been hard. Harder than her first as an untrained, desperate teen all those years ago.

She opened her eyes and took a slow breath. A damp cold shocked through her.

The breeze was briny. Familiar. It reminded her of their seaside cottage.

Where she had left Reina alone.

Her body's instincts screamed at her to go back to her daughter, to reject this likely hopeless search. The pull of the home she had never wanted confused her.

She was here now. The more she fought against the new reality she'd landed in, the harder it would be to integrate herself.

Corinne blinked, waiting for her eyes to adjust to the dimness. She was in a city. Tall lights shed small rings of brightness in the gloom, not quite illuminating a few buildings that seemed to huddle together at one end of the street. Parked vehicles created rectangular shadows. A glut of other vehicles traveled slowly on the wide streets.

A tech level three, according to Network classifications. Better than some of the possible alternatives. Corinne was still not sure she'd made the right choice in coming here, but Jace hadn't left her many other options. This was her last chance to convince him to return to the Network voluntarily. To get the help he needed. If they found him first, and he resisted, they wouldn't hesitate to act for the good of the mission. Reina would never forgive her if she let that happen to him.

For most of her life, Corinne had believed in the Network's mission. Had sacrificed everything for it. Had followed its discipline. Now she wasn't sure what to hold on to, but if Harnett Wellerman was right and Jace was suffering from Reality Disintegration Disorder, his actions threatened to put more than only himself at risk. And the longer he wandered in the multiverse, the greater the danger to them all would be.

Jace would believe she had betrayed him, but if he had RDD, the Network's medical staff could help him. She had hoped all those years without exposure would have put Jace into remission, but Traveling again had to have forced him over the limit.

At least Reina was safe, though Corinne feared her daughter would not see it that way.

It had been so much simpler when Reina was a young child. Now the questions were more complicated and the answers unsatisfying to both of them. Corinne regretted all of the secrets and most of the lies.

"The greatest danger you face Traveling is losing the ability to distinguish between the path you desire and the path in front of you."

Jace's voice echoed in her memory. Long before he had become her lover, he had been one of her trainers. "Oh, Jace," she whispered. His lesson was one she definitely didn't want to think about. They should have been somewhere safe. Together. As a family. Jace, healthy and fully present. But he had left them and hadn't returned. His thread had pulled her here—wherever here was.

Stop. Observe. Reorient. This wasn't the first time she'd landed in an unfamiliar place, alone. Shivering, she forced her swirling emotions aside.

Her first priorities were safety, shelter, and supplies. At the very least, she wasn't dressed for this weather. Exposure could kill as easily as any other danger in Traveling the multiverse.

Where was Jace? Time ran in strange and unpredictable ways across the multiverse. Jace had made his crossing three days earlier, by her subjective accounting. How long that was in elapsed in-world time was a question she couldn't answer. Not without consulting a Network cache.

It would give her data on this instance and a home base from which to search for her husband. And it would reveal her presence to the Network.

In any other circumstances, that's where she would have found Jace, but with his paranoia surrounding anything Network related, he would never risk tripping their surveillance. For years, Corinne had struggled with her divided loyalties. Keeping secrets well had been part of her training and her life for so long, it was disturbingly simple to turn those skills to her own family. Jace had never suspected she'd been back in contact with the Network, and Corinne had thought she'd crafted a balance between all her conflicting obligations. Until Harnett Wellerman found her.

The fallout from her one brief conversation with the senior agent three months ago was enough to bring it all crashing down: her marriage, her place in the Network, and her relationship with her daughter.

She took a few measured breaths. That was all past. She was here in an unfamiliar reality and needed to stay anchored to her purpose. Jace. It didn't matter if Wellerman had told her the truth or sought to manipulate her. She had to find her husband before he hurt himself or vanished somewhere in the multiverse where he risked creating dangerous fractured realities he'd never be able to escape. Even if their trust was well and truly broken, she still loved him, and for the sake of what they had together and for their daughter, she would do everything she could to help him.

A honking car jolted Corinne back to the chilly night. Nearby, a motor growled into life. Red strobe lights and sirens seared her senses. She ducked into an unlit alleyway, just far enough to be draped in shadow but still able to see what was happening. A large van and several small cars screamed their way through traffic. The night returned to silence long before her heartbeat slowed.

Even if it weren't so bone-achingly miserable outside, Corinne knew she wouldn't be safe wandering around aimlessly on her own. As if the universe thought she needed more convincing, she emerged from her hiding place into a fierce gust of wind.

Despite knowing what she was looking for, it took Corinne hours of slogging through the slushy streets to find it. By the time she reached the building where the cache was hidden, the warmth of home was a distant memory and her shoes were completely sodden.

The activation mark was concealed behind the last in a line of ticket machines in a transit hub. There was a notice hung across it in stark lettering; Corinne assumed it said out of order or some other such thing. People swirled around her in a hurry to get from one place to another. There were things about living in a city Corinne missed. That sense of easy anonymity was one of them.

The Network emblem was surrounded by random scratches on the wall tiles. All she had to do was tap the center of the symbol.

That contact would start a countdown. The Network would want to know when a cache was accessed. But there were thousands and thousands of potential worlds, each with caches. Not all of them had real-time monitoring. There was no way to know how closely and how often this world was surveilled.

She reached into the shadow behind the machine. It only took the lightest of touches. Golden light spilled from a tiny crack in the wall that only she could see. The sounds from the station around her receded into background noise as the doorway opened wider.

Corinne slipped past the broken ticket dispenser and slid into the cache. It opened into a tiny and fully isolated stable pocket universe just about the size of the barracks rooms at the Network training facility. Instead of bunk beds and desks for a group of cadets, it was lined with shelves and stocked with the raw materials and the printers to create anything a Traveler might need to survive in a hostile place. The tech that kept it synchronized with the local norms had always seemed like magic to her, but that had never been her area of expertise. She was just grateful for the agents who had deployed it and the automated resources that kept it running.

Leaving her soggy shoes in the short corridor that tied the cache to local spacetime, Corinne walked through to the desk at the far wall and its control console, leaving a ghost trail of wet footprints on the white flooring. At least it was warm inside. Her priorities were a change of clothes, appropriate outerwear, and a sturdy pair of boots. She input her needs and requested the standard resource pack as well. If she was able to find Jace quickly, she wouldn't need the identification card and the local currency, but she had been an agent—and a good one—for a long time. That history kept her sharp. Cautious.

Corinne had finally stopped shivering by the time the sophisticated printer spit out everything she needed. It even created a nondescript carry-all to put the local money in.

She stripped off her clothing from home and put it in the recycling receptacle. The pang of loss that hit her as the cache recycled it into its constituent fibers was fierce and unexpected. Now the only thing that had come with her from there to here was her ring. She spun it around her thumb in a near unconscious habit, hoping that wherever Jace was, he was safe. Warm. Dry.

Dressing in the unfamiliar clothing, Corinne pushed away the inconvenient sentimentality and focused on her job. Right now, she was an agent. Jace was her mission.

The small plastic ID card was still warm to the touch as she secreted it in a zippered pocket. Grateful for the dry socks and warm boots, Corinne glanced toward the small entryway that led back to the transit hub. Now that she was comfortable and provisioned, she would venture out to find a hot meal before returning to sleep in the cache. It was small, but it was safe. And limiting her exposure to an unknown world was wise. Jace should have done the same, but he wasn't thinking straight. He hadn't been for some time, if she was being honest with herself. She needed to find him before he did something even more rash.

A blinking red light on the printer caught her attention.

With rising dread, she stared at the warning message with the light.

Alert: Quarantine in effect. Important guidance to follow.

"Oh, Jace, what have you done?" she whispered, her throat tight.

The printer whirred again and this time spit out a single sheet of paper.

> *Local designation: Earth*
> *Network designation: 7QN11-72*
> *Tech level: 3*
> *Cache Deployed*: NLY3101*
> *Last Surveyed: NLY3101*
> *Status: Interdicted. Level 4 quarantine.*
> *Guidance: No active Network presence. Passive monitoring only.*
>
> **Agent Calloway and Agent Hearne—official status: Missing in Action*

With shaking hands, she turned the page, but there was no other information. Frowning, she reread the few sentences over again. Her mouth dried and she struggled to swallow. In all her years as an active agent, including in her clandestine training work, she had never heard of a level 4 quarantine. It meant a world cut off not only from Network Headquarters, but from Network-controlled realities up to four transits away. This world was essentially isolated within its own bubble.

Heat rose to her face. She dropped the paper and stared as it fluttered to the floor. "Reina," she whispered and fled back into the transit area.

Standing with her back to the scuffed symbol at the cache's entrance and away from its shielding, she sought the thread that had brought her here. It should have been the strongest potential. The clearest Moment. The easiest to follow. Instead, a thick overlay of Moments obscured her senses. The strands of possibility snared her as if she were an insect stuck in the center of a spiderweb.

Everywhere she searched led her back to this here and now. The way home, a tantalizing mirage. A Moment that vanished into fog even as she reached out for it.

Corinne had no idea how long she spent trying and failing to force open the ways between worlds. But she was drenched in sweat and trembling with fatigue. The transit station had fallen quiet. Locals still traversed the inside plaza, but there were far fewer than when she had arrived.

She took a shaky breath.

She had abandoned Reina to follow Jace. And now she was mired in this quicksand world. Alone. Nothing in her training or her missions had prepared her for this. It would be easy to blame her husband, but she was the one who'd made the choices that led her here.

And it was far too late to reconsider the paths she might have followed instead.

Her stomach rumbled. Her body's needs imposed themselves over her misery.

She glanced behind her but couldn't bear facing the emptiness of the cache. Corinne pulled free of the tangle of emotion, strode across the waiting room, and followed a few stragglers out the large doors and into the chill night. By force of habit, she leaned into her training: basic needs first, then plan. No matter what came next, she had to equilibrate to this new world. Embracing it was the best and fastest way.

Personal and community vehicles clogged the thoroughfares at barely a walking pace. The wide ways beside them were filled with people hurrying along. She stood out of the wind and listened to snippets of conversation.

"… reservations for eight thirty tomorrow?"

"… three in a row! My kid's a better goalie …"

"… pick up a half gallon of milk on your way home and I'll …"

It wasn't so different from her home world. It rarely was. People throughout the multiverse worried about the same things; family and safety topped that list. It should have brought her solace. It only sharpened her worry.

δ

Reina Vettel

REINA WOKE IN A HARSH, bright room. Her chest ached. She shivered, feeling hot and cold at the same time. Her head pounded in time with her heartbeat and there was a bitter taste in her mouth. The last thing she remembered clearly was taking the stone from her room before the nightmare of her transit. She shied away from the memory of falling through the icy nothingness and the darkness that followed. Where was she? What went wrong?

"Mama?" The cry only reverberated in her mind. She tried to move, but her limbs felt heavy and dull. Her body and its misery were distant and overwhelming at the same time.

All Reina could see was a slice of a light green wall with a white square on it. A series of squiggly black lines traveled across it—words in a language she'd never seen before. That had to mean she'd Traveled. But where? And what happened to her?

A deep voice reverberated in the room. Sounds pulsed against her ears both as random nonsense and as words full of meaning. It was as if she heard the voice twice, simultaneously. The sounds slowly resolved into sense. "Oh, you're awake."

Someone leaned over her, blocking her view of the wall. It took Reina a moment for her eyes to focus. A light-skinned man dressed in a white jacket over light blue trousers and a short tunic smiled down at her before reaching out to straighten her blanket. Reina felt its weight, its scratchy surface, and the vague sharp scent that rose from it, but as if from far away. She tried to draw breath to speak, but had no control over her body.

The man stood and studied her. "There. That's better."

In the back corner of her mind, she knew she should be afraid, but it was as hard to connect with her emotions as it was to make her body move. Was this some side effect of Traveling between the worlds?

Why hadn't her parents warned her this could happen? Why had they left her here? She struggled to look around, to get any clues to her surroundings, but her eyes could only focus straight ahead. Her thoughts skipped erratically like a stone across water.

Why couldn't she move? Why did everything hurt? The sense of falling returned so fiercely her stomach lurched and her head spun. She must have broken her body when she landed. Why couldn't she remember?

"I need to change your IV bag."

She hadn't realized the man was still there with her. He moved into her field of view again and fiddled with a pouch and tubing on a stand beside the bed. Reina tried to turn her head to follow what was being done, but the strange heaviness persisted. Then warmth flooded through her arm.

"It's a good sign your eyes are open and responding to light." The man smiled down at her. "Dr. Bhavsar will be pleased."

As he kept talking, the strange echo of his voice died out, leaving clear understanding behind.

Could they even fix her? Would they even try?

Over and over again, Reina tried and failed to make some sound—any sound—anything to communicate with her helper. The man kept cheerfully talking to her as if she would answer. It was maddening. If she could just move, maybe it would be okay. Maybe she could heal.

"I'm going to check your vitals now."

The individual words might have made sense, but Reina couldn't force them to have meaning as a whole.

The man pulled what looked like a rolled bandage with flexible hoses from his pocket. He freed one of Reina's arms from beneath the blanket and wrapped the fabric above her elbow. After slipping a cold metal disk under it, the man tightened the cuff. Reina strained to move away from the pressure. Nothing happened.

Fighting to see what he was doing, Reina's gaze finally shifted slightly, just enough to see more clearly to her side, until the wrapped arm was in her line of sight.

It belonged to a stranger.

This arm was not her own.

Reina tried to scream.

Silence.

The odd heaviness of her limbs and the distant sensations suddenly made terrible sense. This wasn't her body.

And she was locked inside it.

Panic finally bubbled up in the space behind where her chest should be. The heart within it raced. A terrible pressure filled this stranger's lungs, trapping their shared breath.

The blaring of alarms filled the room. The man stiffened and his eyes widened. He called out, his words jumbling together so quickly Reina couldn't distinguish them.

Shadows swirled across her vision. The sound of running feet and the babble of urgent voices made a strange music.

A sudden cold spread through her, smothering her emotions.

They belonged to someone else.

Just like this body.

Reina stopped fighting and let the darkness take her again.

Chapter 6

Thorne Truthscryer

POPLAR CAME RUNNING THROUGH the small flap she used to get in and out of their cabin.

"No!" Thorne sobbed as she pressed against his legs. Smoke burned his eyes and throat.

Poplar whined, her mindvoice a thin thread of fear.

He snatched her into his arms and stumbled through the only way open to them now. The crackle of flames behind them fell into silence. A cold wind rushed in to fill its absence.

As Thorne crossed the threshold, it was as if a door had slammed behind him. It shut out the light of the hungry flames devouring his small cottage and sealed him from its terrible heat. A cold breeze whipped through the thin fabric of his coat.

Poplar shivered in his arms. ::it smells wrong::

He held on to her more tightly than she usually tolerated. Thorne didn't have the sensitive nose his dog had, but he felt the same strangeness. This air had winter's bite, even though at home they had not even hit the autumn solstice. The hard surface beneath him stole the warmth from his stockinged feet. He looked up. There was no moon to brighten the dull sky. A thick layer of clouds made it seem darker and colder. Beside him, a building like the ones he had foreseen in his dream loomed over him, vanishing into the night, taller than any structure in the town they had just escaped. A cold lamp hanging far overhead illuminated piles of rubble in a fenced-off square beside it.

Thorne turned in a circle and gasped. A thousand pale lights winked in the distance. Most of them, small white pinpricks. Not overhead like stars, but shining through windows in other, even taller buildings. Wide streets vanished into the distance. Red and green lights hung over them and blinked at slow intervals. It was the alien landscape that had disturbed his sleep. As he tried to make sense of the world he and Poplar had tumbled into, several large wagons propelled themselves down the closest way. Their passing whipped the wind into a frenzy.

He shrunk back against the building behind him.

A stream of urine flowed down his side as Poplar whimpered.

::It's okay, little one. I'm here.::

She was silent in her humiliation.

They needed shelter. From the cold. From the night. From the oddness. He only hoped that day would break in this terrible world. And with it, clarity.

Thorne glanced back at the lit buildings in the distance. Lights meant a town and warmth and people. The warmth would be welcome, but could he trust whoever lived here? What if they were as hostile as those in the place he left behind?

A growl from Poplar raised the hairs on the back of Thorne's neck. "Smell that? It's gonna snow later. You ain't gonna make it out here." A scrawny old man emerged from the shadows to stand in the ring of light from the strange lamp. "It's a good thing Martin likes dogs. It's past curfew, but he won't kick you out."

"Kick me out from where?" It wasn't until he answered that Thorne realized he understood the man's speech and could answer it in kind.

"There." The man leaned down to pick up the bundle of his belongings and lifted his chin at the dark structure behind him. "It ain't fancy, but there's usually extra blankets and shit. Clothes. Food too, sometimes."

Poplar's urine had soaked through his coat and turned it into a soggy, cold mess. They wouldn't last long if the temperature dropped much lower, but he hesitated, the memory of smoke still vivid in his mind.

"Look, man, do what you like for yo'self, but that pup needs to be inside." The lamp overhead made his dark eyes gleam.

Poplar lifted her head and peeked out from the shelter of Thorne's arms. She was still trembling, and still not talking to him, but her fear was not directed at the stranger.

"Will there be food and water for her?"

"I 'spect so. She have a name?"

"Poplar."

"Friendly?"

An image of her fierce hatred of the pastor filled his mind. "Mostly."

He laughed, revealing a mouth full of crooked teeth. "Smart pup!"

Thorne followed the man inside.

"Martin lets me come in late sometimes. Mostly he wants folks to be inside by now. You'd best follow the rules. I'm vouching for you."

The door shut behind them. It wasn't much warmer inside, but they were shielded from the wind, at least. Thorne's eyes strained to see anything in the shadowed space. For the moment, there was nothing but ordinary darkness. None of the looming futures had followed Thorne here. "What are your rules?"

"Ain't my rules. Martin's rules." The man shrugged. "Martin's crib, Martin's rules."

Poplar's small nose twitched rapidly. She let out a bright bark.

::Hush!::

She ignored him and wriggled in his arms.

He set her down with a silent warning. ::Stay here.::

::i smell cheese::

How she could smell anything beyond smoke was a wonder. ::Stay here.::

A small light bobbed in the distance. It was too easy for Thorne to imagine the men and their torches. Poplar was shaking, but from eagerness, not fear. He forced himself to take a deep breath, trust in her keen senses, and let the tension go.

::cheese!::

"Heya, Martin. Didn't mean to wake you."

"Harrold." The voice was part welcome, part warning. "You know the rules. We don't let in strays after hours."

"I know, man, but the dog was shivering and it's gonna snow."

Martin sighed. He shined a metal-clad light at them, letting it linger the longest over Poplar. It brightened their surroundings just enough for Thorne to study their host—a young man with skin a little lighter than his own nut-brown complexion. And in Martin's haggard face, Thorne recognized the same exhaustion and fear that had become his own constant companions.

"Whatever. I wasn't sleeping anyway." He turned to Thorne. "There's no dealing here. No drugs. No gang colors. You leave that shit at the door. You good with that?"

Thorne nodded, as though he understood what Martin was asking him.

"Your dog ain't gonna bite me, right?"

"Not a chance." It was as much an answer as a warning to Poplar.

"She go after rats?"

Poplar let out a sharp bark.

"She's a good enough hunter."

He knelt to the floor and set the light down. Like the streetlamp outside, it made no heat, nor did it flicker like a flame, but it illuminated a wide swath of the floor strewn with paper and other trash. "She like cheese?"

Another eager bark.

"More than rat."

The young man nodded and rummaged in the pocket of his coat. He unwrapped something and held it out to Poplar. Her tail wagged hard enough to move her entire body in a wave. She glanced up at Thorne quivering in anticipation. He nodded.

She stepped forward and lowered her head to gently sniff the prize being offered.

::It's all yours.::

The food was gone before Thorne could count a single breath. Then she stood up on her hind paws to lick their benefactor on the face. His smile was as surprising as Poplar's response. Thorne repressed a surge of jealousy.

Martin patted Poplar's head awkwardly before wiping his hands and standing up. "You can stay. Follow me."

He led them all in a circuitous route through piles of trash and broken furniture to a smooth metal door at the far end of the building. His lamp swept over a stairway that stretched up and vanished into darkness. As they climbed, a wave of dizziness nearly made Thorne lose his footing. Poplar pressed against him, her mind alternating between offering him comfort and wondering if the man with the lamp would give her more cheese.

It was as cold inside the stairwell as it had been outside, but Thorne was grateful for any shelter. The dog would curl up in his coat and share her warmth. At least they would survive until daybreak. And after that? He shook his head. Someone had brought him here. Unless the voice called to him again, Thorne had no idea how he would find them.

Martin led them up what felt like hundreds of steps until they reached another large metal door. It opened onto another open floor, this one lit by the light of flames in metal barrels arranged around the room. Thorne was hit by a fresh wave of smoke and sweat. Poplar sneezed.

It looked like a small village had been created within the large room. Several areas were separated by fabric draped over tall stands. In the open space, small groups of people were arranged in concentric circles around the barrels. Some had low cots. Some were sitting in worn and tired chairs. Many were lying down, wrapped in makeshift bedrolls, probably asleep. A few quiet conversations filled the room with overlapping whispers. All fell silent, one by one, as they walked past.

Martin played his light over Thorne's face again. He blinked in the sudden brightness.

"You sick?"

"No."

"Then you and your dog can camp there with the other single men." He pointed to a pile of unclaimed blankets just at the edge of the fire's light. "Don't stray to the family area or the women's section." He directed the light to a row of boxes against the far wall. "There's some dry clothes and shoes over there. Bathroom's all the way over in the back corner. There's water in a bucket you can use to flush. If you're going to be here more than a few days, you can take a cot or a chair if there are any unclaimed."

While Thorne understood most of the words the young man spoke, their full meaning escaped him. Maybe after some rest, it would make better sense.

"And if the dog craps or pees inside, you gotta clean it up."

Thorne nodded, but Martin wasn't looking at him.

"Keep your hands to yourself. Don't touch anyone's stuff. No one comes or goes until daybreak without my say-so. If you got food, share it. Follow the rules, it's all good."

Poplar bowed her head and whined like a chastened puppy. Thorne didn't have to ask what would happen if they broke the rules. The warning in Martin's voice was enough.

Harrold disappeared into the darkness. Thorne stepped toward his bedroll and paused. "Thank you." There was no answer; Martin had gone as well. No one spoke to them, but Thorne could feel the wariness in the room. It was like walking through the market all over again.

He slipped off his damp coat, and he and Poplar settled into their blankets. He curled up on his side. The floor was hard and chill beneath them, but he'd slept on worse. While the light from the barrels barely reached him, the space was warmer than he'd feared it would be. It wasn't all that much colder than his cabin when the fire was banked for the night.

::You trust Martin?::

Poplar was silent for long enough that Thorne didn't think she would answer. His thoughts drifted back to his confrontation with the pastor and the townsmen and he began to shake.

::he's like you::

If Martin saw the branching timelines, too, then Thorne felt sorry for him.

::not like that:: she said. ::like you::

He saw an image of himself through her eyes. Alone, his head bowed with grief.

::just like you::

That was all she would tell him before pressing into the small of his back. Her presence was a warm comfort, and her steady breathing let him finally fall asleep.

δ

Corinne Vettel

HER DINNER SAT CONGEALING on the otherwise empty desk in the cache. The smell of the heavily spiced noodles and vegetables that had seemed so appetizing when she was waiting in line for it outside the transit building now threatened to make her stomach heave.

Blinking dry eyes, she struggled to focus on the small and unforgiving text of the report crumpled in her hand. She'd been in difficult situations before—hostile worlds, illness, injury, failed missions—but she'd never Traveled to an interdicted world. Never heard of any other agent being lost to one, either. She threw the balled-up paper across the room.

"Oh, Jace, what have you done?" She whispered what had become a repeated mantra. *What have I done?*

Restless, she stood. *Passive monitoring only.* The Network was beyond her reach. Just like the lost agents who had deployed the cache. They were all considered acceptable casualties to the work MTN did across the multiverse.

But if Jace had also become stuck in this chaotic world, then perhaps the consequences of his actions would be contained here as well. And maybe she could focus on trying to find her way out. There had to be a way out.

A memory from her years training new agents broke through her wishful thinking.

Her four trainees had stared around them with near identical expressions of curiosity and wonder. Corinne let them gawk. The brilliant azure sand and the dark waves created a striking landscape. The setting sun created a glittery trail on the water. No other sounds competed with the rhythm of the strange sea.

It only took a few moments for the excitement to turn to an eerie dread. Even so, she waited until darkness fell and a starless night stretched overhead.

"Do you know why we're here?" she asked softly.

No one had an answer. Corinne hadn't expected them to, but she was still disappointed.

"This is an oasis world. Easy to reach. Easy to leave. Simple to change, but your actions here have little to no impact on it. "

"So a playpen." The young man answered, boredom and more than a little disdain in his voice.

"That's one way of thinking about it," she answered. "I prefer seeing it as more of a testing ground."

"I thought this was a real mission," he said.

She heard the smallest of sighs from the woman to his right. Corinne was glad the darkness covered her own annoyed expression. "What is a Traveler's greatest danger?"

The four recited it together. "Losing the ability to distinguish between the path you desire and the path that faces you."

"But do you know what it means? In the moment? When you have to act and make a choice?" She could hear him draw breath to speak and was more than happy to cut him off. "Your teachers have given you theory. You can all hold open a door. You have the skills to move from world to world. You can even reliably recognize the Moment and apply the appropriate push."

"But nothing we do here matters. You said so yourself."

She paused, smiled at the brash student, even though he couldn't see her in the darkness. "Did I?"

Another of the students spoke up, her soft voice respectful of the night. "But it matters to the Traveler, right?"

Corinne nodded to herself. At least one of them had thought this through. "Correct. What you push, pushes you. There are no inconsequential changes. Not even in a place like this. You are here not because we fear you might pose some danger to reality, but because at least in a world like this, we can keep you from posing a danger to yourselves."

Their extensive training had taught Corinne and Jace the skills to protect themselves from the kind of danger she had warned her students about. But every agent also knew their active duty days were limited.

Harnett had tried to warn her that Jace's paranoia about the Network was an early sign of Reality Disintegration Disorder. That any further trips between the world walls would accelerate his fractured thinking and advance the disease.

If she couldn't force her way back home, she had to at least find Jace. She would worry about how to reconcile her loyalties later.

Corinne's oath to repair the broken places in the universe still meant something to her, even if Jace had denounced his. Even if he was right about the danger the Network presented. And despite all the sacrifices, the anger, and the uncertainty, she still cared for him. Believed he cared for her. Knew that Reina was his world. He never would have abandoned her willingly.

And what about you?

Reina was safe. Another chill moved through her body. She folded her arms across her chest. Reina was as safe as Corinne could ensure. Regardless of how they felt about her, her parents would step up for their grandchild. She had to believe that, now more than ever.

At least for the time being, she was stuck here. Jace was here. Somewhere. And maybe, just maybe they could get home if they could join their strengths.

She knew she should rest. Making critical choices out of fear and exhaustion was dangerous. That's what she taught her eager students. But the coziness of the cache had turned claustrophobic and Corinne needed to burn off some of her nervous energy.

Even at this late hour, the transit station wasn't empty. A cluster of young people carrying backpacks jostled and laughed as they headed out toward the exit. Frigid air streamed inside when they opened the doors. Several ragged men and women had pushed chairs together and were sleeping across them, surrounded by bags full of their meager belongings.

If this was how they treated their unfortunate, it was no wonder this reality was interdicted.

The food stalls were closed and locked up. An occasional uniformed guard swept through but didn't notice her. She found a corner of the room where no one else was and sat out of anyone's line of sight. She cleared her mind, took a deep breath, and reached for Jace.

It troubled her that there was no clear ping of his presence. Within a world, even this interdicted one, she should be able to follow the echo of another Traveler's path. She fidgeted with her ring. He wouldn't have gone anywhere near the cache, which meant he'd have to have found shelter elsewhere. But without currency or papers or information, where could he have gone?

Could he have figured out a way to transit through this world? No. She was at least as good an agent as he was. If she couldn't find the right Moment, he wouldn't be able to either. Had he even come here? Maybe she had followed his thread to a dead end.

She rubbed her dry eyes. Weariness made her head pound. He had to be here. Otherwise there was no hope to hold on to.

A Moment hovered nearby. Corinne took a deep breath and centered herself with the familiarity of years of training. The air tingled with possibility, but there wasn't anything she could grasp. In an infinity of Moments, each clamored for her attention. None stayed stable long enough to trace. None carried any hint of Jace.

While she couldn't follow his path directly, there were other ways to track evidence of his presence. Planning beyond that was risky—it opened up too many possibilities.

But as urgent as everything felt, she also knew she would make a critical mistake if she continued to push through her fatigue. Even if she couldn't eat, she desperately needed rest.

Now, more than ever, Corinne had to rely on her Network training, even as Jace was doing everything he could to escape his. In another set of circumstances, the terrible irony might even be funny.

δ

Harnett Wellerman

THE CUSTOMIZED ALERT SNAPPED Harnett to attention. The routine agent reports he'd been tasked to review could wait. Jace was finally on the move.

He tossed the heavy binder aside and scooted his chair closer to the desk shoehorned between his narrow bed and the wall in his one-room flat. It had been several months since he'd lost his quarry after overplaying his hand with Corinne. Which never would have happened if his supervisors hadn't been pressuring him for results. That was a regrettable setback, but Harnett had known it would only be a matter of time until the rogue agent made a mistake.

They always did.

Jace's was to try and raid a Network cache. It was a rookie move and Harnett was surprised. He had trained the man to be more careful than that.

Now it was a matter of leaning on his familiarity with the Vettel family—an advantage Harnett had over everyone else in the Network—to get to Jace first.

Jace Vettel's dossier lay open to the page with an old photo. The son looked so much like the father; they shared the same suspicious look in the narrowed eyes and the frown lines around the mouth. But the father had proven easier to predict than the son. Harnett regretted not acting sooner. He might have prevented the couple from escaping all those years ago.

Then the Network would have them and their child to study, and he wouldn't have the stain of failure on his record.

Jace had been careful. Clever. Harnett had to give him that. He'd been an exemplary agent throughout his entire active career. The only hint of his ultimate rebellion had been the scene at his father's deathbed. Harnett reported his suspicions when Jace had requested a change in supervisor soon after, but they hadn't given his report due credence.

Sipping yesterday's cold coffee, Harnett frowned, not at its bitterness, but at the mistakes the Network made. Mistakes for which they ultimately blamed him.

No more. Finally he could rectify his reputation and gain significant influence by delivering not only Jace, but the whole family. Rare enough to have two Travelers conceive and bring a child to term, this one was Rogar Vettel's grandchild. No wonder all traces of Corinne's pregnancy and the Vettels' disappearance had been classified. Even with Harnett's unauthorized access into MTN files, he hadn't known about the child's existence until recently.

He carefully called up a précis on the world Jace had Traveled to. Now that he had a lead, he could afford to take his time. The alert would continue to track Jace regardless of where he went. He'd placed a second one to monitor any Network activity in the Vettel file. Harnett wasn't going to repeat his own past errors. And even an experienced field agent had something to learn. Preparation was the key.

Earth wasn't a reality he or any of his trainees had ever been assigned to. A near infinity of potentials dwarfed even the Network's resources, and only a small fraction had been fully explored or exploited. Which was probably one of the main reasons Jace had fled there. He must have been desperate to break into a cache. Harnett smiled. Desperate people made mistakes.

The report on Earth opened itself on his monitor. The brief consisted of a single page. Not much more than the heading.

Huh. Jace wasn't the first runner who'd decided to open a way into an interdicted world. They weren't uncommon, but they weren't routine, either. Each was sealed off for a particular reason. Most often for a combination of an aggressive populace, a lack of valuable resources, and limited access to other potentials. Harnett had never seen a reality that rated a level 4 quarantine. It was puzzling: The précis on Earth was terse, even by Network standards. It made him simultaneously curious and uneasy.

Requesting the unabridged report would reveal he had a lead. His supervisors would want to monitor the retrieval. Or take over the operation at a level above his clearance. Harnett drummed his fingers on the desk. He had his own methods and had spent his career carefully excising anything the Network didn't need to know from his reports. Until now, they only cared about his completion rate.

Until Jace, it had been unblemished.

He weighed his choices. Chasing his quarry into a level 4 without appropriate intel or support was less than optimal, especially given how close he was to his lifetime Travel limits. But Jace would be just as hampered. And Harnett was the best at this game. Besides, if he was successful in bringing the rogue in, he could finally step back from high-risk active duty with his record clear.

This was his case. His. No other agent knew as much about the Vettel family as he did. No other agent would be able to get as close to Jace as he could. Last time, he had underestimated the wife. That wouldn't happen again.

He closed Jace's dossier and nodded. Yes, it was personal. Revealing what he knew to the Network was not an option.

The child would be at the right age to manifest their ability and begin training. No wonder Jace had made his move now. He would do anything to keep his child free from the Network. Harnett would do the same to bring them all back.

Chapter 7

Melissa Klein

THE SUN HAD RISEN in the slot between the buildings to blaze directly through the front of her windshield. Melissa winced, her eyes tearing.

What the hell? She was sitting in her car, seat belt latched, the motor in park, idling. Oh, god, had she been driving?

"Stirling?"

She covered her mouth with her hand to keep from whimpering out loud. The ambulance and the EMT she'd been paired with for the homeless count were both gone. The hard, bright blue of a clear winter morning surrounded her.

A vibration in her pocket startled her. She reached for her phone with trembling hands and came away with the device along with a small square packet. It was one of the handwarmers Stirling had given her, now stiff and cold.

Melissa set the phone down on the passenger seat, afraid to look at the display. Instead she stared outside, trying to figure out where she was. Diagonally across from the corner, the scaffolded building they had entered the night of the count rose over the rubble around it. Despite the sunshine, the low structure sat in a pool of darkness. Even the layers and layers of graffiti tags scrawled across all the boarded windows seemed muted.

How the hell had she gotten here? This was definitely not where she had parked when she met Stirling before the count. She shuddered. And how long had it been since she followed the EMT into that building? A few hours? A day? A week?

It had been decades since Melissa had fugued out like this. And what had her body been doing while her mind had gone missing?

The right thing to do would be to call 9-1-1 and have an ambulance take her to the hospital. A neuro exam. An EEG. An MRI. It would be so easy to fall back into the comforting routines of medicine and science.

She shuddered, but it wasn't from the cold. The car was warm. It had to have been running for some time.

Her phone buzzed again. This time, she glanced down at it, recognized the number, swore, and let it go to voice mail. The display glowed briefly with the time and date before dimming. Melissa exhaled. Only overnight, then. Which meant this was Tuesday morning. And she was supposed to be in her supervision meeting. A half hour ago. At least she hadn't missed any patient appointments. This was bad enough, and she'd have to apologize, pay for the missed session with Dr. Maxwell, and reschedule. Later.

First she had to figure out why this had happened now. After all this time. Her "episodes," as her mother had called them, were something Melissa had eventually outgrown, leaving behind only periodic ocular migraines and blistering headaches. Those she knew how to manage. Had been managing them nearly her entire life. But losing time and memories? That triggered a rising fear and shame she thought she'd buried a long time ago.

Stirling. Melissa had to find Stirling. He had been there with her. Maybe he could help her understand what had happened. Her mind kept replaying the wheel of a scintillating scotoma and a child-sized shape falling through its glow. Then nothing. The last time she had seen a doorway open where no door could possibly be, she had destroyed a friend's life. What had she done this time?

The building waited behind her. Perhaps there were answers there, but the thought of going back inside filled her with a dread she couldn't explain or ignore. She'd honestly rather face her therapist.

She also knew she shouldn't be driving anywhere right now. It was nothing short of a miracle that she hadn't gotten into an accident on her way here last night. Melissa turned off the car, cinched her coat tighter, and walked away from the ruined block toward the South End where there would be someplace she could stop for coffee, warmth, and the buzz of anonymous conversations. Even the bright morning sun couldn't chase the chill that had followed her out of the abandoned building. She jammed her hands in her pockets.

Besides the bone-deep weariness and cold, her head had begun to pound. If this followed the pattern of her childhood, a fully-fledged migraine would follow and she'd be good for nothing for hours.

As she walked, the neighborhood shifted from crumbling buildings, empty lots, and tent encampments to tree-lined streets and renovated brownstones with gardens behind ornate wrought iron gates.

She stopped at the window of a coffee shop, staring at the patrons inside. None of them lost time or saw portals to nowhere. Well, maybe some of the folks back at the intersection between Mass Ave and Melnea Cass Boulevard did, she thought mirthlessly.

The door jingled as she opened it. The smells of freshly baked pastries and brewing coffee tangled with the scent of her own fear and sweat, bringing her to the edge of nausea. Another gift of the migraines. Her stomach rumbled. Coffee first, then maybe food. Reach out to Stirling. Contact her therapist to reschedule. Go home. Shower.

Having a plan was good.

The coffee was basic, served in a heavy white china cup. There was a sign on the industrial drip machine: free refills. Not many coffee shops like this one left around town. She sat in a small booth and, for a few moments, wrapped her hands around the warm mug and breathed in the earthy scent. The headache hovered, but at a distance. After she emptied the coffee, Melissa pulled out her phone and found the email with Stirling's contact information. Her hand hesitated over the tiny virtual keyboard. What could she say that would get him to meet her but wouldn't have him show up with lights and sirens and a syringe full of Haldol?

Sighing, she tapped out a brief text: *About what happened last night. I need to talk to you. Can you meet me at...* She paused to glance at the sign on the door. *Sunnyside Up?* Had he told her what his daytime schedule was like? All Melissa knew was that he liked working the night shift. Would he even be awake now?

She gripped the phone so tightly that the buzz of the incoming message nearly made her jump.

You buying, Doc?

It took her three tries to reply. *You bet.*

Then she took a deep breath and composed a careful text to Julian Maxwell. Missing supervision meetings as a clinician was never a good sign. She'd known Julian as a colleague for a long time. He'd initially been surprised that someone with as many years in practice as she had was seeking supervision, but after her parents died, Melissa found herself questioning everything. She'd even considered leaving active practice. He was helping her find clarity.

She glanced down at her message and shook her head at how inadequate it seemed. *My sincere apologies. There was a medical emergency during the count. Do you have any available times today or tomorrow? - Dr. K.* There. At least it sounded rational and sane. She hoped.

Her head jerked up every time the door jingled, and her nerves were completely frayed by the time Stirling arrived. His eyes widened when he noticed her. Melissa had to fight the urge to flee.

"You look terrible, Dr. Klein," Stirling said as he shrugged off his coat and slid into the booth opposite her.

She smiled at his sudden formality. "Why thank you, Mr. Hughes."

Before either of them could say anything else, the waitress glided by with a second cup and the carafe. "I'll be back to take your food order."

"Look, I've been doing the count for eight years and it never gets easy." His voice held a sympathy that Melissa wanted to wrap herself in. He probably pegged her as some sheltered suburban lady freaking the fuck out after her first up close and personal exposure to the destitute population of Boston. If only it were that simple.

"I need to know..." Her mouth was dry and she swallowed hard. "I need to talk about what happened in that building last night."

"Look. You did good. I'm sorry. I shouldn't have risked a rookie in there, but you seemed like you had a handle on it."

Melissa wanted to scream. "Do I look like I have a handle on it now?"

Stirling sighed and studied her. She knew what he was looking at: a middle-aged white woman with wavy salt and pepper hair in a wild mass around a face with no makeup, eyes deeply shadowed, last night's clothes looking as if she had slept in them.

"Please. Tell me what you saw."

He poured a generous helping of cream into his coffee and stirred it until it looked like a mocha vortex. When the liquid settled, he took a long sip. "I left the supplies and headed outside to wait for a minute or two. You were right behind me. All of a sudden you gasped and ran back in. Lady, you must have some next-level night vision. When I got close enough, all I saw was a bundle of dirty blankets. The next thing I knew, you were going all field medic."

Melissa held her breath.

"You really did great, Doc. Before I could even make out what was going on, you started CPR. You probably saved ..."

He paused. Swallowed. She frowned at the odd hesitation.

"...that girl's life. Bought enough time for me to get Narcan in her."

Something shadowed and vaguely human-shaped had fallen through the opening. A girl? She hadn't imagined it. Why couldn't she remember?

"Not too shabby for a shrink." When she didn't answer, Stirling reached across the table and placed a warm hand on her forearm. "Hey, Doc. I was just kidding."

She struggled to summon a smile for him, but the throbbing in her head was worsening. "I think I'm going to be sick," she mumbled, and ran to the bathroom. Trembling, she leaned over the toilet. Saliva pooled in her mouth, but all she could manage was a few dry heaves. Splashing cold water on her face helped bring her focus and clarity. Her new EMT friend had seen nothing more than another near death on Boston's streets. Nothing that would have explained her missing time, the geometric haze connecting here to somewhere else, her rising dread of the abandoned building.

There was a determined knock on the door. "Hey, Doc, you okay? You have an EMT right here. Just saying."

"I'm fine. Be right out." Melissa glared at the tired woman staring back at her in the mirror. "Get your shit together," she warned. "Before Stirling does something you'll regret."

She half expected him to be on the other side of the door, but he'd sat back down at their booth and was now studying her as she walked across the room.

"I'd say that shock can really mess a person up, except you managed like someone who'd seen combat trauma. No hesitation. No fear. You knew what to do and you did it. So why do you look like you've seen a ghost this morning?"

For an instant, she considered telling him about the fugue states. The lost time. Her "imaginary friend," also lost because of her. But as sympathetic as the big EMT was, she barely knew him— and this was not something you laid on a stranger. Especially one with the power and the mandate to report her as an impaired physician. "It wasn't the girl or doing the homeless count. I don't know. Something about that building freaked me out. I'm sorry I wasted your time." She reached for the slim wallet she kept in the inside coat pocket. The least she could do was pay for their coffees and the time they had monopolized the booth.

"No worries, Doc, I was going to text you today anyway. I didn't get a chance to tell you before I transported her, but I took her to the ER at BMC. In case you wanted to check in."

She gripped the edge of the table to keep her hands from shaking. "I don't have admitting privileges at Boston Medical. And I suspect her needs right now aren't psychiatric."

"Still, you saved a life last night. That's never trivial. Maybe seeing her will ease your mind a bit."

Her free hand jingled the keys in her pocket. The pull of a hot shower and her bed was almost overpowering. But Stirling was right. And maybe seeing the girl would help her remember.

"Like I said last night, for what it's worth, I think this is the kind of work you have a calling for, Doc." Stirling smiled at her, a smile with more than a little sadness in it. "Not quite as lucrative or as prestigious as a university position, but still."

Melissa tossed a twenty on the table before she and Stirling slid out of the booth. She laid her hand on the EMT's arm. "Thanks. That means a lot. More than you know."

His eyes focused on her weary face, and for a moment she was sure he saw everything she'd worked so hard to keep hidden. "You have my number. I'm here. Anytime you need a friend."

As he left the diner, Melissa wiped the sudden wetness from her eyes.

δ

Jace Vettel

JACE WOKE FROM UNEASY dreams and opened his eyes to harsh overhead light, a rising din of voices, and the smell of burnt coffee. At least it masked the scent of sweaty bodies and damp clothing. He sat up at the edge of the cot. The thin blanket slid from his lap and pooled at his feet. All around him, men were stirring. Their faces spanned the gamut of shades from pale to dark, but they all shared the same gazes—hard and haunted.

"Good morning," a voice boomed from an overhead speaker. Jace flinched. "The time is 7 a.m. The line for breakfast is open. Please take all your belongings with you. Anything left behind will be discarded."

Some of the men had bags with what Jace presumed were their things. Too many, like him, had only the clothing they wore. So little, yet the people running the Safe Harbor Mission would throw it away. It didn't make sense.

As people vacated their beds, others walked the aisles stripping the cots and tossing the bedding and blankets in piles on the floor. Some gathered the piles into carts and presumably took them to be laundered. Once the cots were bare, the men who had stripped them folded and stacked them against the wall. With a quiet, desperate efficiency, they turned the room into an open space.

No one talked or made eye contact with him as Jace joined the line snaking its way to a room full of toilets and sinks. When he'd been a Network trainee, he'd been housed in a communal dormitory. But it had been nothing like this. He and the other junior agents had had their own beds and small private storage lockers. And as much as Jace ultimately came to hate everything the Network stood for, at the time, the cohort of trainees had banded together to become a community.

He followed the scent of coffee into another room with a line of tables across one wall. The men serving behind the tables looked no less desperate than Jace felt. As he reached the front of the line, someone handed him a disposable cup half filled with black coffee. A second man passed him a tray and a plate. A third dropped a single piece of plain bread and a hunk of bright yellow cheese on the plate.

By the time he returned to the room where he'd slept, it was set up with long tables and folding chairs. He walked over to one that was mostly empty and sat apart from the two men already there. The bread was stale. The cheese had little smell and less taste. The coffee, bitter. Maybe that's what it was like, here. The heat of it was worth the bite on his tongue.

He rubbed his eyes. When he'd arrived last night, he'd been asked by the guards if he had any weapons. They wouldn't have understood—his very presence was a danger. And so was the possibility of unleashing a greater Network response.

Another announcement intruded on his thoughts. "All overnight guests need to exit in fifteen minutes. The medical clinic opens at nine."

The two men at his table grumbled and piled their trash on the small tray from the food line.

"Lenny got roughed up by the cops again last night." The man who spoke had a rasping voice and a thick, ridged scar down the side of his face.

His companion shrugged. He had lighter skin and stringy gray hair that hung past his shoulders. "I warned him. Saw the construction signs go up a week ago."

"You back here tonight?"

"Yeah. Almost got enough saved up for my half of a hostel room. Maybe one or two more days? You?"

"That works."

The long-haired man nodded. "It'll be good to get a hot shower."

"Yeah."

The two men noticed Jace listening and glared at him before pushing away from the table, leaving him sitting alone again. He didn't blame them. Even under the best of circumstances, trust wasn't easy to find. He tore the bread on his plate into smaller and smaller pieces. It was no more palatable. Nothing about his situation was.

He tried to imagine Corinne and Reina sitting at home, having their morning meal, but something of the desolation of this place stole into his heart. Even the thought of Reina's laugh and the intelligence in her bright eyes couldn't lighten his mood.

As if thinking about her was the trigger, Jace's dreams from last night flooded through his mind. There was an old building clad in rusted scaffolding. Reina was trapped inside, pressed under the weight of crumbling bricks. He tried to run to her but was rooted in place as if the stones were weighing him down instead of her. His heart hammering, he screamed her name, but the wind snatched his voice away. Then he was transported to a place he recognized from his early Network days. It was one of hundreds of oasis worlds that were perfect training grounds for new agents. In his dream, the place was a beach; he sat above the tide line as the murky water lapped closer and closer. Corinne was walking up the beach toward him and he called out her name. But she was already speaking to someone else. A stranger Jace didn't recognize. When the two of them reached him, he tried to catch her attention, tried to warn her about Reina and the danger she faced, but Corinne walked right by him as if she didn't or couldn't see him. He woke before the water could swallow him.

Dreams were just fictions. They had no true power in the multiverse, but seeing his daughter struggling and hurting, being helpless to rescue her, broke something in him and he laid his head in his hands on the cold metal table. He never should have left them.

"Sir?"

Jace started and glanced up. A dark-skinned young man wearing a bright white shirt and gray pants stood across the table from him. The quiet intensity in his gaze reminded Jace of a junior agent he had once trained. Too earnest for his own good, just like his long lost protégé.

"The clinic is starting. If you need any medical services, I can put you on the list." He held a clipboard in his hand.

"I don't need any help." Jace's voice sounded harsh and overly loud in the now empty room and he winced as the man gripped the list close to his chest and stepped away from the table. His gaze flicked over to the door where several large guards stood. "Thank you. I'm fine," Jace said, more gently this time, keeping his hands relaxed in front of him. "I was just leaving."

He nodded and backed away.

Jace waited until he had gone before standing. The guards stared at him as he emerged outside into the raw and gray day.

The Boston streets were thick with vehicles. People crowded the walkways, veering around him as if he didn't exist. Everyone seemed to know where they were going. Jace was already shivering. He regretted not snagging one of the thin blankets from the shelter, though the guards would have probably seized it. This place was cold in so many ways.

He had to make a choice. Standing here wouldn't get him any closer to Corinne and Reina. The guards were still watching him as if loitering near the shelter was some sort of local crime. Jace picked a random direction and started walking. At least it wasn't snowing.

Struggling to keep his anger and frustration in check, Jace studied his surroundings. He'd kept track of the route the taxi had taken last night and realized he'd been heading back to the library. It would be warm and dry there. And if shelter was all he needed, he could at least survive for a time. He had done so with less before. But never with so much at stake.

The sun streamed through breaks in the clouds as he walked, finally warming his chilled and weary body. Two days of trying and Jace was no closer to opening a way home. He couldn't wait any longer. There was nothing at the library, despite all its stored knowledge, that could help him now. The Network cache and its resources were his only hope, regardless of the danger.

He was long past worrying what might happen to him. From the moment Reina had begun to show her ability, he knew he'd had to act. And that he would risk everything to ensure her a future free of the Network. He twisted the ring on his thumb. Useless now, either as a focus for Travel or to retrieve the proof he had collected. But he could use himself as bait. Lure the Network to follow him, keep them from finding Corinne and Reina. If only he had one final chance to explain it all to them. But they could hate him or believe he was as deranged as his father had become—it would all be worth it if his family was free.

Perhaps there was an alternative world in which they all found their way to safety. If he'd been a better man, imagining their lives otherwise might have given him at least some kind of comfort; as it was, it only sharpened his resentment of what could have been.

A cold wind whipped around the nearest building and set him shivering again. Jace walked faster, trusting his training and his senses. If this was where the interstitial space was thinnest, this would be where the Network had seeded a cache. As soon as Jace stopped fighting to stay hidden, it was as if a beacon began to ping at a painfully high pitch. He followed the vibration through the serpentine streets of Boston. The closer he came to the cache, the more anxious he felt and the worse the pain in his head became.

He stumbled to a stop at a busy intersection to catch his breath. The pressure was a steady drumbeat now. It wasn't too late. He could still walk away. The Network would never find him here. But he would be trapped, separated from Corinne and

Reina forever. Leaving them at the mercy of the Network. And Harnett Wellerman.

"You promised to get him help!" Jace had shouted at the man who'd once been like family to him. Behind him, the doctors covered his father's body with a clean white sheet before leaving the room.

"There was nothing we could do." Harnett Wellerman stood near the bed, his perfectly tailored suit in stark contrast to Jace's clothes, rumpled from sleeping in the chair next to his father's hospital bed. "By the time you called us in, it was already too late."

Jace collapsed into the chair in the corner of the room, his cheeks burning. He couldn't bring himself to look at the shrouded body of his father. "And whose fault was that?" There was always an assignment. Always a critical need for Jace to be deployed in the field. And always Wellerman's promises. "I should have been here for him."

"We did everything possible. He was comfortable to the end."

Before he had any conscious awareness of his own actions, Jace had leaped from the chair and punched Wellerman square in the face. As blood poured from the agent's nose, three hospital orderlies seemed to materialize out of nowhere to crowd the room. Two of them tackled Jace and pinned him to the ground. The third handed Wellerman a towel.

"It's okay. Let him up," Wellerman said. "I suppose I deserved that."

"What the hell?" Jace shouted as one of the orderlies pulled a syringe from his pocket.

"That won't be necessary." Wellerman turned to Jace. "Will it?"

Was that what they had done to his father? Jace swallowed hard and shook his head. The orderly glanced back at Wellerman before slipping the drug back in his pocket. He and his fellows faded down the corridor, but Jace knew they weren't gone. This was a Network facility, and he was a Network agent. If they deemed him a danger to himself, others, or the mission, they wouldn't hesitate to act.

He couldn't bear the thought of Reina or Corinne in some hospital room, powerless to escape.

Giving up and abandoning them wasn't a choice. The resources he could access in the cache might give him the edge he needed to save them. He had to hold on to that hope.

People flowed around him on the busy streets. No one made eye contact. No one even brushed past him. It was as if he didn't exist. And in some ways it was true: Even before he had made his escape with Corinne, he had already vanished from his own life.

After his father died, Wellerman had arranged for two weeks of compassionate leave and grief counseling. It wasn't for Jace's benefit but for the Network's. They had to ensure he wasn't showing any signs of the disorder they claimed had killed his father. The irony in needing the Network's resources to determine that was abundantly painful.

Maybe everything would have been different had Jace escaped the Network then, but he had been determined to find proof that they were responsible for his father's illness and death. A few months later he'd met Corinne. The price of keeping his increasing dread of the Network a secret from her in the years that followed is what stranded him here, alone. And possibly about to make the biggest mistake of his life.

A car speeding by sent a wave of icy slush over his legs and feet. He knew it was a bad sign that he barely felt the added cold. This world could kill him as easily and as casually as the Network. To survive long enough to lead them away from his family, he had to find the resources to fight both.

And that meant risking the cache. Every choice involved risk. It was something he taught the agents under his training. *What you push, pushes you.* It was a lesson he'd do well to remember now.

It felt like he'd been walking for days, but judging from the shadows, it had only been a few hours when he found himself in front of a large, brick-faced building that took up most of the block. A constant stream of people moved in and out of multiple doors. The pressure in Jace's head suddenly vanished. The cache was here.

Chapter 8

Harnett Wellerman

SWEEPING THE COMMS DEVICE from his desk, Harnett glared as the rugged machine bounced twice before rolling under his bed. The message from Aisa Oswald was couched as a routine communication, but its timing was unmistakable. Either his query had raised an alarm or she had placed her own tracker on Jace Vettel and wanted to ensure she got to the rogue agent first.

Harnett had to be careful. Ignoring the summons was not an option. He gathered up all of the material he'd collected on Jace and his family and stashed it away in the tiny cache he'd modified. Let them come and search while he was occupied with Oswald. They would only find what he wanted them to find.

He took the time to change his clothes and check his appearance before stepping into the stable Moment that linked his apartment to Network Headquarters. It deposited him at the front steps of a building that was meant to be imposing: a large white marble structure, a line of columns around its perimeter etched with historical scenes from critical events across the multiverse. A reminder of the power and influence of the Multiverse Travelers Network. A logo with its stylized lettering–MTN–was everywhere. Harnett suppressed a smirk. The way the acronym evoked the word *maintain* had always struck him as the height of conceit.

Carved into the steps was the Network's motto: Guiding the Greatest Good. Even as a young trainee, he had seen the propaganda for what it was. It amused him to notice how the words had been scuffed and erased in some places.

Inside the ornate doors, an enormous lobby space vanished into deep shadows at the edges of the room. Agents in identical gray suits moved across the terrazzo floors, their shoes clicking against the tile, until they reached one of a near-infinite number of stable Travel corridors and disappeared into silence.

No concierge or contingent of guards was necessary. The building itself was far less important than the nexus of mapped Moments within it. Those were the real power, and only Network agents would be able to Travel to headquarters. Once inside, just those specifically summoned would be given access to the relevant administrative section.

Harnett remembered his first visit here after Aisa had recruited him. How confident she seemed to be as she explained the purpose of the Network and showed him how to navigate the bewildering space. How awed he had been. Of her. Of the building. And of those who controlled the ways through the multiverse.

He had craved that sense of control. And the Network had used his weakness to their advantage. He had been young. On the run. Filled with a heady mix of triumph and fear after escaping his father. They barely had to do anything to convince him. He was one of the few. The gifted. But even then, he had understood the importance of keeping his own secrets.

Harnett smoothed the fabric of his jacket and strode toward the way provided for him.

There was the briefest instant of disorientation—perfectly designed to keep an agent humble—and then he was through, stumbling to a stop in Aisa's new office. Like her, it was free from ornamentation or distraction. A single large desk took up the center of the room. Smooth and black, it looked like it had been carved from stone. It was lit from above, creating a cone of brightness that illuminated only its empty surface, leaving the rest of the office draped in darkness. Harnett set his jaw and waited, his hands clasped behind him. This was a game where he didn't set the rules.

"Harnett." Aisa Oswald's voice emerged from the darkness an instant before the light shifted and she appeared, sitting in a high-backed chair made from the same inky material as the desk. He wondered what reality it had been harvested from. She was dressed in a sharply tailored black suit flecked with subtle silver accents that shimmered slightly as she leaned forward. Aisa had come a long way since she had been Harnett's handler. Now she supervised a cadre of senior agents and reported to those who made the critical decisions for the Network's future.

"Aisa." Harnett nodded. It appeared as if she'd finally crossed some invisible divide that reminded him he would always be on his side of that line. But this could also be an opportunity: the higher she rose, the less connection she would have with the work on the ground. His work.

She set down a slim folder before folding her hands together. "We have an assignment for you."

Of course she did. Either she knew he'd located Jace or she was fishing for a reaction. It didn't matter which. Harnett needed to play his part regardless.

Aisa pushed the folder toward the front of the desk. Harnett stepped forward to take it, but she didn't relinquish the slim folio. He stiffened, his fingers inches from hers. She locked her ice-blue gaze on his. There had been a time where they had been, if not close, than at least collegial, but it was clear she had chosen to cut those ties.

"There is some concern among senior leadership about your recent performance."

"Yes, ma'am." That was as close as she would come to directly mentioning his failure to bring the Vettel family in. He had already explained himself in the official reports. There was nothing to be gained and too much to lose in trying to justify his actions. He kept his gaze low, still able to watch her eyes in his peripheral vision.

"There are some who wished to see you assigned elsewhere. I have personally vouched for you to remain in this division. Don't make me regret my continued support."

The last time she had "vouched" for him was after the disaster with Vettel's wife. Aisa had had him demoted. His seniority, the case he'd been working on for years, stripped from him. The basic fieldwork he'd been assigned to could have been completed by the most junior of agents.

"No, ma'am." Harnett struggled to keep his voice calm and even. Aisa seemed as controlled as ever, her silver-streaked hair in a tight bun at the nape of her neck, her expression and her body language quietly confident. And yet, even through his anger, Harnett could tell something felt off. She would never risk her position for anyone unless it benefited her. What could she possibly need from him, if not Jace Vettel?

She lifted her hand from the file, and he picked it up.

"I will, of course, expect regular reports."

"Yes, ma'am." He didn't so much as glance at the folder. That would have to wait until he was dismissed.

Her lips quirked into a slight smile that Harnett would have missed had he not been studying her so intently. It both piqued his curiosity and raised the level of his concern. Whatever task this folder contained, it wasn't simply busywork to sideline him while they collected Jace. That would have been too simple for Aisa.

If she were making a play for an even greater leadership role in the Network, Harnett might be able to use her ambition to his benefit.

He slipped his orders under his arm and bowed his head briefly.

The light overhead dimmed. Aisa vanished. The abrupt dismissal was a message, too. Just like every part of this meeting, from summons to assignment. From here on, Harnett had to act as if every move he made was being tracked. Which made his next steps that much more difficult.

Whatever this file contained, Harnett wasn't going to let Jace or his family slip away again.

δ

Melissa Klein

HER PHONE BUZZED AS Melissa walked out of the diner and into the cold harsh day. The terse reply from Julian Maxwell was more or less what she had expected, but it contrasted with Stirling's warmth and concern. *3 p.m. Today.*

When she got back to her car, a bright orange ticket was tucked under the windshield wiper. Melissa was oddly grateful to be annoyed by something so normal. She was grateful, too, for the hospital web portal that let her reschedule the few patients she was seeing during her sabbatical without having to speak to anyone.

As much as she would have loved to go home first for a shower and a change of clothes, she knew that once she got there, she'd stay there until her therapy appointment. At which point, Melissa was going to have to figure out what to tell Julian that didn't end up with her being reported to the medical board.

Maybe Stirling was right. Maybe seeing the girl she'd saved would help. Her hands shook as she slotted the key in the ignition and started the car. According to the GPS, it would take her twenty-five minutes to get home to Belmont. Ignoring the familiar directions and the buzzing of messages and voicemails on her phone, Melissa drove to the Boston Medical Center instead. And as if the universe were supporting her nonsensical choice, she found a parking space with a broken meter on the street just a block away.

Grumbling to herself, she grabbed the spare lab coat she kept in the back seat and dug into her glovebox for her ID lanyard. While it was true she didn't have admitting privileges at BMC, she did supervise students during their rotations there. And visiting a patient wasn't a HIPAA violation.

She silenced her still-buzzing phone and shoved it in the bottom of her coat pocket before tossing the coat into the car. There would definitely be fallout from canceling the day. The back of her head started to throb. First see the girl. Then collapse. Then damage control.

As she walked into the hospital lobby, she hesitated. Their Jane Doe didn't have a name, as far as Melissa knew. Hard to ask for a patient when you didn't know who the patient was. She waved to the receptionist and indicated her ID before turning down the hall to the ER.

The waiting room was relatively quiet for a city emergency room. That would likely change later. Melissa walked up to intake. A young Black woman with a coiled mass of braids woven around her head looked up from her terminal.

"Good morning. I'm Dr. Klein. We brought a young girl here last night from the homeless count. Do you know if she's still here?

The receptionist raised an eyebrow. "Do you know how many John and Jane Does come through here in a night?"

"No. Not really." Stirling would definitely have known. Her face heated. She should have known.

"Too many." The woman sighed. "What time was yours brought in?"

Melissa had to reconstruct the timeline. They'd gotten to that last building around eight thirty. "Sometime between nine and nine thirty."

She nodded and bent to her terminal.

"Oh, the one Stirling brought in."

"Yes."

"You working with him?"

"Yes."

The woman's face softened and she nodded. "Stirling Hughes is good people. Yeah, she's still here. Her name is Daniella Lopez. Room 7. Dr. Bhavsar is the attending physician today."

"Thank you." Melissa's breath eased out in a sigh. CPR in the field was often a crap shoot. The girl got lucky.

She hesitated again before walking into the ER. The dissonance of hospital monitors had formed the soundtrack of her parents' final year and the slow-motion disaster of trying to manage it all. It was becoming harder and harder to push those memories away.

Most of the treatment cubicles were empty, their curtains pulled back. A few staff members clustered at the nurses' station.

Aside from a brief glance and a nod from a nurse, no one paid any attention to her. Melissa felt uneasy about walking in to see a girl she had no memory of treating, but now that she'd come this far, she couldn't back out.

She took a deep breath and asked for Dr. Bhavsar. A young man turned toward her. His dark hair and skin contrasted with the starched white lab coat. He hardly looked any older than the first-year medical students she lectured.

"Sanjay Bhavsar. Hospitalist and ER doc." He held out his free hand.

Melissa shook it. The man's hand was firm and well calloused. Not overpowering. Probably a first-year attending, but without the bravado and bluster so many of them showed. "Melissa Klein."

He squinted at her ID. "MGH?"

"Psychiatry. I have a teaching appointment there."

"What can I do for you, Dr. Klein?"

"Please, call me Melissa."

"Well, Melissa, what brings you to my ER?"

She felt less certain of herself by the minute. "The young woman transported last night from the homeless count? Daniella Lopez? I'm the one who found her. I wanted to check in on her."

"You stabilized her on the scene?"

Did it count when she couldn't remember? "Yes."

"What's an academic doing saving lives on Boston streets?" His voice was filled with warmth and genuine curiosity.

"Midlife crisis?" She gave a sideways smile and shrugged. It was as true an answer as any and simpler than anything she was willing to share outside a therapy session. "How's she doing?"

"Between your quick response and the Narcan the EMT administered, she's alive. She coded again last night, but I think she's through the worst of it." He shook his head. "She shows signs of long-term drug use and anorexia. Hard to say what the effects of the drugs, the malnutrition, and the code have had on her cognitive status."

"What will happen to her?"

Bhavsar sighed. "She's stable now. We're still hydrating her, but we'll need to discharge her soon."

"Back to the streets?"

"We have Social Services working to contact any family she might have. Otherwise, we'll release her to an emergency foster placement."

"I'm not sure I did her any favors."

Bhavsar set the chart he was holding on the counter of the nurses' station with slow deliberation. "That's not for any of us to determine, Doctor."

Shame heated her face and she turned away from the dark intense eyes of the young attending.

"Do you want to look in on her?"

Melissa nodded, even though her palms were slick with sweat and her stomach was knotted up.

Bhavsar strode toward a cubicle and pulled the curtain aside for her. "I'll give you a minute."

Get a grip on yourself, she thought. You're a doctor. You know how to do this. After a pause, she walked in, hoping habit would help her find the right words to say.

The beeping of a heart monitor was the only sound aside from soft, rhythmic breathing. The girl was asleep, nearly dwarfed by blankets. Both side rails were up. Someone had tied back her wavy brown hair from her face. Melissa stared down at her, willing her mind to latch on to something it recognized. Anything.

She sat on the chair beside the bed and laced her hands together. "I'm Doctor Klein," she whispered. "I found you last night." Maybe the words would have the power to make her remember. "I don't really know why I'm here, but I wanted to make sure you were okay."

The girl's eyes hadn't opened and her breathing hadn't changed. Nor had the steady rhythm of her heartbeat. "I sorry. I don't know anything about you," Melissa whispered. With a trembling hand, she reached out to touch the girl's face.

"Maybe someday you will."

The ER doc had slipped into the room behind her. Melissa startled and snatched her hand away. "Thank you for your time, Dr. Bhavsar."

His face softened. "Sanjay. Please."

She nodded and left him to look after his patient, wondering when she had lost that passion and spark. Perhaps he would be able to hold onto it longer than she had.

δ

Jace Vettel

JACE GLANCED AROUND THE transit terminal, hesitating. No one paid him any attention, but he still had the lingering sense of being watched. It set the hair on his arms and the back of his neck tingling in a primitive warning. He took a steadying breath. Once he triggered the sigil, the Network would be alerted to his presence. Nearly thirteen years of hiding and sacrifice, obliterated in one desperate act.

The entrance to the cache revealed itself. His heart raced.

Memories of missions on countless worlds came flooding back. Each cache was identical: A short corridor opened into a rectangular room with the data center and printers that produced whatever an agent might need. It allowed for maximum efficiency, especially in cases of emergency. For the smallest of moments, the years rolled away and Jace was a junior agent again, on his first solo trip, preparing to enter a reality just a few degrees of separation from his own.

He stepped inside the narrow entry that anchored the pocket dimension.

A gasp shattered his concentration. It was too late. The Network was here. Waves of hot and cold moved through his body. They had found him. It was over. He growled softly. No. Not over. They hadn't gotten to his wife and his child and they wouldn't. Ever. Even if it was the last act of his life. He glanced around, not seeing the bland surroundings, but searching for something, anything he could use as a weapon.

"Jace!"

He shook his head. Corinne's voice in his memory was so strong. He kept reliving bits of the last conversation he'd had with her. An argument. He regretted that, but he had to stay focused in the here and the now.

His hands curled into fists. Whoever was here had to move past him to get out of the cache. Jace wasn't going to let that happen.

The scrape of a chair on the hard floor. They were coming. The back of the cache was in shadow. They were coming.

"Show yourself!" His voice echoed harshly off the polished walls.

"Jace, it's me."

No. It couldn't be. No. She couldn't be here. Jace started to shake. Sweat dripped into his eyes. He tried to blink them clear as his enemy walked toward him.

CJace."

The hand that brushed his fist was cool, smooth, familiar. It eased open his fingers and pressed gently palm to palm. Their twin rings clinked together softly.

"Corinne?" His voice cracked and he swayed on his feet. "No. You can't...this isn't..." He gripped her hand, hard.

Her amber eyes were bright, shiny with unshed tears. Her lips were pressed tightly as if she was holding back the years of frustration from all their past arguments. Jace had to look away from the anger in her expression. Then he frowned at the empty room beyond her. "Where's Reina?"

"You went away without us. We waited. You didn't come home." She snatched her hand away from his.

"Where is Reina?" he asked slowly, carefully, as if she hadn't understood his question.

"She's safe. You know I couldn't risk her making the transit. She wasn't ready."

"Alone?" Jace's voice cracked. "You left her alone?"

"Of course not. My parents are taking care of her."

"Your parents abandoned us."

"No, Jace. You abandoned us." Corinne emphasized each word as if it were its own universe.

Jace's cheeks burned. "I had no choice. Everything I've done was for you. For her. You told me you understood."

"Jace—"

He shook his head, cutting her off. "We have to get out of here. Somehow. Get back to her. Try again. It might not be too late." He reached for Corinne, but she stepped away.

"You have no idea what you've done."

"What *I've* done?" Jace couldn't control the fury shaking his voice. When Corinne had confessed she'd secretly returned to the Network, it had nearly broken their marriage. Keeping Reina safe was the one thing—the only thing that had kept them together. Was she lying to him now? "Why did you come here? What have you told the Network?"

Her face flushed and her eyes narrowed, but he didn't give her a chance to speak.

"Because of you, Wellerman has had months to sniff out a trail right to us. And you left Reina without anyone to protect her."

"What did you expect me to do? Lie to Reina until she realized you were never coming back? Or wait for you to trigger some catastrophe across the multiverse?"

"Even after everything, you still don't understand." Jace hated the note of panic in his voice.

"I understand you love our daughter." Her reply was so soft, he feared he'd imagined it.

"If you never believed me, why did you run away with me all those years ago? Why protect her from the Network?"

Corinne opened her mouth to speak, then snapped it shut before taking a deep breath and starting again. "I couldn't—I couldn't lose you. Reina couldn't lose you. Not like you lost your father." She choked back a sob. "And if there was even the slightest possibility you were developing RDD, I couldn't take the chance that it would affect Reina, too."

Everything in him wanted to reach out to Corinne, to gather her in his arms. "But you hedged your bets. Kept your contacts with the Network. Was that all you did? Or were you spying on us for them?"

"How could you say that? I gave up everything for you."

"If you had, truly, then we wouldn't be here." That was the crux of it. The core of their trust, once unshakable, now fractured beyond repair.

Corinne paced the short side of the room's rectangle, her cheeks flushed, her jaw clenched. "Do you really want to have this argument again? Here? Now?"

"Fine." Jace's anger cooled to an icy fear. He needed Corinne. Now, more than ever. They weren't safe. This would be the first place Wellerman would come. They needed to grab whatever resources they could and maybe together, they'd be able to force their way home. "But we don't have much time. I don't like the idea of Reina alone." She was far too vulnerable. If someone from the Agency found her, they would convince her to go with them. Even Corinne couldn't want that.

He turned toward the cache's printers. She gripped his arm with surprising strength and spun him around to face her.

"Did you know?"

"Know what?"

"This." Corinne thrust a crumpled sheet of paper at him. "If it's all true, we're trapped here."

"What are you talking about?" He didn't want to take the report. The Network had compiled it. Jace remembered studying dozens and dozens of précis just like this, in the concise, carefully neutral language of MTN analysts.

"Read it." Corinne wouldn't let him go, wouldn't shift the report away from his face.

"We can't trust anything they tell us. Just standing here is a risk. We need to go."

"Not until you look at this."

He tried to turn away, but her gaze was too insistent. "They're trying to force our hand. Make us panic."

"Oh, believe me, I'm far past panic." She shook the report with every word. "This is an interdicted world. Quarantined to four levels. Did you know that when you planned all this?" Her eyes were fever bright.

"No. It can't be." He took the sheet from Corinne's hand and quickly scanned it. All the warmth drained from his body. He couldn't stop shivering. No wonder he couldn't find a way back. This was a quicksand world that would swallow careless Travelers and leave no trace behind. "They're lying."

"Did you even try to come home?"

"Of course I did! I would never leave you and Reina! I told you I'd be back." He met Corinne's gaze and flinched from the pity and pain he saw in it. And the anger. "You shouldn't have followed me."

"What did you expect me to do? You made a promise to Reina. I couldn't keep lying to her."

"Now we've both failed her."

Anger flared in her eyes. She snatched the report and tossed it across the cache. "You may have given up, but I won't. Not now. Not ever."

Chapter 9

Reina Vettel

VOICES CAME AND WENT. Light and shadow flickered through the window. Reina drifted, trapped in a state that wasn't quite awake, but wasn't asleep either. The fear was still there, but its edge was blunted. A discordant beeping made it hard for her to think clearly, but she knew she needed to find a way out of this place.

Reina's mind kept replaying her journey. The nothingness of the void between worlds. The whirlwind. The vertigo. The terrifying, endless fall. The memories wouldn't stop. She had done everything her parents had taught her. If she concentrated, she could feel the edges of the stone she had chosen as an anchor, but in this here and now, she knew her hand was empty.

A sharp throbbing in her wrist pulled her back into the room where nothing made sense. Not the signs on the wall, not the harsh brightness of the light in the ceiling, not the body that wasn't her own.

The skin on this stranger's arm was darker than hers. The muscles of the forearm, more defined but also scrawnier. The fingers were longer and more delicate. The nails had dirt beneath them, and the cuticles were ragged. A small tube stuck out of the skin. If not for the pain, Reina could believe she was simply looking at someone else's body. But her mind's reaction insisted this was her arm. Her hand.

She knew she should be terrified, and somewhere in the back of her mind she could catch the echo of her own voice crying out. But it was as if her emotions were being smothered under a heavy winter quilt. Maybe it was better this way. Reina thought if she started screaming, she might never stop.

The pressure to move built and built until Reina thought she would scream. But that would bring the people back, and the alarms, and the terrible twilight that brought the dark dreams.

If she could only shift the position of her wrist, then she could rest and breathe. Reina's whole world narrowed down to the creased brown skin and the clear tube. She'd never had to think about moving before. Her body had always just done what she wanted it to do. But this wasn't her body.

What had happened to the person whose skin she now wore? Was her body walking around with some other person animating it?

Her father had warned her about the dangers of Traveling through the world walls. He'd never said anything about this. When they Traveled, they physically moved from world to world. Reina must have done something wrong. Did that mean this was her fault?

Hello? Are you there? Reina strained to hear a response. Anything. A change in breathing, a cry, a movement. Anything. *I'm sorry. I don't know how I got here.* A pulse of terror broke through the numbness. Was her own body dead?

Please. Help me. I don't know what to do. Her voice echoed in the cavern of her mind.

Heat swirled in her chest. Tears streamed down the stranger's cheeks in response. Reina felt their warmth at a distance. They were hers, yet not hers.

There was no one else. Reina was alone in a hollow shell.

A sob burst from her, the strangled sound loud against her borrowed ears. And still the arm throbbed. If she could just move it. Her vision blurred, but she couldn't wipe away the tears. She squeezed her eyes shut. Frustration silenced the pain. The urgency eased. Her wrist straightened and the throbbing stopped.

It was replaced by a flood of sensations so strong Reina nearly drowned in them. Her breath and the pulse beat of her heart were the howling of a storm's wind and the rumble of thunder. Her limbs felt thick and awkward. The muscles cramped. The throbbing in her head had returned, this time combined with a dizziness so profound she was certain she was falling. For a terrible moment, she feared she had slipped between worlds again.

She opened her eyes to painful brightness. Everything around her seemed outlined in thick, dark ink. A metallic taste filled her mouth. Reina swallowed blood and nearly gagged.

"Here. Let me help you."

Her head thrashed around on the pillow as Reina tried to find the source of the voice. Her body flopped on its side and almost slithered through the rails lining the sides of the bed. Someone leaned over her, eclipsing the glare from the overhead light. She couldn't identify the shadowed figure, but the woman's voice seemed kind. The hand that wiped Reina's mouth with a towel and helped her back into bed was as gentle as her mother's.

"Do you want to sit up a little?"

Reina nodded.

The woman pushed a button and the head of the bed moved. The room spun around her for another moment before the dizziness faded.

"I'm glad you're awake." In the light's glare, Reina could only see a round face surrounded by a nimbus of curly, dark hair. "I'm Alice Pearlmutter from Social Services. Do you know where you are?"

The odd doubling of voices remained. The sounds were a string of meaningless noise before they resolved into words she could understand. If Reina could make this body talk, would they understand her? Would she understand herself? And then what? The tears threatened to spill again. She shook her head.

"You're at the Boston Medical Center emergency department. They brought you in last night after your overdose."

She shook her head again.

"Your brother is here, but before we discharge you, I wanted to give you some resources for drug counseling. There's a group that meets in the hospital twice a week. There's no charge. Just show up. Okay?"

Reina blinked in confusion. Brother? She had no brother. Only a mother and a father who had vanished between the worlds. Or maybe it was she who had vanished from them. Everything about her transit had gone so wrong. There was no way to know if the Moment she'd followed had brought her to where they had gone. How could she have been so reckless?

She picked at the blanket with awkward hands. Then she turned them over and stared at their palms. Intersecting the lines on the left hand was a crescent-shaped scar. The same scar in the same place that had marked her real hand, her own hand as a child. A chill slid down her spine. "I don't understand," she whispered.

"I'm sorry." The woman set a sheaf of paper on the table next to the bed and sighed. "The nurse will be in soon to go over discharge instructions with your brother." She paused as if she wanted to say something more, but then shook her head and ducked outside the curtain to call someone.

Brother. This body had a brother. Would he help her? What would happen when he found out his sister was gone, replaced by a stranger?

Another sob broke the silence. Would she be trapped here forever? The tears that followed felt all too familiar.

When the curtain slid aside next, another pale woman wearing shapeless white pants and a long overshirt hurried in, talking to someone behind her Reina couldn't see. Like almost all the other helpers who had come to see her, this one also had a listening bell around her neck and a rectangular badge attached to her shirt pocket. "Make sure you fill that prescription before you leave the hospital."

A slender brown-skinned man holding a large bag slipped in behind her. His eyes widened and his lips trembled before he pressed them tightly together.

"It's important. She's going to need it to help with the detox."

He nodded.

This must be the brother. How could she tell him his sister was gone?

The woman helper turned to Reina. "Hello, Daniella. I'm Maryanne—the day nurse. I'm going to remove the IV now and talk about what you need to do next. Just keep your hand still, okay, hon?"

Daniella. This body had a name. She rolled the word around her mind, but nothing about it felt familiar. Reina finally nodded, not trusting the control over her voice, and watched the woman tug the tubing so she didn't need to meet the brother's gaze.

The nurse pressed some kind of bandage against her hand and covered it with tape. "There. Hold here. The bleeding should stop in just a few minutes." Then she turned away, lecturing the brother with complicated instructions Reina was helpless to understand. That strange word "detox" was mentioned more than once.

All through it, he kept nodding.

"Do you need help getting her dressed?"

"No," he said, his voice overly loud in the small room. He winced and softened. "I can take care of her."

Even Reina could see the nurse's skepticism.

Finally the woman left, and Reina had no choice but to look at him. The brother. He had wiry black hair cropped closely to his head and a dark beard and mustache. His chapped lips were pressed in a grim line. Sad eyes, full of disappointment and relief, stared at Reina from beneath heavy brows.

"Let me help you," he said. His voice had a soft lilt. It sounded kind. Reina hoped he would be kind. Even after she told him who she was.

He emptied his bag onto the edge of the bed. With gentle hands, he helped her put on soft pants and a top, short stockings and shoes. Then he wrapped her in a thick coat.

Reina waited for him to say something to her—anything—that would help her figure out how to talk to him. He only broke his silence to say "Let's go home."

Home. That was the small house near the sea she shared with her parents. Full of warm light from large windows and the accumulated knowledge of her parents' Traveler experience. A terrible clarity burned through her, and she knew she'd never return.

She stood to follow him out of the small room and stumbled. He stepped back and steadied her with a wiry but strong arm.

"Daniella, you promised me you were done with the drugs."

What did he mean? Drugs were what medics dispensed. Then she shuddered. Daniella. What had Reina done to his sister? Tears gathered in her eyes.

"It's gonna be all right. I'm sorry. Please don't cry. I'm not mad. It's just...I almost lost you the last time. I can't take that again."

Reina opened her mouth to speak, but closed it again, with no idea what to say.

"I swore I would keep you safe."

She turned away from the naked emotion on his face and followed him through the building, her eyes focused on the backs of his legs. It was the only way to handle the overwhelming strangeness of this place. There were more people in the hallways of the treatment facility alone than she usually saw in the course of a full day back home. The too-bright lights made her squint and created afterimages that were disturbingly like the Moment when the walls between the worlds thinned. How was she going to find her way out of here? Her strange body fought all her habits. Its strides were too long. Its footfalls too hard. Its breathing too labored.

He guided her to a rigid chair in a room filled with other waiting people. Reina stared at the floor.

"Don't move," he said.

As if she had anywhere to go.

Snatches of conversation made little sense and she let the words swirl past her. It felt like forever since he had left her here. Maybe he wasn't coming back. Maybe that was for the best.

"Okay. I have the stuff." His voice startled her. "Are you okay? Do you need a dose before we go?"

She shook her head. None of this made sense. Of course she wasn't okay.

He helped her up and led her with a steady hand at the small of her back, steering her past obstacles and outside into air colder than Reina could imagine. She gasped at the sharpness of it as it seared her lungs, and she coughed so hard her middle cramped. A light coating of snow covered the ground. Her eyes watered. Back home, it had been spring.

"It's okay. We don't have to walk. Stirling's waiting for us on the corner."

She didn't understand, but he was expecting some response so she nodded and kept walking. Cold crept up from the ground to chill her feet. Her legs felt heavy and stiff.

"There he is."

Reina bumped into him as he stopped abruptly. Looking up, she shuddered, but this time not from the temperature. The sun was a distant, pale orb that sent its harsh illumination down to a scene of utter chaos. Vehicles raced down a wide thoroughfare with barely a hairsbreadth between them before screeching to a halt under swaying lights. A wave of vertigo swept through her, and she emptied her stomach on the dark ground.

"Awww, shit," he said and steadied her.

She leaned against him, panting heavily.

Another man appeared at her side. "Here, let me."

His voice was rich and deep. With gentle, confident hands, he guided her toward a waiting vehicle. She stiffened but didn't have the strength to resist as the two men settled her on a seat and fastened a buckle across her body. It was a testament to her misery that Reina didn't even gasp as the vehicle roared into the road, narrowly missing ones on either side of it. The nausea threatened again. Shuddering, she closed her eyes.

"How did she find a new source, Martin?"

So that was his name. At least she didn't have to ask him.

"I don't know!" There was a sharp tone in his voice and Reina cringed. They were talking about her. Or the person they thought she was. "It's been over a year. She never missed a meeting. If I find out who slipped her that shit, I swear I'll kill them."

There was a moment of silence. The loud grumble of the vehicle filled the cabin.

"Don't do anything rash. She won't survive out here without you."

"She almost didn't, even with me."

"You were lucky this time. If we hadn't been there—"

"You don't think I know that?"

Stirling sighed. "You could return to the shelter."

"No." Martin's voice was grim, final. "They would split us up. You know they would."

"What about transitional housing? There's a new program…"

Martin snorted. "And how long are the waitlists for that? Five years? Ten?"

"This is no way to live."

Reina tried to follow the conversation, but there was too much about this world that didn't make sense. What she did understand was Martin cared about his sister. A surge of guilt brought fresh tears. She buried her face in her arms so they wouldn't hear her.

The two men fell silent. The roar of the vehicles all around them drowned out Reina's harsh breathing and her racing heart. Where were they taking her?

"Are you hungry?" Stirling spoke again. His resonant voice rumbled through the moving vehicle and made her feel safe. "I have a little while before my shift starts."

"I can take care of her!" Martin's reply cut through Reina's momentary comfort. Why was he so angry? "Just drop us and go."

"Martin—"

"Don't. You think I don't know how charity works?"

Reina frowned. Without charity, a community died. For all that her family had isolated themselves, they were still part of their town. Still offered and accepted help when help was needed.

"Thank you, Stirling. There. I said it. Good enough? 'Cause I'm not really feeling it today."

The vehicle rocked to a stop. Reina risked looking out of the window. A tall building stood etched against a painfully blue sky. Next to it, piles and piles of crumbling bricks lay within a tall metal fence. This was where Martin lived?

"I'm sorry, man." Stirling glanced back at her briefly before turning to Martin. "Look, you don't have to take any of it, but my church donated a box of warm winter clothes. Gloves, hats, scarves and stuff."

When Martin didn't answer, Stirling continued.

"If you don't want it, the little old ladies who did all that crocheting and knitting are gonna feel bad."

Martin's rigid shoulders eased. "Don't ever piss off aunties."

"Amen."

They both unbuckled their harnesses. Reina fumbled with hers, but couldn't figure it out. Martin leaned over her. A click, and she was free.

"Um, Stirling?"

"Yeah?"

"Can you grab the box? Leave it in the lobby. I'm gonna help Daniella."

"You got it."

δ

Martin Lopez

MARTIN STEERED DANIELLA THROUGH the cluttered lobby and to the stairwell without a glance back at Stirling. A twinge of guilt nearly turned him around. He knew he owed the big man an apology. More than that. If it weren't for him and that doctor last night, he would have lost his sister forever.

His hand briefly tightened on her arm. He forced himself to relax. It wasn't Daniella he was angry with. Martin was going to find the dealer who nearly killed his baby sister and make sure he couldn't hurt anyone ever again. Stirling didn't understand. This was Martin's home, and someone in it had broken his trust. That could not stand.

He knew every single person who sheltered in this building. With the exception of the new man and his dog. But they had come in long after Daniella had OD'd. Still, Martin would talk to him first. It would be easier on everyone if the dealer wasn't one of their own.

But first he had to get Daniella settled. She looked like shit. Even worse than she'd looked last year when she'd been actively using. Her eyes were a dull brown. The bags underneath looked like bruises. Her hair was a snarled mess. And she still hadn't said a word to him.

He guided her up the stairs to the little room they shared, away from the large open space where everyone else slept. "Room" was probably an exaggeration. It was just a corner, carved out and separated by a makeshift barrier of stacked crates and sheets hung from the open ceiling framework. But it was theirs. The only thing in this world that belonged to just them. And nothing was going to make Martin trade it for whatever false security Stirling thought they'd get from a shelter or some Social Services program.

As he settled Daniella on the ragged sofa, he thought he heard her sob, but when he glanced into her face, she stared at him with an expression so blank it made Martin shudder. "Are you okay? Does anything hurt?"

Daniella shook her head. Martin wasn't sure which question she was answering.

He pulled out the bottle of medicine from his pocket, trying to remember exactly what the nurse had told him. Stirling could help him understand the confusing instructions on the bottle, but he wasn't going to ask. No way was he going to give the EMT one more reason to push his way into their lives. Martin took a deep breath as the nurse's voice replayed in his head: three tablets four times a day for the next week.

He sat beside her, the ragged sofa creaking with the added weight. "It's gonna be okay. I'm not mad at you. Just tell me who you got the shit from."

"I don't know—" A coughing fit cut off the rest of what Daniella was going to say.

Martin reached for a water bottle from the supply crate next to the sofa, opened it, and handed it to her along with three pills. "You need to take these."

"I don't..."

"If you don't want them to take you away, take the damn pills."

Flinching, she glanced up at him, her eyes wide, before taking the medicine and chugging down all the water. She took a deep breath and Martin forced himself to wait for her to speak. She would have to tell him the truth in her own time. He knew that. It still wasn't easy.

"I don't know who you are."

"Daniella?" Martin's stomach dropped as if he'd been pushed down an elevator shaft. "What are you talking about?"

"I'm not her. Not Daniella. Not your sister."

He gripped her hands in his. "Cut it out. That's not funny."

She fought against his hold. "You're hurting me!"

"Fuck." Martin released her hands as if they had burned him. "I'm sorry. I'm sorry." He wondered if he could reach Stirling. Would he even come back? And if he did, would he take Daniella away for good? No. He had to handle this. Himself. "It's the drugs. They shoulda kept you in the hospital longer. You just need more time to get that shit out of your system."

Tears streamed down Daniella's face. Martin felt sick.

"You need to rest," he said finally, before standing and turning away from her. "Let the medicine work. Here." He dragged over a blanket from a pile of bedding in the corner and wrapped it around her. "Just sleep. There's something I have to do. I'll be back soon."

He paused by the curtain they used as a doorway and scrubbed the moisture from his eyes. What he needed now was the anger, not the pain.

δ

Corinne Vettel

JACE TURNED HIS BACK on her and started methodically raiding the supplies in the cache.

Corinne stepped between him and the well-organized shelves of basic clothing. "What are you doing?"

"We can't stay here," he said.

An all-too-familiar anger twined with fear, making her reply sharper than she intended. "Do what you need to do. I'm not leaving until I find a way back to Reina." She had given in to his disordered thinking far too many times.

The harsh lighting in the cache threatened to give her a headache. Corinne rubbed her eyes and wondered how much time had passed for her daughter. Reina must be furious. Repairing their relationship would have to be a priority when Corinne returned. Her heart skipped a beat. If.

"Corinne, please. He'll come here first."

He. Wellerman. Jace's first handler. By the time she and Jace had gotten together, he had already switched handlers. It wasn't common, but it also wasn't completely unusual. He was still reeling from the death of his father. Wellerman had also been his father's liaison and she understood why Jace might have wanted to work with someone else.

"You're not listening. No one from the Network is going to risk getting entangled here." The biggest danger—and Corinne was afraid to even voice it—was not being able to get to Reina. And if even the smallest part of Jace's ravings was true, their daughter was vulnerable.

"Someone set up this cache. And they have to be monitoring it. It isn't safe."

Neither was wandering through an unmapped world with a paranoid partner. The cache was likely the safest place for them. Once deployed, it ran autonomously, keeping the resources current and culturally appropriate. The unlucky agents who first scouted out this reality probably either assimilated into this world long ago or jumped through random Moments trying to get to a stable instance with a patent Network connection. That was the last choice Corinne wanted to make. The further you jumped, the weirder it got.

"Look, whoever they were, they're not here now." She tried for reasonable, but heard the familiar annoyance in her voice that came out when Reina had asked the same question for the thousandth time.

Jace was nearly vibrating with anxiety. There was no reasoning with him in this state. Corinne swallowed her rising fury and resentment, a sudden terrible realization breaking through: In literally any other set of circumstances, she would walk away. The man she loved, had worked with side by side, her life partner and father of their child, had become a stranger.

She wanted to weep with the futility of it all. Being trapped here with the only other person who cared about Reina's safety as much as she did and not being able to trust him was evidence of the capriciousness of the multiverse.

"Corinne, we need to go."

There was a finality to Jace's voice that chilled her. She stepped out of his way. "So go. I won't stop you."

"Do you have an ID?"

His sudden switch from agitation to efficiency nearly gave her whiplash. "What?"

"An ID. So we can secure lodging somewhere."

In his mind they were a team again. Corinne sighed. "Yes. Of course."

"Currency?"

"I have what looks to be a few days' worth, along with a payment card." This was the most basic of basic agent training. How could he not trust her to have done this first thing?

"Good. I don't want to spend any more time here than absolutely necessary."

"Fine. Take what you need." She tossed the gear bag toward him.

"What are you doing?"

She ignored him. It wouldn't be the most comfortable, but she could stay put. And then what? The cache wasn't actually part of this reality. It existed as a liminal space only tethered to it. She had to be physically present in the world outside in order to locate any potentials. The more she integrated into this reality, the better her senses would become.

Maybe Jace was right. Maybe finding lodging away from the cache made sense. It would make it easier to find a patent

Moment. To somewhere. Maybe the Network had missed something. She ignored the small voice in her head that warned about wishful thinking and moved toward the infostorage unit.

Jace frowned at her. "You know they can trace anything we request, right?"

"So what? For the last time, Jace, no one is monitoring this world. Why would they?" How could he not be focused on a way home to Reina? Corinne needed every advantage she could get. She had hoped that included Jace, but that was also wishful thinking.

As Jace hurriedly changed into warmer clothes, Corinne printed out a set of local ID for him. It was the least she could do. When the additional currency was ready, she shrugged into her coat and the boots she'd left to dry by the cache entrance. She could slip away. Disappear into the world and never look back. But she would never leave her daughter behind.

She squeezed her eyes shut on tears she had no time to shed and reached for the door into the transit area.

"Wait. Please." Jace's voice had softened.

Despite herself, she paused.

"I'm sorry. About everything."

Corinne shook her head. Apologies wouldn't unmake her choices or his. Wouldn't help her get home to Reina.

"If this report is real, then I...we'll be stronger together."

He sounded so reasonable.

"I can't undo the past. But I would do anything in my power to help Reina. If you believe nothing else, you have to believe that."

The pain in his voice matched her own anguish. How could she not pledge the same? Even if that meant working with Jace again. "I know." It wasn't trust and it wasn't forgiveness, but it would have to be enough.

He strode out of the cache, through the transit area, and into the city's streets with purpose. Corinne hesitated, then hurried to catch up with him. "Where are you going?"

"I found a library. We can search for local lodging there."

She nodded. It was a good choice to blend into a target population as much as possible. Corinne glanced at the people of the city. Fairly homogeneous, but part of that was the cold. Everyone looked the same, bundled up in bulky coats and hats. The cache-provided outerwear was in line with what others had on.

The walk helped Corinne focus and lean on her training. Her concern for Reina was background static in her mind. But if she could think of this as a mission, she could function.

"We're here."

Jace's soft voice pulled her from her thoughts.

The library was a stunning and impressive building. This world must prize knowledge. That seemed like a good sign. So why was it interdicted? Too many questions and not enough data. She followed Jace up the stairs and inside.

He seemed to know his way around the building and was using the local tech without any apparent difficulty. Corinne sat in a comfortable chair close enough to keep an eye on him, but far enough away that no one would assume they were working together. It was so simple to fall back into their old partnership. But could she trust him to do his part?

She studied his lined face. Had Wellerman been right? Did Jace have Reality Disintegration Disorder? All agents were trained to watch for the signs. Mood swings, fear, and paranoia often came with an inability to hold to a core timeline. At different times, he had shown all of them.

Despite the Network's best research efforts, no one knew if there was a genetic predisposition for the condition, but the risks seemed to increase with exposure to new realities. No agent was allowed more than four hundred total lifetime trips over a sixteen-year span. Plus, there were mandatory annual workups starting at year ten.

She'd been sure Jace was one of the lucky ones. He'd already successfully served the maximum sixteen and had been settling into his career as a supervisor when Corinne became pregnant.

When everything changed.

When her supervisor had found out, Corinne was pulled from active duty, isolated from her team, and reassigned to a desk job at Network Headquarters. It had felt like a demotion. It didn't help that Jace pressured her to resign. As her pregnancy progressed, he became more and more agitated, until Corinne felt as if she was at the center of a three-way tug-of-war between the impending birth, her responsibilities to the Network, and her concern for Jace.

At the time, she'd convinced herself he just needed a leave from the stresses of work. That a brief hiatus would be good for both of them. That he couldn't possibly have RDD since he had passed his mandatories.

He insisted they take a complete break from the Network, and she reluctantly agreed, at least until their baby was born. They shifted through several stable mapped realities until they found an instance with appropriate prenatal care and without an active MTN presence. By unspoken agreement, neither of them spoke about their work or what they'd left behind.

Despite her long estrangement from her parents, Corinne wanted to return to her home reality for the delivery. She was sure everything would be better after the birth. Certain her parents' joy over becoming grandparents would make up for the conflict that had only grown between them in the years since she'd left their church. Certain that Jace's anxiety would resolve once they'd had a healthy baby.

For a time, it seemed as if she had been right. Jace was as caring and attentive a father as she could have hoped for. Her parents had relented and visited, bringing gifts for Reina. But it wasn't long before they began to relitigate all their old family arguments. When they tried to insist she and the baby leave Jace and return to their congregation to beg for forgiveness, she formally broke ties with them. And when she needed Jace most, he isolated himself in a quest to prove the Network had been responsible for his father's death.

Alone with an infant, Corinne abandoned the idea of returning to active missions. Even if she'd had appropriate child care, it felt too risky. But she never lost hope that she could return to the Network someday. Regain the life she had given up everything to achieve.

Jace pushed back from the terminal and nodded to her. For a brief moment, Corinne considered simply closing her eyes and staying in the library. It seemed the kind of place where she wouldn't be bothered. She could rest here. Other patrons were ensconced in reading areas. Some were even napping.

Jace stopped at the exit and turned back, an unspoken question in his eyes.

She donned the warm coat before trailing him out of the library.

He waited until they had walked a few blocks in the blustery sunshine before turning to explain. "We have a room at a local lodging. It's just a short walk away. If this world is as poorly monitored as you say, we should be safe there for a little while."

It was hard not to react to the mistrust in his voice. She shrugged. "Fine. We need a base of operations. Somewhere we can rest and refuel." His face looked haggard, lost. "How much sleep have you had in the past few days?"

This time he shrugged. That wasn't a good sign.

Warmth. Food. Sleep. Those were the priorities. Then she would assess her resources and make a plan. She knew the path she desired. How much it diverged from the path she faced was a problem for later. There were plenty of other dangers for unwary Travelers. Making decisions when exhausted, on poor intel, and out of fear were close to the top of that list.

For now, her needs and Jace's ran together. "Let's go."

Chapter 10

Poplar

Poplar woke from a dream of running. Not the usual joyful one where she was chasing prey through the woods, but one filled with fear and burning. She whimpered and pressed into the warmth of Thorne's sleeping body, hoping to find her way to rest again, but everything was wrong.

This place they were in was as strange and jarring as her dream, filled with unfamiliar sounds and scents.

The smells were definitely wrong.

Not the sweat and burnt food smell so common around people, but the way everything overlapped with something smoky. No, that wasn't right. Poplar knew the smell of a cook fire. How it was different from trees burning in the woods or the ash of a nearly cold fire-pit. This was all of that and none. Acrid. Stinging. Her nose filled with the cold of steel and the damp of mold. The rot of dead animals and the spoor of live ones. Everything in such a profusion, a single sniff threatened to start her sneezing.

She buried her snout in the one familiar thing in all the strangeness that helped calm her overwhelmed senses. Thorne murmured in his sleep, but the words and the random, slippery thoughts he shared meant nothing. Usually his dreams were comforting, but not now. His dreams, like hers, were filled with fear and danger and death.

Just like the world around them.

Her fur prickled with warning and she couldn't separate her unease from Thorne's. It would be easy to wake him. Just a lick across his face would do it. But then what? This was just as strange to him. She knew that, even as he tried to hide his worry from her.

Poor Thorne never understood that she didn't need his thoughts to read him. Translating body position and intention was a simple thing. People were ridiculously easy to understand without their incessant language.

There was movement and noise around her. Poplar froze, but none of the people milling about the large room seemed to notice her. So many people! It was like market day, only without the market.

And what part of the day was it? Inside, it felt like perpetual twilight. There was nothing in the air that gave Poplar any hint to the passage of time.

Her belly cramped with hunger. Missed meals, then. How many had they slept through?

There was a pressure in her hindquarters to pee.

She could wake Thorne up, but he smelled like exhaustion. His dreaming mind was too far away to reach. Retracing her way to the area they had used to relieve themselves last night, Poplar added her scent to the overlapping others, then she started back to Thorne's bedroll.

A high keening caught her attention. Her ears flicked up to try to capture where the sound came from, but it wasn't anything carried through the air. She shivered. From the first memories she still retained from puppyhood, Thorne's steady mindvoice was the only one she ever heard. There was no one else in all the world she shared this kind of communion with. It was beyond pack or mate.

Would he sense it too? Should she try to wake him?

It was such a tiny voice. Nearly lost in the sensory barrage of the bodies moving in this large room. Poplar worried she would lose the thread if she turned her attention from it, even for only a small moment. Swallowing a whine, she moved away from the promise of warmth from Thorne's body toward this new source of pain and fear. People were strange. So large. So strong. So capable. But in such need of the small comfort her kind could provide.

Right now, someone's need and distress were stronger than Thorne's.

That was a thought that unnerved her even more than the unnatural world surrounding them.

δ

Reina Vettel

THERE WAS NO WAY REINA was going to be able to rest. She tossed and tangled herself in the blanket Martin had given her. It smelled of sickness and mold. She pushed it to the floor. This whole place reeked of unwashed laundry and too many bodies crammed into a small space. How did people live here?

This body felt heavy. Warm. Its nerves buzzed with irritation and restlessness. She wanted to run, but where could she go? It was too cold to wander outside, and as uncomfortable as it was in here, it was out of the wind. Her stomach gurgled but she was still too nauseated to even think of eating. At least the little tablets Martin made her swallow settled her insides a little.

Martin said he'd be back soon. What was she going to do then? He had looked so lost. Shame and guilt flooded through her again. There was nothing left of his sister in this body. Reina struggled to find some way—any way—to tell him what happened, but she didn't understand it herself and anything she could think of would only make his hurt worse.

Still, she closed her eyes and searched every space, every thought. She called and called for the other woman. All Reina found were vague sense-impressions. They weren't even clear enough to be called memories, but when she thought of Martin, he seemed familiar. This room, too, felt less alien now. It was as if this body found solace being here.

It would bring no consolation to Martin.

He was right. She was exhausted. Maybe everything would make more sense after she rested. Or if not, then at least she would have the strength to find the right words to tell him his sister was gone.

Ignoring the smell, she reached for the tattered blanket and wrapped it around herself. She lay down on the lumpy sofa, staring up at the dingy sky through the bare window. Buildings stacked on buildings seemed to march all the way to the horizon. A world without trees. A world without her parents. Could she find a doorway back home? Even if she did, what then? Either she dragged someone else's body across with her, or she found a way to separate her core from it and return the way she'd come. But what if her own body wasn't waiting for her?

As weary as she was, her tortured thoughts wouldn't let her sleep. She hurt in unexpected places. And burned with what felt like a fever. Her skin vibrated with the energy of a beehive. Her legs twitched, finding no ease.

How could she live like this?

The pressure built up in her chest. If she let it out, it would emerge in a howl that would bring Martin running back. She wasn't ready to face him again.

Instead, she kept it trapped inside. Her cry echoed through her mind as tears soaked the worn cushions beneath her head.

Reina had no idea how much time had passed when she felt a tiny warmth pressing against her fingers. She gasped, pulling her hand back. A soundless whimper filled her thoughts. As her eyes adjusted to the dimness, Reina saw the small dog looking up at her from the floor.

"Hello, little friend," Reina whispered. "Where did you come from?"

::you hurt. i came::

She bolted upright and the blanket fell away letting cool air rush in.

"You understand me? What—what are you?"

::poplar::

"Poplar?"

The dog jumped up into her lap and nestled there. In a habitual motion that felt right to both her mind and body, Reina's hand briefly rested on the crown of the dog's head before stroking the wiry fur from crown to tail. Poplar sighed and settled in more deeply.

::better?::

The dog's mindvoice had the feel and cadence of a bark, but the meaning was as clear as if it had somehow learned to speak aloud. She focused on sending her own thoughts directly to the dog. ::How is this possible?::

Poplar stiffened. ::ow! no shout!::

"Sorry," Reina whispered. Did all the animals in this strange world communicate like this?

::not from this place::

::No, I'm not. I don't know how I got here.::

The dog shook its head in a very human gesture of frustration. ::thorne and me come from another where::

"Wait. Are you...trapped? Like me?" The thought of another Traveler here should have brought her relief. Instead it was muted by horror. What if she'd landed in an animal? It was shocking enough to have woken up in a stranger's body, but at least it was the same kind of being she'd left behind.

Poplar stared at Reina with the pink of a tongue lolling out of its mouth. The voice in her mind was laughing. ::dog i was before dog i am still:: The laughter faded. ::trapped though wrong smells wrong everything:: The dog hung its head. ::i followed a trail of wrong to you::

Reina scratched behind Poplar's ears. She could only imagine how much worse this place and she must smell to the dog.

Poplar sniffed her delicately. ::smell sick but only on the outside::

::I guess that makes sense. I'm not from this place either. Well, this body is. It...She was sick. Dying. When I came through the world wall, I... ::

One moment she had been standing in her house, the shimmering curtain of the Moment coalescing around her. The next, tumbling in a silent whirlwind. Then the hospital. Then here. Had it all been just one day? ::can you open the way between the worlds, too?::

Maybe they could work together. Maybe Poplar could help her find her parents, or even get her back home, though she had never heard of a dog being able to Travel. Or speak inside a mind. Yet here they were.

Poplar whimpered and turned aside.

::what is it?::

::home is gone::

There was an echo of a mournful howl in the dog's thoughts.

::What do you mean?::

Sensory impressions barraged her mind: smoke, fire, darkness, voices raised in anger. And through it all, fear. Poplar's fear.

::It's okay. You're safe here.:: She had no business making assurances like that, but she couldn't let the small thing suffer.

The dog cut off its mental sending with a sharp bark. It grabbed the material of Reina's pants and tried to pull her off the sofa.

"Stop that!"

::come see thorne help:: Poplar kept repeating the jumbled thought over and over. Reina couldn't figure out if she was meant to help Thorne or Thorne was meant to help her. Or if Thorne was a person or another animal. Either the dog couldn't or didn't want to explain. Instead, Poplar herded Reina out of the little makeshift shelter and out into the large room she had crossed with Martin earlier.

She had felt so queasy after leaving Stirling's vehicle, Reina had barely noticed her surroundings. The room was vast. Plain columns interrupted it at regular intervals, but there were no interior walls. Everywhere she looked, silent people huddled together in what seemed to be campsites. Bedrolls and blankets were arranged roughly in concentric circles. At the very center, a small bonfire burned in a tall metal barrel. The smoke roiled at the ceiling and streamed toward cracks in the high windows. At least the smoke masked all the other noxious smells

"What is this place?" she whispered to herself.

"What did you give her?" a deep voice shouted from the far side of the room.

The dog at her feet responded with a low growl.

::Poplar?:: She crouched beside the animal, trying to soothe it with a gentle pat.

The dog didn't respond. Its whole body quivered and the spiky fur stood up in a line from neck to tail.

Reina followed its gaze. Martin stood, confronting a tall shape in the shadows.

"Rules ain't complicated. No gangs. No dealing." Martin slammed his hands into the other person's chest with each phrase, forcing them back against the wall. If they gave a response, Reina couldn't hear it.

"You're lying! It had to be you!"

Nails clattering on the bare floor, Poplar weaved between the resting bodies in the most direct line to where Martin stood and launched itself at him in a mass of snarling and bared teeth.

"Poplar! No!" The shout that filled the air was from the man standing opposite Martin. It echoed her own cry.

The dog latched onto Martin's sleeve, his growl muted by the fabric of his jacket.

"Son of a bitch!" Martin yelled as he shook off the dog and grabbed his wrist.

Poplar slid into a post with a dull thud and yelped.

A shared shock of pain broke Reina's momentary paralysis and she ran toward the dog, nearly colliding with the man Martin had been arguing with. He cried out—an almost animal-like whimper—and cradled Poplar against his chest.

"Are you Thorne? Is Poplar okay?"

The man turned to face her, his expression hard and tight. "How do you know our names?"

"And you! Stay away from him." Martin grabbed Reina's arm. "You promised me you'd stay clean."

Poplar growled again and struggled to free himself from Thorne's hold.

"It's okay. I'm okay," Reina said to the dog as she shrugged off Martin's grip. There would be time later to sort out what he was talking about.

Thorne followed her gaze to Poplar and back. "I've never seen you before."

"Fucking liar!" Martin punched the wall. Reina winced.

"I don't understand," Thorne said.

The intensity of his gaze was painful. "Your dog—Poplar told me who you were." It sounded ridiculous. Even to someone who had walked through the world walls. But it was the truth and she wouldn't shy away from it.

"What?" He clasped the dog even tighter.

Martin turned to Reina, his eyes shining with unshed tears. "Just tell me. I won't be mad. Is this the man who gave you the drugs?"

Before Reina realized what she was doing, she had stepped between the two men, keeping them at arm's length. She gave Martin a sharp look before shaking her head. If this Thorne and his dog were Travelers, they would never have done anything to hurt the girl whose body she wore.

"She spoke to you?"

"What?" Oh. Reina realized Thorne meant the dog. She. Not it.

"What?" Martin repeated, confusion softening the anger. The flush had drained away from his cheeks and his breathing had slowed.

All around them, hushed conversations resumed. The rustling of shifting blankets and the crackle of the fire were loud, now that the shouting had stopped.

"Daniella, please. Tell me the truth. How do you know this man?"

Reina shook her head again. His sister was gone and she didn't know how to make him believe it. "I don't. The dog came to me. She knew I was hurting." She took a step closer to Thorne and reached a hesitant hand out to the dog. Her fur was warm and her breathing, rapid but regular. "Will she be okay?"

"Poplar is a scrappy thing. She's had worse." Thorne stared at Martin. There was a challenge in his eyes.

"Stop it!" Reina commanded.

Thorne opened his mouth to argue, but Poplar stirred in his arms.

"That thing nearly took a bite out of me!"

Reina swung her head to Martin. "You were attacking her person."

"I wasn't! I was just..." The dog whimpered. Martin shifted his gaze between Reina and Thorne, and his newly rekindled anger drained away. "I'm sorry. I didn't mean to hurt your dog."

Poplar huffed and turned away.

Now that the intensity of the moment had passed, Reina's fatigue returned with full force. Her legs buckled beneath her. If Martin hadn't caught her, she would have fallen.

"You need to be back in bed." He glared at Thorne before curling his arm around Reina's shoulder and steering her across the room.

"Wait. We need to talk."

"Later. After you rest and eat something."

With the last reserves of her strength, she stood her ground and nodded to Thorne and Poplar. "No. All of us. Need to talk. Now."

"I don't understand."

Reina swayed into the support of Martin's body. "I know. And I'm so, so sorry."

His eyes filled with the fear that lived just beneath the anger. He paused to stare into her face for a moment before turning to Thorne and Poplar. "Fine. Fucking fine."

δ

Harnett Wellerman

WHATEVER GAME AISA WAS PLAYING, she had to know Harnett wouldn't allow himself to be her unwitting pawn. And yet, here he was, her orders tucked into the folio he couldn't risk studying until he was somewhere secure.

He took the open corridor back to the lobby. As far as any observers were concerned, he was just another agent carrying out the Network's agenda. Only Harnett knew this was Aisa's agenda. If she was in a position to concentrate even more power beneath her, it would be in his best interests to stay in her good graces.

Bringing in Jace Vettel and his family would advance his standing in the Network. It should advance Aisa's, too. But she had maneuvered to pull him from the case. There had to be some reason, some advantage she would gain either through their disappearance or controlling their capture.

His fellow agents, in anonymous gray suits, crisscrossed the lobby on their way from here to there. As one vanished through a portal, another seemed to take their place in a kind of controlled choreography. Harnett had been dancing to the Network's tune for long enough to know it was all illusion.

He navigated the mapped ways back to his apartment, set Aisa's folder on his desk, and sat down as if nothing at all unusual or unexpected had happened. The agents who had searched his rooms in his absence were good. Just not as good as he was. The air held a subtle shimmer that told of a recent passage. Probably two or three individuals had moved through here within the past half hour. It was even possible that they planted surveillance equipment.

Searching for it would only call more attention to himself. Which meant Vettel's file had to remain hidden. No matter. He had committed everything within it to memory.

He paused before opening the folio Aisa had given him. Had she sent the agents here? What were the ramifications if they were working for someone else?

Perhaps her information would provide, if not answers, then at least better questions.

Harnett set a privacy shield over his desk and carefully removed the three sheets of paper inside the folder. Harnett arranged them in a triangle, placing the photograph at the top.

He picked it up and frowned. The MTN director, Calder, stared a challenge back at him. The single most powerful individual in the Network, Darius Calder was also the most enigmatic. Harnett could recall only a single event where he had met the man in person. Whoever had taken the photo had completely captured his intensity. Harnett set the photo face down on the desk and turned to the other data Aisa had given him. The first sheet of paper was a printout from Calder's personal calendar, with his appointments for the next several weeks. The second contained Harnett's reinstatement codes to full senior agent.

Aisa had given him the stick during their meeting. This was the carrot. Presented to him in such a way that she could maintain complete deniability. Was this an elaborate setup? But that wasn't really Aisa's style. Or at least it hadn't been for all the years they had worked together.

Regardless of the outcome of this mission, he would take the fall. Aisa had to know he realized it. Did she think his loyalty included self-sacrifice? Harnett shook his head.

The only thing that made any sense at all was that Jace Vettel and his family were still rogue, and it was still his job to retrieve them.

He slipped everything back in the slim folder. Darius Calder would have to wait for now.

Time to get to work.

Chapter 11

Thorne Truthscryer

POPLAR SQUIRMED AGAINST THORNE'S hold, but he was afraid to ease his grip on the dog. When he'd woken earlier, chilled and alone, the fear that something had happened to her had made his blood run cold. He could face anything—even this alien place—as long as Poplar was there to anchor him. If the boy had harmed her—

His dark thoughts were interrupted by a murmur in his mind.

::not worth it::

::Poplar?::

::who else?::

::I thought I'd lost you. Why did you leave?::

The dog sighed. Her emotions had no real translation except to convey a vague confusion and need. ::she called me::

::I don't understand.:: A flare of jealousy rose up from his chest, nearly choking him.

::she's from elsewhere too. like us::

"What?" Thorne only realized he'd spoken aloud when both the boy and the girl turned to glance at him. "Nothing," he mumbled. ::Poplar?:: But she was either too tired to reply, or more likely had thought that was all she needed to say. Still, he pressed her. ::Poplar? What do you mean?::

She yawned and curled her pink tongue over sharp white teeth. ::hungry. more cheese?::

That was all he would get until he'd found something to offer her. Thorne turned his attention to his new companions as he followed them toward the far corner of the large and now crowded room. The girl had wanted them to talk. He had no idea why. The two seemed to know one another. The boy—Martin— had called her Daniella. Were they lovers? No. Their body language said they were close, but not intimate in that way. Siblings? They certainly looked enough alike.

Martin paused in front of a long, dingy curtain. "Are you sure?"

She sighed and nodded.

"Fine." Martin led them all beyond the small partition. It was not much different from the larger space outside it, but it was clearly more of a permanent home than the makeshift camp. A faded couch stretched across one wall. Folded blankets were stacked in the opposite corner. Two wooden chairs, mismatched, sat around a leaning table. Supplies were neatly stored on pallets beside it. Poplar stirred.

::cheese! bread!::

His stomach growled in sympathy. How long had he slept? How long were the days in this place?

"Sit." Martin pointed to one of the chairs and waited until Thorne had obeyed. "You too, Daniella."

::not daniella::

::what?::

Poplar merely sniffed and settled back down in his lap.

"I'm sorry. I didn't mean to hurt her." Martin said again. He stood with his back against the wall next to the sofa. "Dog gonna be okay?"

She lifted her head. ::better with cheese::

Thorne smothered his laugh in a cough. "She hopes there's no hard feelings and wants to know if there's more cheese."

::not what I said::

::Hush.::

Frowning, Martin shifted his gaze between Thorne and Daniella before settling on Poplar. "Seriously? Like I'm going to believe you speak dog?" He rolled his eyes.

"More like she speaks person." Thorne shrugged. "Believe me or not. It doesn't really matter. Understand this: I will protect her. She's all I've got."

He expected Martin to bristle at the implied threat, but his shoulders slumped and he buried his face in his hands. His muffled voice seemed full of frustration and surging emotion. It was hard to stay angry at him, even after what he did to Poplar.

"If you didn't slip Daniella that shit, then who did?"

"She's your sister?"

"Yeah."

The girl flinched as if in pain. Poplar gave a nearly inaudible yip before jumping from his lap and crawling into hers.

::Poplar?::

::she needs me::

Thorne clamped down on his resentment. It wasn't fair. Daniella had Martin. Poplar was his.

::not daniella. lost. like us::

It was not the first time Poplar said it. Which made no sense. The girl lived here. In this world. With her brother. Poplar had to be confused.

::not::

And he had to do a better job guarding his thoughts from that dog.

She sent an image of herself, open mouth grin, tongue lolling to the side. What was going on?

"Is your dog right? Are you a Traveler?" The girl's dark eyes stared at him, full of pleading. "I need your help. Please."

"Traveler?" He cocked his head and for an instant saw himself through Poplar's eyes. It was the exact same posture she mirrored when she was confused.

"World walker? Reality bender? Do you call it something different where you're from?" Still that desperate note in her voice.

Martin looked at her as if she had turned into a complete stranger. "Daniella? What the hell are you talking about?"

She reached up to him and took him by the hand. "I keep trying to tell you. I'm not Daniella. My name is Reina. I'm from… somewhere else."

Martin pulled his hand from hers as if he'd been burned. "No. No. You're not making sense. It's the drugs."

"I'm sorry. Something happened when I found the Moment and came through. When I woke up, I was in here." She took a deep breath. "My name is Reina and I'm very far from home." Tears shined in her eyes. "Tell him, Thorne. You understand. Help him see."

What she was saying didn't make much more sense to him, but as she spoke, Thorne could see multiple futures stretching out from the choices the girl would soon have to make. Choices that would change everything for him and Poplar. He swallowed against a sudden lump in his throat. Borrowing pain from possibilities wouldn't help any of them. And Thorne knew better than to try to use his sight to warn anyone.

"You! Everything was fine until you showed up." The anger was back, but Thorne could tell how desperate Martin was to hold on to it, how behind it was an enormous well of fear in which he was terrified of drowning.

For a moment, Thorne was lost in the memory of his cabin. Or memories. All the possible futures he had seen were stacked together like a tower of scrying cards. In most of them, his body and Poplar's lay dead and unmourned in the ashy remains of his former home. Not a single one had led him here. How could he have missed it? Did that mean that he hadn't seen all the potentials?

Perhaps there was some hope, after all. He frowned, watching the girl stroke Poplar's wiry fur.

The dog yawned delicately and rested her head on her paws. ::is good here::

Not for the first time, Thorne wished he had Poplar's ability to revel in the present moment. She opened her eyes to give him a brief look of smug satisfaction before sighing and settling more deeply into the girl's lap. Why was Poplar so attached to her?

Thorne struggled to see past his petty hurt. And remembered a cry in the night. "Wait. It was you. You were afraid. You called me. Then there was a door and I came through." He glanced at her wide eyes. "I think you pulled me here. I didn't know that was possible." Did that mean each of the potentials he saw were actually different worlds with different versions of him and Poplar, not just possible futures? Following that thought led to a chasm he would never be able to leap across.

"You're not a Traveler?"

He didn't know what she meant. "Back home I am called Thorne Truthscryer. I see possibilities that hinge on the smallest of changes and try to find the paths of safety. But I never foresaw this place. Or you."

"This is fucking crazy." Martin backed away from the two of them shaking his head. "Talking dogs. Other worlds. I don't... I can't..." He glanced back at the girl he desperately needed to be his sister before turning to flee through the curtain.

Reina and Thorne stared at the makeshift doorway in shocked silence long after Martin had gone.

"Do you believe me?"

"I have seen futures stranger than this."

Tears welled in her eyes. "I don't know what to do."

Poplar whined and they both turned to the small dog.

::eat first. yap later::

Usually her single-mindedness would have driven Thorne to distraction. Now he was grateful for her pragmatic concern. ::When her brother comes back. I promise. We'll go and find you food::

::smell food here:: Poplar stretched her body long and licked Reina's face.

::it doesn't belong to us::

The dog's sigh was dramatic.

"I guess it belongs to me. Or Daniella. Go. Feed Poplar. Take what you need." Reina stood and set Poplar on the ground. "I have to go find Martin."

"You don't know where you are. You don't know where he'd go." Thorne glanced out the window at the city's massive dwellings. "I think he needs some time. This is his home. He'll come back." He had no right to make promises, but he couldn't stand to see her so distraught.

"Have you seen it? Will he really be okay?" The hope in her voice nearly broke him.

He wished he could give her the assurance she needed, but that was never the way his gift worked. He spread his hands wide.

"What if I killed his sister?" Her face was dull gray; her eyes, wide and glassy.

Was that even possible? Before this, Thorne had never known other worlds than his existed, much less that he could move between them. He and Poplar arrived here as if they'd fallen through a gate. A strange, wavering gate made of light and color, but he had stepped from there to here. What had happened to her, he had no way to explain or understand.

He could only answer her the way he had always answered his own deep doubts. "All we can do is face what is and seek the truth." It wasn't comfortable, but it was what he had.

δ

Martin Lopez

THE SHARP WINTER AIR BIT into Martin as he fled the sanctuary he had built for himself and his sister. It had always been just him and her. Even when their mother had been alive, she had spent more time looking for her next fix than thinking about feeding or caring for either of her children.

Martin thought the most awful moment of his life was when they got split up by Social Services and placed in different foster homes. Every single day over the years that followed, Martin relived the memory of her screaming and crying when they pulled her away from him. It was his fault. He had promised to keep her safe.

But his amazing, funny little sister had hung on in that horrible system long enough for him to age out when he turned eighteen and come find her. And for a little while, it was the two of them again, giving the world a big fuck you and surviving.

Until that day when he found her strung out and out of her mind on drugs in the alley behind their building. Seeing her nearly turn into their mother just about broke him. But nothing was as wrong and as painful as this.

This time, the shit had destroyed her mind.

Martin paid no attention to where he was going or how long he had been walking. He was beyond caring about being cold. It had been stupid to walk out without his coat, and now that the initial panic had settled into a heavy dread, he knew he might die out here. Shadows were lengthening and the afternoon was shading into evening. He needed the dark and its anonymity like some kind of drug. But it still wasn't enough to outrun the terror. Neon lights flickered, catching his attention. It was one of too many generic package stores that were the last weak anchors for neighborhoods some Boston corporation would soon buy up and redevelop, ensuring endless supplies of desperation along with upscale cafés and boutiques.

When Daniella had beaten the drugs and put back the weight and regained her strength, she was still the same goofy kid who'd spun wild stories to make him laugh during the long nights when their mother prowled the streets for a score. Who saved him from his own demons. Who gave him a reason to steer clear of the gangs. Who made the unheated squat he'd broken into their home. She was the one who insisted they take in others—the lost and the forgotten like them. She was his only family, but she belonged a little bit to everyone who sheltered there as well. It had taken him a long time to make his peace with that.

And now he had lost her forever.

The door of the packie buzzed as he entered. The one employee sat behind a clear barricade. Martin wondered what he looked like to the spy cams peering down like giant purple eyes from each corner of the store. Just another homeless kid searching for a few hours of oblivion. He pulled out a few wrinkled bills and some coins from his jeans pocket. It was enough to buy a handful of nips. It would have to do.

The clerk never even looked up from the security monitors and grunted something unintelligible as he counted Martin's money and gave him a few coins back in change.

"Keep it." Martin tucked the tiny bottles in his pocket and headed back into the cold.

At least the alcohol would give him the illusion of warmth.

He kept walking until his face and toes were numb and his legs heavy. "Shit." His random path had taken him back home. It would be warmer inside. He turned away and ducked through the break in the fencing until he stood in the middle of the empty lot next door. The pile of bricks and twisted steel was the rubble of the life he'd struggled to build.

He stumbled against a partially standing wall and found a place to sit out of the worst of the wind.

It took three of the nips before he stopped shivering. The seven little bottles lay spread out around him. He methodically smashed them all with a rock. First the empty ones, and then the unopened ones. The vodka inside made dark puddles on the bricks that looked like blood.

"Feel better?"

"Fuck you, Stirling. What are you doing here?"

"Looking for you."

"How did you find me?"

"I came to check in on Daniella. She said you'd run off. She's worried."

"She's not!"

"Martin—"

"She's not Daniella. Not anymore. She doesn't even know me." He glanced up at the big Black man. Stirling's eyes shone in the moonlight. Fucking Stirling. Always there. Always trying to help them. "Why?" Martin demanded. "Why the fuck do you care?"

"Because I'm human." Stirling crouched down beside him.

Martin squeezed the rock he still held until his hand cramped. He wanted something or someone as a target for all his rage, but Stirling just waited in silence.

"What happened?"

The tears that Martin had worked so hard to hold back spilled down his face, leaving ice-cold tracks on his already frigid cheeks. He didn't want to tell him. Didn't want to tell anyone, but the words, like the tears, weren't under his control anymore. He told Stirling everything. All the crazy shit she and that man— Thorne—had said. The world walls. The body snatching. The fucking dog. All of it. And when he was done, Stirling pried open Martin's hand and eased the stone out. The EMT took off his coat, then helped Martin to stand before wrapping it around him.

"Whoever she says she is, she still needs you."

Martin shook his head but didn't resist when Stirling led him back home.

Dusk blurred the sky as they walked inside. Martin shuddered beneath the weight of the EMT's winter coat. His fingers buzzed now that he was out of the wind and in the relative warmth of the old building. Frostbite could kill as easily as the violence on the streets. He should have known better, but he wouldn't let Stirling examine him. The man was impossible as it was.

Stirling had been looking in on them for almost three years—ever since a 9-1-1 call brought his ambulance here in the aftermath of a knife fight. After the cops cleared out the building and boarded it up for at least the third time, Martin and Daniella had come back and set up shop again. Somehow, Stirling found out and had made it his business to keep tabs on them.

At first, Martin distrusted the man. He had to want something. Everyone did. But when Daniella started using that first time, he had no one else to turn to. At least no one who wouldn't report them to Social Services or worse. Ever since, Martin had done everything to keep Daniella safe—had nursed her through detox, gotten her to Narcotics Anonymous, kept her clean. After all that, someone got her hooked again.

He glanced at Stirling. As grateful as he was, he couldn't risk him getting the system involved this time. Martin shook off Stirling's coat and let it drop to the floor. "Thank you." His voice was formal. And final.

"You're welcome," Stirling said, stooping to pick up the coat and continuing across the lobby to the stairwell.

Martin swore quietly and followed him. "You're not going to leave, are you."

"Nope."

"I think this is something even you can't fix."

"Let me be the judge of that."

"Don't make promises you can't possibly keep," Martin snapped. He let the stairwell door swing shut. Stirling stopped it with his shoulder.

There were times Stirling's pious optimism really pissed Martin off. But the man was one of the rare believers. He peddled hope like it was a drug, and Martin would be lying if he said he didn't crave it. He paused at the curtained-off area that was his and Daniella's. "She's different. It's bad."

Stirling nodded, but Martin knew he didn't understand. Wouldn't understand until he heard some of the crazy shit she'd been saying. The big EMT tried to give his shoulder a squeeze, but Martin ducked the man's touch. He didn't need anyone's pity.

"Hey," Martin said softly at the curtain to their room. "It's me. Can I come in?" He gritted his teeth. This was his house.

The white-haired man who'd been with Daniella earlier pulled the curtain aside and walked out. His small dog pattered after him. Martin glared at him. This old man was part of whatever delusion had gripped his sister.

"I'm sorry," he said. "I didn't want to leave her alone until you got back."

"Get the hell out of my house."

The man's shoulders drooped. Even the dog looked sad.

"Fuck you and your dog. Everything was fine until you showed up." Martin bumped past him and pushed through the curtain.

Daniella was sitting on the sofa, her face lit by the battery-powered lantern perched on top of their storage crates. It highlighted her sunken eyes and the sallow cheeks. Martin wished this had all been some kind of joke, but he'd learned a long time ago how dangerous wishes could be.

"Daniella?" She turned and looked up at him as he spoke, and for a moment he let himself hope. But her eyes were sad, and she just shook her head. Martin swallowed the lump in his throat. "Can Stirling take a look at you?"

She met his gaze with a terrible blankness in her expression. It was all Martin could do to stand there and watch the stranger who had once been his sister. But if he didn't stand by her, who would? He pressed his hands into his eyes, waiting for Stirling to give him something, anything to hold on to.

δ

Melissa Klein

MELISSA SNAPPED AWAKE FROM incoherent dreams into the darkness of her bedroom. The muscles in her hips and neck protested as she rolled over. A dull throbbing in the back of her head reminded her of a college hangover. Served her right. Daytime naps had always disoriented her.

The rest had helped, but not nearly enough. She reached for her phone and struggled to focus on the display. Six nineteen. There were seven new messages in her voicemail queue. Six nineteen. Shit. Shit. Shit. She'd missed her makeup appointment.

At least one of those messages had to be from Julian Maxwell.

She contemplated hiding the phone beneath her pillow.

Avoidance. "One of the hallmarks of anxiety and depression, Doctor." Talking to herself wasn't any part of being crazy, but seeing portals to nowhere probably was.

Her stomach growled loudly in the silent apartment. The last time she'd eaten was an early dinner before the homeless count. Maybe she could grab something from the Thai place on the corner. She stared at her phone again, unable to summon the will to make choices and manage even the online ordering app.

After a cup of strong coffee and rummaging for some ultimately tasteless leftovers, Melissa was no closer to getting a grip on what happened than she had been walking out of the ER this morning. She was going to have to actually call Julian Maxwell, and that wasn't going to be pleasant. At least with a day's separation, her fear of the abandoned building had lessened to a persistent unease. She could work with that.

Clinical distance was the key. And acknowledging her emotions. It's what she helped her patients with and what she needed to do for herself.

If she'd been one of her patients, she'd recommend an urgent counseling session. If one of her psych residents had come to her this unmoored, she would have them in for formal supervision. Melissa retrieved her phone and scrolled through her contact list. Julian was an excellent clinician. She'd referred many of her own patients to him during her sabbatical, but what would she say to him that he would even remotely understand? She was certain he couldn't help. Not with this.

The irony didn't escape her: She was about to do something that from any clinical perspective should definitely make her question her own judgment. And yet.

Making a silent promise to call Julian soon—later—tonight, Melissa left her condo, took the elevator to the parking garage, and drove to where it all started. If there were any answers, she would find them there.

In most cities, heading downtown after the work day would have meant only light traffic, but there was almost never a time where Boston streets weren't a nightmare of reckless drivers and short tempers. Melissa typically cursed her fellow commuters, but this evening she barely noticed them. Instead, she grappled with her fragmented memory, trying to link the shimmering, round portal with the girl from the hospital.

How were they connected? How was she connected with them? And why had her childhood ghosts come back to haunt her now?

The storefronts and coffee shops gave way to dilapidated brownstones, and then she was there: the block circled by fencing, filled with mostly rubble, with one lone building rising up near the destruction. She parked at an open space and sat, clenching the steering wheel.

This was a bad idea. She could practically write the story herself: White suburban doctor's body found in abandoned structure—film at eleven. "Get over yourself," she muttered. Her biggest risk was probably contracting tetanus or the building falling down on her head. But if she was going to do this, she really should let someone know.

Her phone woke up still displaying the contact information for Julian. She could leave a message on his voicemail, but that would mean explaining something that she barely had a grasp of herself. So was her reluctance avoidance or rationalization? Swearing softly in the privacy of the quiet car, she knew it was probably both.

"Fine. Don't call your shrink." He would try her again, soon enough. She would have to deal with the consequences and somehow convince Julian she wasn't a danger to herself or anyone else. For now she scrolled through her recent texts. Which of her friends could handle the trip down this particular rabbit hole? She paused at Eleanor's contact information, but her oldest friend was thousands of miles and three timezones away. Then

Stirling's voice echoed in her mind as she saw his name pop up: *"You have my number. I'm here. Anytime you need a friend."*

"Okay, then." Before she could change her mind, she sent Stirling a brief message telling him where she was. It would take practically a dissertation to explain why she was here, so she didn't bother. At least she wouldn't be some unsolved mystery if she vanished. Though that would end her problem with Julian.

Out of habit, she slipped a few quarters in the meter and laughed at herself. What good would an hour of legal parking be if a portal to nowhere swallowed her up? At least then she wouldn't have to pay the parking tickets.

She shook her head. Humor. Another defense mechanism. Damn, she hated shrinks.

Melissa yanked on her gloves. The cold winter evening was uncharacteristically silent. No honking horns or distant sirens. Even the light traffic had stilled, leaving her in a strange lacuna. She glanced back at her parked car as if it were a life raft and shook her head. Denial had taken her this far but no further.

This was her choice. There was no turning back.

The building's front door swung open at her touch. Fumbling with her phone, she managed to find the flashlight app to light the space ahead of her. Scattered piles of trash had been indistinct blobs in the other night's darkness. The box that had contained Stirling's supplies stood empty and overturned in the middle of the lobby.

"Hello?"

No response came, but Melissa had the strong impression of being watched.

"I was here the other night. With an EMT. We brought blankets and food."

A soft rustling came from the shadows. It was probably rats. She suppressed a shudder. Someone had to be here. "I'm a doctor. I'm trying to find out about the girl I saved."

"Why?"

Maybe it was because the man's soft voice was anonymous or maybe because it was direct and curious that she found herself responding to him as if he were a therapist and not a threat. "I saw something and I need to figure out if it's true or if I'm crazy." She didn't like using the "c" word like this, but that was the heart of the matter: Either there were doors between realities, or she had lost her grip on hers.

"Why can't it be both?"

In the darkness, Melissa laughed. Ellie had always answered a question with a question. Her college roommate would have been a great therapist herself, but her flavor of curiosity sent her to rabbinical school instead. Maybe that's what Melissa needed now. Less shrink, more rabbi. "Good question."

Another rustle caught her attention and she lifted her phone. The light illuminated the shape of a small white dog with irregular splotches of brown on its wiry fur. It reminded her of a Jack Russell her family had once owned. She stopped herself from leaning down to greet it. Strays were mostly harmless, but the last thing she needed was a bite or a scratch.

"Poplar!" The man's voice called out, and the dog stopped short and lay down at her feet.

"Your dog?"

A tall white-haired older gentleman stepped into the small cone of light from her phone. For a moment, her breath caught in her throat. It was her father's face. And it wasn't. She knew it wasn't. But that didn't stop her hands from shaking or her from taking a step back toward the door.

"Mostly she's her own." The man shrugged. Even that gesture felt familiar. "But she travels with me."

She shook her head, hoping to clear away the ghost-image of her father, but when she looked at the man again, it was still there. Her father hadn't been that clear-eyed for at least a decade before he had passed. Nor had his face been as dark or weathered. "And you are?"

He gave her a curiously formal bow. "Thorne Truthscryer. And she is Poplar."

The dog barked brightly as if introducing herself.

The tightness in Melissa's chest eased. Her father was dead and it had been a long time since she had believed in any kind of afterlife. "Melissa Klein. Dr. Melissa Klein."

"Pleasure to meet you."

He sounded kind. But how much of that was her transference? Melissa forced herself to focus on what she'd come here for. "You live here?"

"I am here now."

It was an interesting non-answer. "What do you know about the girl?"

"I'm not sure you'd believe me if I told you."

Anger—quick and unfamiliar—burned its fire through her. "You have no idea what I've been through. What I'd believe."

His eyes widened briefly before he dropped his gaze and spent a long moment looking at the dog. "You're right," he said. And she could have sworn he was talking to the dog. Then he turned back to her. "My apologies, then. Best you speak to her yourself. Follow me." He turned and vanished back into the shadows.

Chapter 12

Reina Vettel

REINA TOOK A DEEP SHUDDERING breath as Martin entered the room and stood like a statue by the curtain, his eyes downcast. The man who had driven them from the hospital—Stirling—moved past him.

"Daniella, can I take a look at you?" Stirling asked.

"Please. It's Reina. I know that you're some kind of healer, but I'm not ill. At least my mind isn't." She glanced over to where Martin was staring out the window. He flinched but still wouldn't meet her gaze. "Don't make me go over this again. I've hurt him enough already."

Stirling glanced at Martin before concentrating on her again. "Okay, Reina, I just want to make sure your body is better."

Reina knew that tone of voice. Adults used it when they felt they had to lie to you and were being as kind as they could in the process. She shrugged again. Nothing he could do would make any difference.

He knelt next to the sofa and gently placed the disc of his listening device on her chest.

"Your heartbeat is strong and regular. Fifty-one beats per minute."

He may have been talking directly to her, but she knew it was meant to reassure Martin.

She winced as he shined a light in her face. "Your pupils are normal sized and reactive to light. Your skin is dry. That's all good. How are you feeling?"

Blinking away the afterimages, she sighed. "Do you really want to know?"

Stirling nodded.

She stole another quick glance at Martin. It was easier than looking at the strange body she wore. "I can't stop my hands from shaking. Sometimes out of nowhere, my heart races. I get cold, and then hot. Eating makes me queasy."

"That's from the detox," Stirling said. "Are you taking the medicine they prescribed for you?"

"I'm making her take it," Martin snapped. "She's not due for another dose for a few hours."

She sighed. "But worse than all of that, I'm scared. Confused. I don't understand what happened."

"That makes two of us." A woman strode into view through the curtain. Someone who looked familiar, though Reina was certain she'd never seen her before. Older than her mother, she had close-cropped hair that was mostly drab brown and silver. Fine lines fanned out from the corner of eyes that seemed more comfortable squinting than smiling. A pair of spectacles hung around her neck on a beaded chain.

Thorne and Poplar followed her in to crowd the small room. Reina caught the dog's gaze and sent a question toward her. ::Who is she?::

::she is for helping:: Poplar answered, a smugness in her mindvoice.

"I told you to leave," Martin said, glaring at Thorne, "and who the hell are you?" He moved to block the woman's way.

"I'm a physician. Dr. Melissa Klein." She handed Martin a small card. "I was here with Stirling the other night." She glanced toward Reina. "I'm the one who found her."

Martin crumpled the card and shoved it in his pocket before folding his arms across his chest. "Fine. Come in. Why the fuck not."

"She saved your sister's life," Stirling said.

The doctor started. Her mouth fell open and her eyebrows drew together. "Stirling? I just texted you. What are you doing here?"

"He snoops on us," Martin said.

"Wait. You know these people?"

"Hi, Doc. It's complicated." Stirling sighed and stood. "My church considers this place part of their mission. I guess I do, too. I've been looking in on Martin and his sister for a while now."

"Are you on the clock now?"

"Not exactly."

"Is that why you didn't tell me you knew who she was?"

Stirling spread his hands wide. "Like I said. Complicated."

The more the woman spoke, the more familiar she seemed. And then Reina remembered. "I saw you," she whispered. Reina stared at the doctor, her eyes open wide, seeing the chaotic darkness of her broken transit. "Before I fell. Before..." She trailed off and shook her head before continuing. "Before everything."

Poplar jumped onto the sofa next to Reina and nuzzled her face gently.

::can help:: Poplar was looking at the doctor, her eyes bright.

::Do you really think so?::

::yes! help. is a little like us.::

::A Traveler? Like me?:: Hope surged through her. If she could only find her parents. They could all get home... .

Snippets of conversation between Dr. Melissa and Stirling floated through the room. They were talking about her, but paying no attention to her.

"...drug overdose leading to such a persistent delusion."

"During the episode? Especially if the drug used was a stimulant—sure. But after?"

"Could she have schizophrenia?"

"...the right age for it to manifest."

"What about admitting her through the ER?" Stirling asked softly.

"No!" Martin shouted. "She's not going anywhere!"

"At least let the doc do a mental status check. We're trying to help."

"Fine. It's all fucking fine." Martin folded his arms and turned to the dark city outside the window.

None of it made sense to her. She studied the doctor as she came closer. Was Poplar right? Could this woman help her?

"I saw you, too. You fell through a doorway made of light."

::see? I told you. See?:: Poplar's mindvoice was smug and triumphant.

Reina's heart raced with possibilities. "You can see the world walls. You're a Traveler, too! Do you know my parents? Will you help me get home?"

The woman stared at her, unblinking, her eyes glassy. All the color had drained from her stern face. She swayed on her feet, looking like she was about to faint.

Reina jumped up and guided her to the sofa. "Hey, are you okay?"

She shook her head. And then her knees buckled.

δ

Melissa Klein

SHE SAT RESTING HER FOREARMS on her legs and leaned forward, hoping that would stop the dizziness. The girl beside her placed a hand on her back. The dog poked her leg with its snout. The physical contact helped more than Melissa wanted to admit. "There was a ring of light. And then you were at my feet. You weren't breathing."

"First Papa left and then Mama went after him. She warned me not to follow, but I couldn't...I couldn't. They left me. And it all went wrong."

The girl was on the edge of tears, her breath shaky, cheeks pale.

"I did everything Papa taught me. I did everything right, but something happened. It hurt so bad. I wanted it to stop. And then I woke up, but I'm not me."

The girl wasn't making any sense. Maybe Stirling was right. Melissa's head throbbed in synchrony with her heartbeat. *Not now. Not again.*

"Dr. Melissa?"

She pressed the heels of her hands against her eyes as if that would stop the dancing dust motes. The girl was ill. She'd had multiple codes. Substance use disorder. Anorexia. Of course she was confused. Of course her mental health was impacted.

It would be so easy to dismiss it all in terms that were defined so narrowly and neatly in the DSM. A chill moved through her. Something happened in the lobby on the night of the count. Something Melissa couldn't reconcile. Not with all the armor of her predictable, ordinary, rational life.

The looking glass was real, and there were worlds on the other side.

Julian was going to have a field day with all of this.

"Hey, Doc?" Stirling's voice was full of concern and something more. "Everything okay?"

Like "safe," "okay" was a relative term. A few days ago, okay would have meant a good research day and all of her patients showing up on time. Today? Today okay was not passing out on the floor of a homeless encampment. She lifted her head and shrugged. The room didn't spin. So far, so good.

"What do you think? Does she need a more thorough evaluation?"

How the hell did you evaluate this?

Martin stomped over to where Stirling stood and glared at both of them. "I can take care of Daniella here."

"No one's trying to take your sister away from you," Stirling said.

"You people all lie. Get the hell out of my house. Now."

The dog lifted its head from the girl's lap and started to growl. She tried to soothe it. Melissa focused on the way the dog stared at the girl when she spoke. The way its hackles smoothed and it sat back down with a sound like a human harumph. She let

Stirling and Martin's argument continue in the background. It was only a distraction. The girl was the center of it all.

"Daniella?"

She sighed. "Reina. My name is Reina."

"Who's Daniella?"

Reina shook her head. "It's complicated."

Melissa glanced across the room. "And that's your brother?"

Her eyes welled up. "I don't...he's not. He was her brother, but she's gone now."

The girl wouldn't meet her gaze. Melissa spoke quietly, as much to keep her calm as to keep what she was saying private. "You asked me if I was a traveler. What do you think that means?"

"You really don't know?"

A vague unease moved through her, along with memories Melissa had suppressed for far too many years. The echo of what she'd always thought of as a visual aura—the sign of an impending migraine—glowed in the harsh light from the single fixture. She shook her head again. The image didn't clear.

"But Poplar said you—" The dog whimpered and Reina silenced it with a touch. "It doesn't matter. I'm trapped in here now. I don't know how to find my way back."

"Back where?"

"You won't understand," the girl said.

Melissa was tired of people telling her that.

The men's voices rose again, anger filling the room. Melissa forced herself to ignore them and tried to blink away the geometric shapes dancing in her periphery. The first time she'd seen them was when she was five and a half during a family vacation to Spain.

It had been raining the day they visited El Alhambra. Her mother had wanted to cancel the tour, but they'd already paid for the taxi and the guide. Melissa had been happy—her parents let her run around the formal gardens while they stood under an overhang, waiting for the weather to clear. Unlike so much of what had come after, this memory was as vivid as the day it happened.

It was almost a relief to let herself relive it.

The clouds had parted, turning the downpour into a sunshower. Melissa loved the way the water droplets glinted in the air. Wished she had someone to share the magic of it with. Out of the corner of her eye, she caught a shimmer she thought was a rainbow, but when she turned, there was a golden fiery wheel spinning in front of her.

A dark-haired, dark-eyed little boy in long pants and a tunic stood just inside the ring of light. As Melissa watched with wide open eyes, the things around the boy seemed etched with a painful brilliance. The raindrops bent around him. Melissa blinked, but the vision had remained, shimmering in the silence.

It was a doorway into a summer day. To a garden almost the twin of the one she was standing in, down to the mosaics and the fountains. Except on that side of the door, all the flowers were in bloom. She slipped her arm through.

One moment, raindrops plinked on the mosaics in this garden. The next, sunshine warmed the palm of her hand, even as her hair dripped with rain.

The boy laughed and clapped his hands, gesturing for her to follow.

She blinked in the strange sunshine, trying to see past him. Then she looked back toward her parents and the rainy garden. They were deep in conversation with their tour guide. Probably getting ready to drag her through another boring museum. The boy waited. Playing with him would be way more fun. She stepped into the brightness.

A woman in a white dress stood between her and the boy, blocking the opening, her eyes wide in shock or fear. She shouted in a language Melissa didn't understand before grabbing the boy's arm to yank him away. He started crying. Before Melissa could say a word, the shimmer in the air vanished like a soap bubble, leaving her in the rain alone and furious. She ran back to her parents babbling about the boy and the doorway, the other garden, and the mean woman, struggling to get the words out when her head began to throb, the garden spun, and she threw up at their feet. The next thing she knew, Melissa was in a Spanish hospital, undergoing round after round of tests and examinations.

It was the first time she had met what her parents had named "her imaginary friend." The first time she'd experienced the crippling headaches her doctors finally called atypical migraines. It wouldn't be the last for either.

"That isn't your call!" Martin's fury broke through Melissa's memories. "Take your doctor friend and get the fuck out."

Time must have slowed while she'd been trapped in her past. The two men were still arguing, their voices getting even louder and more insistent. The promise of violence hung in the air. Anger was always the default for a man's fear.

Melissa's internal voice—the one she'd cultivated, full of amused cynicism and clinical distance—shook through her: *And what about your fear, Doctor Klein?* There would be time for that later. She promised herself.

"I can't just walk away, Martin. She needs our help."

Melissa knew all too well what that kind of help looked like to a young girl who talked about doors to nowhere and lights that no one else saw shining in the air.

Martin glared between her and Stirling. His hands were balled into fists. Then he turned to his sister. From her perch on Reina's lap, Poplar growled softly and stared at him as if stalking prey.

"Fine. If you want to be Reina, I'll call you Reina. I just need you to be okay."

The anguish in his voice stirred something in Melissa's heart, and she blinked back tears.

Reina tightened her hands in the dog's fur. It sighed and nestled into her. "I need to find my parents. I need to go home."

"Our parents are dead. You are home." Martin pressed his palms to his eyes.

Reina placed her hand on Melissa's arm, startling her. "Please, Doctor Melissa, If you can't help me, at least help him understand. I'm not his sister. And I don't belong here."

Understanding was different from accepting. It was hard enough for Melissa to believe there were other worlds. Somehow, once upon a time, she'd touched an opening from here to there. In an instant, her well-ordered life had become a fiction—a story she'd made herself believe for all these years. And if there were worlds within worlds and people who could travel between them, why not this? If Reina was to be believed, the girl Martin called Daniella was gone. What could she say to him that would in any way ease his loss?

She turned to look at the girl, trying to formulate the questions that crowded out all the other concerns. How did this "traveling" work? What was on the other side of the ring of light she so often saw as a child? Why wasn't her friend Borys able to escape home?

Before Melissa could speak, the doorway she'd been trying so hard not to see burst open between them. A glistening wheel began to spin in the air. The sounds in the room faded into the distance.

Melissa choked on a sob she didn't dare let loose. "I didn't make it up." Not last night and not as a little girl. It wasn't a seizure or a migraine or any of the things that made sense to her parents or the specialists. And if she hadn't imagined the doorway or Borys, then she also hadn't imagined what had happened to him later, after he came through the portal that had opened in her own house.

"Doc?" Stirling was still waiting for her to examine Reina.

She looked up at him, struggled to focus on him through the visual distortion. To be the expert he expected her to be. "There's nothing wrong with her that either of us can fix."

"What do you mean?" the EMT demanded.

Bright shapes continued to dance everywhere she looked. "It's complicated."

She struggled to separate out the then from the now. Blurs still bent the air all around them.

Poplar barked sharply. Reina cried out. Someone shouted her name. The world spun in in a kaleidoscope of light in front of her, impossibly hard, impossibly bright.

δ

Thorne Truthscryer

THORNE TRIED TO SHIELD his uncharitable thoughts from Poplar. He knew she hadn't really abandoned him. It was just hard not to feel jealous, watching her curl protectively into Reina's lap.

The dog twisted her head to give him an over-the-shoulder glance, complete with a toothy smile.

::You're enjoying this, aren't you?:: Thorne said to her, ignoring the argument about the girl raging around them.

Poplar leaned in to give Reina's hand a lick. ::maybe…::

He was about to make some sarcastic retort when the air around him thickened into a haze, as if the smoky fire in their small home had caught up to them somehow. A doorway, like the one he had seen there, yawned open in the center of the room. The glare made him wince. Thorne's throat tightened. Poplar gave a single sharp warning bark, and the room fell eerily silent. The doctor cried out from her place sitting beside the girl.

Potential futures splintered out from this current moment, from the doorway between worlds, like fractures across glass. There were too many to track. Hundreds of ways where he and Poplar died. Worse were the timelines where Poplar was gone somewhere he couldn't see, couldn't find, leaving him to mourn alone. Everywhere he looked, grief followed. Sometimes his. Sometimes Martin's, sometimes Reina's. There were jumbled realities where the doctor was locked away in a small stark room, her face slack with confusion and remorse.

His hands shook; a sob lodged in his throat. He couldn't do this. He wasn't strong enough. There wasn't a way through.

A low growl pierced the fog in his mind. Thorne opened eyes he hadn't realized he'd closed. Looked down. Poplar had a mouthful of his trousers and was trying to shake him. As soon as he saw her, the link between them opened more fully that it ever had before. Her fear, her concern was a flood that diverted his focus away from all that pain.

He picked her up with shaking hands. Poplar licked his face and he realized he'd been crying.

Thorne's heart was still racing with the aftereffects of his vision. It had never been that bad before. Why here? Why now?

"Doctor Melissa!" Reina's voice tore through the room.

The doctor was on the floor, trembling from head to toe. The big medic was kneeling by her side.

The portal shrank to a pinprick as intense as the sun before vanishing. Thorne blinked rapidly, his eyes tearing.

Stirling. He wasn't in any of his visions. Why wasn't he in any of the visions?

::you have to tell them::

::Tell them what?::

::dangerous. bad things will happen. tell them::

Bad things were always going to happen. That was what his curse gave him: the ability to see it all, along with the futility of avoiding any of it.

::not true:: Poplar growled for emphasis. The taste of cheese, the nap of soft blankets, and a mélange of smells he imagined would be pleasant were he a dog filled his mind. And in every image, he was there.

If only it were that simple.

"What the hell is going on?" Martin moved closer to Reina, ignoring the warning bark Poplar gave him.

Thorne jerked his head up and stared at him. "Did you...did you see it?" Maybe it wasn't his burden to carry alone.

The boy gave him a puzzled look. "What's wrong with her?" He pointed to the doctor.

"She opened a way," Reina said, her voice an astonished whisper. "She can do it. She can help me get back to my family."

As if Reina's words were a trigger, possibilities flooded through Thorne again. And time after time, disaster followed.

"No," Thorne said. "It's all wrong."

No one heard him. They were clustered around the doctor. But the woman wasn't the pivot around which the universe turned. And he knew he needed to find out who was. He clutched

Poplar close to his chest. Normally, she didn't like being held that closely, but this time she didn't even make a whimper.

The vortex of possibilities waited for him, whether he wanted it or not.

Thorne took a deep breath as if he were about to dive into a cold, deep lake.

Poplar's warmth and the rapid, steady beat of her heart comforted him.

He opened himself to the future. Futures. All of them. Even the ones where he ended up alone.

It was too much. Drowning would be simpler. For a brief moment, the memory of his long dead teacher came back to him. If he drowned, then who would care for Poplar? Thorne forced himself to swim against the current. Back, to before any number of ways Poplar vanished, back to first one branching point and then another. At each nexus, he tried to rest as the potential futures shriveled and died away.

And then he knew.

It was Reina.

If she reunited with her parents, he would lose Poplar.

He could see nothing more beyond that.

Chapter 13

THEY HAD HAD NO TROUBLE checking in. The two of them seamlessly reprised their old roles as agents, presenting as polite and eminently forgettable. The room was serviceable. He'd stayed in far worse and after last night in the shelter, the private bathroom and the large double beds felt like the height of luxury.

Corinne had insisted they eat and get a few hours' rest before making the attempt to open a way. Despite the urgency like a lump of ice in the pit of his stomach, he knew she was right. She chose the bed closest to the window and fell asleep instantly.

Jace had tried to do the same, but as exhausted as his body was, sleep eluded him.

His failures replayed in the darkness behind closed eyes. The Network had taken everything from him. His father. His purpose. His wife. He couldn't let them have Reina.

All his attempts to open a way had ended in failure. So had Corinne's. What made him think this would be any different? They were trapped here. Reina would be alone. Helpless. The

Network would find her, and everything he had sacrificed for all those years would have been for nothing.

He fought for control over his panic. Corinne was still asleep or at least feigning it. If he woke her, then his demons and doubts would only poison any hope she might still have. She had followed him out of the cache and across the city when he had been sure she wouldn't. That was hope, wasn't it?

Jace tossed, his restlessness driving him to do something. Anything. A sour odor wafted up from his body. A shower would clear his mind, help ready him for what came next. Part of him chafed at even a moment more of delay, but the multiverse punished the unprepared.

Hadn't it already punished him?

He let the flow of the hot water wash away the sweat and the fear. It wasn't rest, but it would have to do.

He got dressed in the spare set of clothing from the cache and stepped out of the bathroom, toweling off his hair. The remnants of the bland food they'd eaten as the fuel it was, had been cleaned up. The bed Corinne had claimed, remade.

She was gone. Jace's heartbeat raced. The damp towel dropped from his suddenly cold hands. He shivered, all the borrowed warmth of the shower, gone.

"No, oh no," he whispered, his throat hoarse as if he'd been shouting.

The click of the lock disengaging on the door was as loud as a gunshot. Jace froze.

Corinne stepped into the room, two steaming cups of coffee stacked in one hand, the other pushing open the door.

Jace shivered with the release of tension. She hadn't left him, though he had given her far too many reasons to.

He swallowed hard and nodded his thanks as Corinne handed him one of the coffees. She took hers with her to the bathroom.

He rolled the foam cup in his hands and inhaled the nutty aroma as he stood by the window. The city glowed with twilight. A gentle snow was falling, the flakes illuminated in the dim streetlights. Despite the hopelessness he felt, despite the evidence of its cruelty, this world also had stark beauty.

Corinne emerged from the bathroom followed by a billow of steam, dressed in her Travel clothes. Her damp hair hung past her shoulders. Even after all these years, she still had the power to take his breath away. When was the last time he had told her how lovely she was? How long ago had it been since they reached for one another in shared passion?

If they got out of this, he swore he would do whatever he could to repair the rift between them. "Are you ready to try?" he asked softly.

Corinne glanced at him, sighed, and looked away. She seemed as reluctant as he was to talk about their poor chances. "I'm ready."

Jace sat at the edge of her bed, set the coffee cup on the night table, and held his hand out to her. His ring gleamed in the dim light.

It seemed an eternity before she sat next to him and took his hand. Her ring clinked against his. While it was true that all Travelers moved alone through the multiverse, working together should make it easier to visualize the strands of possibility and push their way through to the correct one. He had to believe that.

Jace cleared his mind of everything but his connection to Reina. Corinne nodded and gripped his hand harder. He opened his senses to the flow of the paths around them. Even in this room, there were a myriad of potentials. Most were highly unlikely and easily ignored. Many held some kind of flashy disaster—an explosion, a meteorite hit, a tornado—all below the threshold of the probable and most barely—if at all—possible.

Beyond the noise of what could be, Jace struggled to listen for the echo of his passage here so he could trace it back to his daughter. He could sense Corinne doing the same. It had been a long time since they had done this as a team. The comfort of it was a promise he knew he couldn't rely on.

Unease gripped him and he lost focus, his awareness falling back to the drab room, musty carpet, and scratchy bedspread. Possibilities slammed shut even before they coalesced into anything solid. He slipped his hand from Corinne's and wiped his sweaty palms on his trousers.

Corinne frowned at him.

"I'm sorry. Let's go again." What he dared not say was how hard this was for him. How each transit rattled his sense of self and certainty. But he owed it to Corinne and Reina to try. They needed to be somewhere safe, even if it meant he lost himself.

She gently took his hand again and Jace felt an upwelling of gratitude. They were stronger together. He had almost forgotten that. Had let his fear nearly drown him.

Time slowed. A single intense memory burned through him: the day they nearly lost Reina to the ocean. The day they pulled her small, limp body from the water and got her breathing again. The day Jace realized there were threats other than the Network that could take her from them.

Corinne's steady presence had been by his side that day and she was here now. Jace opened his mind again to find the connection to their daughter. He heard the steady cadence of his heartbeat and his breath. A thousand possible moments coalesced into one bright thread.

"I see it," Corinne whispered.

It would take every bit of their combined will and discipline to force their way back from this interdicted reality into their own. It would be like trying to run up a steep and rock-strewn slope.

"Go," she urged.

They reached for the highlighted Moment together. Jace held onto the memory of his daughter, safe in his arms, shivering, seawater dripping off her hair and her clothes to soak him. He could almost smell the briny air. Taste the adrenaline on his tongue.

Crosscurrents of alternate timelines buffeted him, but he faced the strongest headwinds and battled his way through, pushing forward with every breath. He knew Corinne was beside him, but he no longer felt her hand in his. The hotel room was a thin and fading tapestry.

We're coming for you, Reina, he thought fiercely. His daughter's name was a light in the chaos. Every step was a battle. Through the darkness of his transit, Jace could see a distant soft glow. He only hoped Corinne saw it, too.

The illumination strengthened as Jace fought closer. Home. His daughter. Safety.

He could see the outline of their white clapboard house and its rambling garden against a rain-lashed sky.

A flare of lightning seared the air. All the strands of possibility twisted into a writhing tornado, a force with its own inexorable pull. It dragged him away as if he had been the one who'd nearly drowned in the rip current instead of Reina. His vision cleared. Showed him a trash-strewn street. A dark, brooding building loomed in front of him. Scaffolding covered most of the front, and all the windows were boarded up.

The wind rose again, howling, and scattered his thoughts. His concentration shattered.

His body hit the floor as if the storm had slammed him there.
The generic hotel room slid back into focus.
Beside him, Corinne sobbed quietly.

δ

Harnett Wellerman

THE IRONY WASN'T LOST on him—in a very real sense, he was about to go as rogue as Jace had. Harnett's disappearance would be duly noted, but he wasn't too worried. They wouldn't resort to tracking him yet, especially if Aisa had his status as on active duty. By the time she realized he'd abandoned her mission for his own, it would be too late.

It was worth the risk for the chance to acquire Jace and Corinne's child—who would be twelve now and a third-generation Traveler, if the classified reports were to be believed. That would explain why the parents had run. Soon Harnett would be able to complete all the blanks in the official forms and clear the failure from his record. Once he succeeded, Aisa would be forced to publicly take credit for his actions. Which would only enhance his position within the Network.

He opened the drawer in the middle of his desk and took out a small wooden box. It had been hewn from a species of tree that he'd long forgotten the name of. As well-crafted as the container was, it was less important than the item nestled inside: a dull metallic key on a worn lanyard.

The door the key unlocked had been left behind, along with the rest of his life before the Network.

Harnett placed the key in his left palm and wrapped the lanyard around his hand three times. The feel of the cold metal against his skin and the ritual nature of the action grounded him. The familiar flutter of anticipation let him know the Moment was approaching.

The air around him chilled as if a storm were swirling. His mouth dried and his breathing quickened. No matter how many times he'd Traveled on Network missions, the memory of opening his first portal never faded.

He had woken up bruised and bloody on the morning of his fourteenth birthday knowing one immutable fact: His father would never beat him again. The key to the man's gun closet pressed into Harnett's leg through the thin material of his pants pocket. The next time his father loomed over him, he'd be ready.

Harnett limped over to the shack that contained his father's makeshift still, workshop, and armory, barely caring if the man heard him coming. He wiped his nose; fresh blood smeared over the discoloration on his wrist from where his father had nearly ground the bones together with his rage-fueled grip.

Luck had been with him: His father was passed out on the shack's floor, using a sack of grain as a pillow. Harnett stepped over him, partly relieved, partly furious the confrontation he'd been playing over and over in his imagination wasn't going to happen.

The past didn't disappear, but it wasn't a distraction anymore. For the most part, he had been able to seal it off in the same way the portal he'd accidentally opened had sealed him off from his father. Harnett wasn't sure he even needed the key anymore, but he'd been using it as his focus for so long now, he couldn't imagine making a transit without it. And it was far from the only object he could move from instance to instance. It made him particularly useful to the Network as a courier and ensured he would never arrive somewhere unarmed and helpless.

He slipped his favorite knife into its concealed pocket, along with the wrist restraints that would prevent Jace from opening a portal. No, this particular rogue wasn't going to escape again.

In his time pursuing strays—agents in the throes of acute RDD and ones who had simply gone rogue—Harnett had learned ways to obscure a passage. Techniques he had chosen not to share with his supervisors. Techniques that died with the clever agents who had discovered them.

He was ready.

The pressure wave crested over him, and the Moment crystallized. Harnett stepped from here to there with the ease of long experience. When the universe coalesced around him again, he was standing in the midst of a city. The air tasted of snow. He opened his fist, carefully unwound the lanyard, and slipped the key into his pocket.

He stood in an open space—likely what passed for a park in this reality. Moderately tall buildings surrounded him, lights winking from most of the windows. If Jace was still using the cache, this might be the simplest retrieval Harnett had done in a long time. He closed his eyes and cast about for the Network signal. It was loud, steady, strong. The cache was nearby.

Good. The less time he spent here, the better. And a quick success would justify the orders he was—if not disobeying outright, then at least delaying. Harnett let himself be the needle in a compass, turning toward the slight disturbance in the fabric of reality that was the cache's presence here. The sudden pressure wave that hit him was as unexpected as it was painful.

Harnett's knees wobbled. He would have fallen had it not been for his long years of training. Gritting his teeth, he cast about for the new signal. Another rent in the world, this one not carefully planned or even more carefully balanced like the cache. There was definitely something wrong here.

Could it be a natural phenomenon? Is that why this world was interdicted? Harnett shook his head, trying to clear it. The echo of the portal was fading, but his head still rang loudly enough to mask the subtler signal from the cache. There would be no finding it now. He would have to seek out the source of this unauthorized opening and try to seal it off before he could finish the mission.

He recalibrated to the attenuating signal, wondering if Jace had anything to do with it. This should be interesting, he thought.

Chapter 14

Melissa Klein

A SEARING LIGHT CUT THROUGH the throbbing in Melissa's head. She tried to turn away, but something kept her from moving.

Not again.

Her heart raced. Acrid saliva filled her mouth.

No. Not again.

She whimpered and squeezed her eyes shut.

"It's okay, Doc, just making sure you're still with us."

"Stirling?" Her voice was a harsh whisper.

"One and the same."

She stopped struggling as her mind fought to reconstruct memories of the past few minutes. The EMT was examining her. The light was his penlight, not the start of another episode. She blinked away its afterimages. Her eyes watered and refused to focus. Stirling was a dark blob kneeling beside her. Wait. How did she get on the floor? "Help me up?"

"I'm not sure that's a good idea, Doc. I'm thinking I should take you to the ER."

"I'm okay. Really." She shifted sideways and pushed up to sitting. The room stayed put. Mostly. The two of them were alone in the small curtained-off space in the shelter Martin had fashioned. Melissa fought past a moment of panic. Where had they all gone? Did the portal swallow them up? "Where is everyone?"

"I sent Martin to get some dinner for"—Stirling cleared his throat and swallowed—"Daniella."

She let out a deep exhale. "Reina. Her name is Reina." An image of the frightened young girl sharpened in her mind. She had to talk to her. Find out what she knew about the doorways. How they worked. Where they led to. Questions Melissa had suppressed for nearly her whole life. If they could be answered, maybe she would finally be able to understand what had happened to Borys. And then, maybe, start to forgive herself.

Stirling frowned.

This would be a lot easier if she knew what he was thinking. Had Reina tried to explain any of this to him? That would probably have made things worse. But at least it wouldn't be only Melissa talking about doors into other worlds. Of course, mass hysteria was an option.

"Can you tell me what happened? One minute you were talking to her, the next thing you were on the floor. Out cold."

Between this morning and tonight, he must really be wondering what the actual fuck was wrong with her. To be honest, that was taking up most of her mind, too. What happened? A really good question. One that Melissa wasn't ready to talk about. Definitely not to Stirling. Certainly not to some random ER doc. Soon, she would have to face Julian. The consequences of the missed appointments alone would be big.

Add the rest of the weirdness? She didn't want to think about it.

It was definitely time for some damage control. At this point, Melissa would take any kind of control at all. Scrambling up to the ratty sofa, she smiled reassuringly and leaned into what she had learned to do as a child. "Really. It's nothing. Something must have triggered another migraine. I've had them on and off since I was a kid." She stared at Stirling, almost daring him to challenge her. "I'm fine. Promise. I'll go home and head right to bed. First thing in the morning, I'll call my neurologist. Okay?" She kept her gaze steady, willing him to see her as the put-together psychiatrist she presented to the world every day. "But I need to talk to Reina as soon as possible."

"It's late and you're in no condition to drive." There was steel in Stirling's voice that made his words a command rather than an observation.

And as much as she wanted to believe otherwise, he was right. The actual headache wasn't the real problem. The ocular symptoms were. Despite willing it away, she could still see the slight sparkle dancing in her peripheral vision. The headlights from oncoming cars would turn into sharp-edged prisms. "It's fine. Really. I'll call a cab or something." Maybe her car would still be there in the morning.

"In this neighborhood?" Stirling got to his feet. "Come on. I'll take you home."

She absolutely needed to find a pleasant way to ditch him. Not only to have the opportunity to talk to Reina alone, but also to dodge all the difficult and awkward questions he was bound to ask. "Don't you have a shift starting soon? Besides, you've done more than enough."

Stirling winced and turned from her. "If that were true, Daniella wouldn't have OD'd."

You couldn't take responsibility for other people's choices. It was a hard lesson he would have to learn before he burned out from his job and his ministry. *And how's your therapeutic distance doing, Doc?* Melissa shook her head. Now was not the time to have a full-on argument with herself.

She was still trying to find the right words to either comfort or distract him when he turned to her with his hand outstretched.

"Keys."

Panic fluttered in her heart. She needed to stay. At least until Reina got back. "You really don't need…"

"Doc, you're in no position to tell me what I do or don't need. One more word and I will call for that ambulance."

She'd pushed him too far. She could see it in the narrowing of his warm brown eyes and in the stiffness in his expression. Keys it was. But it didn't mean she was going to talk on their way.

Stirling offered her his free hand and even though Melissa didn't think she needed it, she let him help her up. Her head throbbed with the change in position. Once she was safely home, there were meds she could take that would help. Or at least guarantee her a long and dreamless sleep. She glanced around the empty room that was Martin's home once more. First thing in the morning, she was coming back to talk to Reina. "Will they be okay?"

"Define okay."

Melissa sighed. It was the same demand he'd made of her on the night of the count. Somewhere between then and now, her definition of the word had definitively changed.

As they drove, only the stilted voice of the GPS broke the silence. Stirling parked where Melissa pointed. He shut off the car and they sat in the quiet darkness, the car's engine softly ticking, each waiting for the other to say something. Melissa sighed, unbuckled her seatbelt, and exited the car. Stirling followed. "What about you?" Melissa said. "How will you get home?"

"I have an overnight shift. I'll take a ride share to the hospital."

Melissa tried to lighten the mood. "In this neighborhood?"

He shot her a look she couldn't interpret. "I'm going to check on you after my shift. Text me when you've talked to that doctor of yours."

She didn't need a babysitter, and she surely didn't need Stirling to add her to his ministry, but she was too spacey to argue. If this followed the pattern of other episodes, the headache would get worse until she could medicate and sleep. "Deal." She held out her hand for her keys.

Stirling placed them in her palm and gently encircled her hand in both of his. "You sure you don't want me to take you to the ER?"

Melissa had had enough scans of her head for several lifetimes and had dealt with far too many physicians convinced they would have the magic cure for her constellation of symptoms. Symptoms. She turned a nascent laugh into a cough. There was no medicine for seeing doors between worlds or for the children lost among them.

Blinking back tears, she walked away from Stirling, the keys rattling uncontrollably in her shaking hands. Shrinks who claimed to see things that weren't there ended up as patients.

The visual distortion made the apartment hallway stretch out ahead of her into an impossibly distant vanishing point.

She struggled to focus as the swirling air threatened to become portals to nowhere. "Toto, I don't think we're in Kansas anymore," she muttered to herself, but the humor she'd relied on to deal with the intense pressures of her medical training wasn't helping now.

It took her five tries to unlock the door to her condo.

Intrusive memories from childhood broke free of her tight control in a barrage of fractured images. Her imaginary friend. The shining door from his *there* to her *here*. Red and blue emergency lights.

The past merged with with the present. The nothingness that had fallen through the crack between worlds and into the dying body at her feet had weight. It pressed down on her. Made it hard to breathe. She was a helpless kid again, sobbing as they took her friend away in a police car. Powerless to save Borys or Reina or herself.

Melissa struck the edges of furniture that had suddenly jumped into her path on the way to the bathroom. She fumbled in the dark for her migraine meds. The childproof cap nearly broke her. When she finally got it loose, half of the bottle emptied itself all over the bathroom counter. *I'll deal with that tomorrow,* she thought as she dry-swallowed several of the capsules. Even through the haze of pain and confusion, she knew there was no making sense of this. Not now. Not tomorrow. Maybe not ever.

But the meds would make her sleep, and that was as good as she could hope for at present.

She stumbled to the bedroom and flopped fully clothed across the unmade bed, waiting for chemical oblivion to quiet her whirling thoughts.

δ

Harnett Wellerman

HARNETT STRODE THROUGH THE STRANGE city's streets listening for the echo of the unauthorized opening. It was like a wound through reality—but more of a clumsy slash instead of the surgical precision of a Traveler's entry. Had Jace lost all of his skills? Perhaps he was showing signs of RDD after all.

If this incursion had been Jace, then it was more critical than ever that he locate the man. At least keep the agent from doing something catastrophic the Network would have to fix.

The cold was an inconvenience, but Harnett had decades of experience on difficult missions. Jamming his hands into his jacket pockets, he slipped through groups of other walkers until he'd tracked the signal to an abandoned street. Good. Fewer witnesses meant fewer loose ends. Fewer complications. Especially critical given his unsanctioned crossing.

The signal weakened and finally silenced as Harnett reached a dark building, its windows boarded over. An abandoned structure would make a decent hiding place for someone who didn't want to attract any notice. Which assumed that Jace was thinking coherently. A big assumption. Actually, two big assumptions. It might not have been Jace at all.

Not having the right data on this world was more than problematic. Could it be that people here had already developed the ability to Travel, albeit in a clumsy fashion? That would be one good reason it was interdicted. The Network preferred to find worlds without their own access to the multiverse, or at the very least, on the cusp of grasping it. It made it far simpler to control the flow of information and resources.

Harnett moved closer. A knot of people gathered near the entrance. Well, so much for no witnesses. He was going to have to risk some kind of contact.

They were a ragged bunch. Rough-looking men dressed in cast-off and mismatched clothing huddled around a metal can flickering with a fire. A thin thread of smoke wavered in the still air. Harnett looked down at himself and nodded. Given how ill-prepared his clothing was for the climate, he would easily fit in with these desperate few. Just in case, he grasped the hilt of the knife hidden in his pocket.

As he was trying to determine what to say, one of the men looked up and waved him closer. "Too cold to be walkin' around like that."

That was too easy. Harnett nodded and stepped closer to the fire. It put out a surprising amount of heat, and he was grateful for it. "Thank you."

A sharp barking startled him. He looked down to see a dog as ragged looking as the men around the fire, yapping at him. Its head and tail were lifted, and it stared at him with a predator's eye. A line of raised fur lined its back. Harnett shifted his weight to his back leg, preparing for the confrontation.

"Poplar!" One of the men darted forward and scooped up the animal before Harnett could kick it away. "She's harmless," he said, staring at the dog and not him.

I'm not, Harnett thought and nodded at the man. He took his hands from his pockets and slowly reached out to the fire. "Smart creature to be wary of strangers."

"She is," the man said.

Harnett wasn't sure which part of his statement he was referring to.

The man gave him a long, uneasy look before he and his still growling dog picked their way through icy patches and mounds of trash toward the door of the building behind them. So it wasn't abandoned. Perhaps what or who he was looking for was right inside. He turned to the other two men still at the fire. "What's in there?"

"You new around here, too?" The man who answered him was the one who had invited him to their little circle. His dark skin gleamed in the firelight. When he smiled, shadowed gaps showed where he was missing several teeth.

"I guess I am," Harnett said.

"Martin runs a safe house here. No comings or goings between ten and six. No smoking inside, neither. So smoke 'em now if you got 'em."

The third man chuckled and took out a stub of a cigarette. He patted through a few pockets and his hand emerged with some matches. The smell of the lit tobacco brought back memories of his father Harnett had thought he'd locked away long ago. In a near unconscious movement, he patted the pocket that held his key.

He edged away so he could keep both men in his sight lines. Wary was good. Distracted was not. "Was the man with the dog Martin?"

The gap-toothed man laughed until he coughed. "Nah. That was Thorne. And Poplar. They new here, too. Martin would be inside, seeing to everything. Keeping the peace."

The smoking man took a few deep, rapturous puffs before putting the cigarette out and stowing it back into a pocket. "Gettin' to be that time," he said in a voice like rough gravel.

"I'll be along, Jack. Let Martin know there's another one in need of some blankets." He turned to study Harnett. "You ain't thinking of sleeping rough, are you?"

Well, he didn't even need to ask. This couldn't have worked out better if he'd planned it.

"No, sir. And thank you."

"Sir." He cackled again before shaking his head. "You definitely ain't from around here. I'm Harrold." He held out a hand. Leathery fingers poked out of threadbare gloves.

"Harnett."

After a brief hesitation, Harrold pulled his hand back. "I'm what you call the con-see-urge of this place. Been squatting here since before Martin cleaned it up and organized it. Account of that, he lets me come and go. Bring in new folk."

Harnett nodded as if this all made perfect sense.

"But if I bring you in, I'm sayin' you okay. So keep to the rules."

He nodded again. All that mattered was getting inside and finding whoever had opened the gash in reality. If it was Jace, so much the better. He'd spent nights in worse places.

Harrold frowned up at the sky. "Looks like it might get a lot colder pretty quick tonight. Let's get you settled."

Not even bothering to glance at what few unfamiliar stars might outcompete the city lights, Harnett followed the old man into the waiting building.

A slight young man stood just inside the door, blocking their way. His dark eyes were narrowed, his face haggard. "Another of your strays, Harrold?"

"That's Martin," Harrold whispered, as if confiding a secret to a friend.

"This isn't a good time for strangers," Martin said glancing at Harnett, and then at the door. "Sorry. There's a shelter not far from here."

It would be simple enough to push his way past him. Whatever authority he had was clearly not based on size or strength, but Harnett didn't want to brute-force his way in. At least not if he had any other option.

"C'mon man. It's gonna be bad out there," Harrold said.

Martin shook his head. "We're full up."

"You're going to go there? Really?"

"Harrold, I can't save the fucking world." Martin's words were angry, but he looked fragile, close to tears.

His fisted hand concealed in his pocket, Harnett gripped his knife. He had to get inside. He had hoped to gain these people's trust, but there were other ways.

"I'm sorry, man," Harrold said. And it seemed like the old guy really was.

As much as direct force might be more satisfying, there were likely too many other people in the building. He didn't like those odds. Harnett let his shoulders and head droop while studying the entry, already planning his next move. It didn't look like the door had a working lock mechanism. Easier to feign defeat, then break inside in a few hours, when the inhabitants would be sleeping. Would they post guards? Even if they did, Harnett knew he could handle them. Especially with surprise and stealth on his side.

"Hey, you tried. I get it," he said, turning toward the street.

"Martin!" A girl's outraged voice filled the room.

He turned back to see the boy's cheeks flush and his eyes flash with anger. "Daniella, go back to your room!"

She walked up close to him, her body language pure challenge. "I thought you didn't turn anyone away."

Martin backed away from her. "This doesn't concern you." His voice was thin, wavering.

"Just because you're mad at me doesn't mean it's okay to hurt someone else."

Interesting. There was something off about their dynamic. Martin seemed afraid of this thin and fragile-looking girl.

"I'm not...I just..." Martin shook his head. "Please. Just go back upstairs."

"I'm not her. I can't be her. But for her sake, please, don't do this."

The flush started at Martin's neck and spread across his cheeks to his forehead. Harnett was certain he was going to explode in rage and that the girl would be his target. Instead, the boy turned his face away, his shoulders shaking. The girl hesitated long enough to catch Harrold's attention.

"Get him set up for the night, okay?"

The man nodded and motioned for Harnett.

As if she was uncertain of Martin's response, the girl slowly placed her hand on the boy's shoulder. A shudder rippled through his body. She sighed.

"He gonna be okay?" Harrold asked.

"I wish I knew," she whispered.

Harnett slowed to study her as they walked past. As their gazes met, it was as if a vibration hummed between them, but she didn't seem to notice. He stopped. Harrold tried to grab his sleeve and Harnett shook him off.

It was her. Decades of training Travelers had made Harnett exquisitely sensitive to the subtle signs of the ability. Did she even know what she had done? Maybe there was a way Harnett could still turn this to his advantage. He might not have a lead to Jace, but if this reality was creating native Travelers, the Network would want to know.

Harrold latched onto him more tightly and pulled him toward the back of the room and another door he hadn't noticed until now.

One mystery solved. A new one in its place. Something to work with.

Chapter 15

Melissa Klein

THE GAUZY REMNANTS OF DISTURBING dreams fogged Melissa's brain as she reached for the clock on her night table to silence its alarm. Slamming the snooze did nothing for the rhythmic pulse flooding her ears. She swiped at it again, her clumsy arm sweeping it from the table and yanking the plug from the outlet. The noise kept droning.

Fuck. The phone.

It had fallen from her coat pocket to the floor by her bed. Now that she was at least somewhat awake, she realized it had been ringing on and off for some time. She stared at it in fascinated horror as it stilled for a moment, only to start up again with that overly cheerful electronic music that had seemed the most innocuous ring tone when she'd gotten the new device. There would now be nearly three days' worth of calls, texts, and notifications waiting from a world that she hadn't really been a part of since entering the homeless encampment with Stirling.

Her mind shied away from everything that had happened there. Denial was like splurging on credit, and Melissa was painfully aware the bill was coming due.

She ran her hands through her snarled hair, struggling to reorient herself. Time: morning. Place: her condo. Person: That was a harder one to answer at the moment. At least the sharply edged wheels of light weren't following her gaze anymore. For now.

She had promised Stirling that she would call her doctor in the morning. But not a neurologist. She knew who she desperately needed to talk to: the one person in all the possible worlds she didn't want to face.

Ignoring all the notifications on the phone, including ones she was sure were from Julian Maxwell, she opened the messaging app.

She'd now missed two appointments with him. Knowing how much she'd inconvenienced him was enough to flood her with acute embarrassment. But that was the least of her problems. What could she tell him that made any sense at all? Her own experience sounded unhinged, even to her—and she'd lived it.

She started typing. *I'm sorry. Something happened.* She deleted that last word. *Something is happening to me that I don't understand.* Understand wasn't the right word, exactly, but she didn't know how else to put it. *I need your help.* She watched the letters glow on the screen and deleted that last sentence, imagining him reacting with a call to 9-1-1. Not optimal. Okay, then. Instead, she replaced it with something slightly less alarming. *I need a session with you.* Then she paused, watching the cursor blink, not sure what else she could say in a message that would arrive without context. *It's urgent.* Urgent was a good word. Urgent said important, not a full blown disaster or emergency.

Emergency meant lights and sirens. Urgent meant today. Or at least she hoped that's what it meant to Dr. Maxwell.

If he called her back, she wasn't sure she'd be able to talk coherently. The dancing dust motes had put away their ballet shoes for now, but that didn't mean they wouldn't return. *Please message me with a time at your convenience.* Just as she was about to hit send, she hesitated. He would be concerned, just as she would be if their positions were reversed. Two missed appointments with no communication spelled acute crisis. *I'm home and I'm safe.*

It was done.

No taking it back now.

Melissa flopped back on the bed, dreading the buzz of a reply.

It came almost immediately in the ringing of her phone. Fuck. She hit accept and put him on speaker. Harder to glean someone's emotional state with the added background noise. She hoped.

"This is Dr. Klein," she answered, in her best professional tone.

"Melissa..." Dr. Maxwell let his voice trail off, giving her space to answer.

He was such a good therapist, she wanted to scream. Instead, she took a deep, steadying breath and let the truth fly. "Something happened on the night of the count. Something I'm still struggling to process. If you had time to see me today, I would be very grateful."

There was a brief pause at his end that felt like an eternity. "I can fit you in at eight. That's thirty minutes from now. Can you make it here by then?" He spoke slowly and carefully as if he was concerned she wouldn't process his words.

Something tight unwound in her chest. "Thank you. Yes."

"Melissa?"

She stiffened. "Yes?"

"I'm worried about you."

Same, Julian, she thought, same. "Thank you. I'll be there."

"Good."

She ended the call and took a ragged breath. Thirty minutes. Fifteen to his office, which gave her ten to get presentable. No time for a shower. Not even time for coffee. She washed up and put some subtle eyeliner on, hoping she didn't look like a hungover raccoon. Changing into a fresh set of clothes left her five minutes to spare. There was a Dunks drive-through on the way. Caffeine was definitely medicinal for migraines.

She made it to Maxwell's in under ten minutes, the traffic lights working out in her favor for a change. Sitting in her car in the designated space next to his home office, she sipped the coffee, grateful for its warmth and for giving her something to do with her hands. Would he see it as the crutch it was if she brought it in with her?

Probably.

Definitely.

Melissa decided she didn't care.

She walked up to the front door of the big old Victorian home, painted in cheerful shades of blue and purple. It was a bright spot against the heavy gray sky and dingy snow covering the dead lawns. The neat sign on the door instructed patients to press the button on the doorbell and head inside. The door to his office opened almost as soon as she'd sat down in the foyer he'd transformed into his waiting room.

"Come in," he said, softly.

Julian looked exactly like the character a director would invent if they needed a shrink in a movie. Tall. Slightly stooped. Short hair gleaming with silver strands. Wireframe glasses. Bow tie. Tailored button-down shirt. Cardigan sweater. The mental health version of Mr. Rogers.

Melissa stood and her coat dumped off her lap. She managed to hold onto the coffee, at least.

Without saying a word, Julian leaned over and picked up the coat before hanging it on the antique coat tree in the corner.

So much for camouflaging her state of mind. She followed him into the cozy den, complete with the dark wood desk free from any hint of clutter and the ubiquitous soft leather chairs whose presence said "therapy appointment".

"Make yourself comfortable. Can I get you something to drink?"

Melissa hefted her coffee. "All set." She didn't mind the pleasantries. As soon as they were over, she was going to have to rip open her soul. Suddenly that didn't seem like such a smart idea.

He sat back in his seat and steepled his fingers together. "What's on your mind?"

"It's complicated." She gripped the smooth wooden chair arm with her free hand. "I don't know where to start."

"I generally find the beginning to be the best place."

The beginning. That would be Spain, when she was six. Even if Julian had cleared his whole schedule for the day, there wouldn't be enough time to start there. But maybe she could connect the dots from there to here. "Two nights ago, during the homeless census, something triggered a massive ocular migraine. The first one I've had in a very long time."

Julian sat with his head slightly tilted to one side, his eyes focused slightly past her, listening intently. He was definitely a good listener. She wondered what he heard in the words she wasn't saying.

"According to my EMT partner, I ended up doing emergency CPR on a girl in a homeless encampment. Saved her life, actually."

"According to?" Julian raised his eyebrows.

"I don't remember it. I don't remember anything that happened after the scintillating scotoma began until the next morning. I came to sitting in my car nearby."

"Ahh."

This would be simpler if she were only a patient. Instead she could see her own techniques being used, well, not against her, but definitely in a way that made her acutely aware of her own distress. "I haven't lost time like that since I was a kid."

Julian nodded.

She had disclosed her medical history to him years before, but it hadn't really been relevant to the work they did together—a combination of therapeutic supervision and occasionally some personal therapy related to it. A good clinician was a self-aware clinician, and the work often triggered issues from one's own past. Julian had been her supervising psychiatrist for years. Even long past the point where supervision was required, she continued to see him. She trusted him. But could she trust him with this?

"I would imagine a neurologist might be more helpful with your migraine issues."

"I can manage the headaches. I've been dealing with them for a long time." Inwardly she cringed at how defensive she sounded. But really, she'd seen every top neurologist in the Northeast over her lifetime. Not one of them could help her with the real problem.

"You said you needed my help. Urgently."

Melissa took a deep breath. Nodded.

The soft hum of a humidifier was the only sound in the room.

Julian broke the silence. He must have taken pity on her. "So why have you missed the past two appointments with me?"

She winced and blurted out, "When I was six, I had an imaginary friend. Except he wasn't." Her body went into adrenal overdrive, not knowing whether to fight, flee, or freeze. Her heart raced and sweat beaded on her forehead. She sneaked a glance at Julian, who hadn't moved from his intense listening pose.

"He was real. He came to play from time to time. From a door to another world."

As if finally saying it out loud were the magic to summon her memories, his image blazed in her mind. A slight boy with intense brown eyes and dark unruly hair. A single dimple on his left cheek when he smiled. A warm laugh that seemed made to share. Julian remained silent and Melissa kept talking to fill the space between them.

"His name was Borys. And one day, my mother found us playing together." She sneaked a quick look at Julian. "We weren't doing anything wrong. He was just a strange child, impossibly in our home. Who didn't understand or speak English."

Her mother had been confused at first. How had he gotten there? Where were his parents? Then Melissa tried to explain that he was her friend from Spain. The boy she had met through the portal at El Alhambra. The portal everyone believed she'd invented. Where her troubles had all started.

"My mother began to yell. Borys started to cry. I was afraid."

Tears spilled down Melissa's face. Julian leaned forward and silently handed her a box of tissues. Sobs racked her body, despite her struggle to keep in control. All the while, Julian waited. As her breathing calmed and the crying eased, she heard the quiet ticking of the grandfather clock. Melissa didn't know how much of their session she'd already burned through with nothing accomplished except for falling apart in front of her therapist.

His voice as gentle and even as it always was, Julian asked, "What happened then?"

She drew in a tiny gasp and looked up at him. He hadn't challenged any of what she'd said. Didn't insist she was making it up or letting her imagination run wild or simply lying for attention—all things doctors and therapists had told her through her childhood. Relief mixed with the fear she'd held onto so long, and it took a long moment to control the fresh upwelling of raw emotion so she could speak again.

"When it became clear that my mother couldn't communicate with him and that he had no identification, she called Social Services." The rest of that afternoon was a blur of sirens and strangers and Melissa crying and screaming until a massive migraine left her incapacitated for days. From her mother's viewpoint, it was the only logical and appropriate action to take. Looking back all those years, Melissa could even acknowledge that, but it didn't change how wrong it had been. How guilty she had felt ever since, even as she'd tried to forget. Her hands shook and she clasped them around her coffee cup in a fruitless attempt to hide how rattled she was from Julian. "I never saw Borys again."

"What do you think happened to him?"

She shook her head. There were times when she had been certain Borys hadn't been real. On the few occasions she'd worked up the courage to ask her mother about him, Melissa ended up undergoing more rounds of tests and therapies. For her headaches, they'd always said. It was safer to believe what she'd been told. "A social worker took him away. I couldn't stop her. It was my fault." Borys probably spent his life swallowed up by the foster care system. And if he were lucky, survived to age out into living in the streets. Like Martin and many of the people he sheltered.

"You know as well as I do that repressed memories find a way out. You've also been struggling with prolonged grief surrounding your parents' deaths, and a sense of stagnation in your work. All these things are undoubtedly connected. Isn't that what prompted your sabbatical?"

She nodded.

"And you just spent an intense night among Boston's most vulnerable. It's probably no coincidence it was that night that brought your past flooding back."

Julian had used his most calming professional voice. A voice like a warm blanket. Or tomato soup and grilled cheese on a raw day. Such a reasonable tone joined to the most logical of conclusions. She could just about hear his thought process: one lonely, imaginative girl with ocular migraines. One homeless or lost boy—likely autistic or traumatically mute—who wandered into her yard. It only made sense that she would conjure up portals out of the ocular distortions that looked like something otherworldly to explain his sudden appearance. The visual aura is what linked him to what she had believed she'd seen in Spain. And her parents' deaths brought up Melissa's unresolved guilt from losing her childhood friend.

Simple. Logical. Tidy. Mystery solved.

If only.

None of that explained Reina, or Thorne and Poplar. Or the fact that Melissa was able to see what looked like worn places in the fabric of reality, and that openings seemed to follow her wherever she went.

The sound of clock chimes brought her back to Julian's den and the solid reality of his supportive presence. It was 8:45. Time to wrap up their session. Time for Melissa to shove her past back in its box and assure Julian that she was perfectly fine now. The session ended up being better than she could have hoped for—as far as Julian was concerned, she wasn't having delusions or hallucinations. Just ordinary childhood trauma.

"I'd like it if you came back tomorrow for another session, Melissa. I have a cancellation at nine a.m. And I'm going to recommend you take a brief leave from seeing patients."

She nodded. Both things made sense. Even if Julian's assessment was simplistic and not remotely close to the truth.

"I also want you to inform me when you experience another visual aura. If we can process your emotional reaction to them in real time, they may have less power over you."

That would be a lot of texts or phone calls, but if she didn't want to lose her license, she was going to have to work with him.

"I also think you should get a fresh neurological workup." He held up his hand as she drew breath to speak. "I know. You've been down that road, but there's been a lot of new research and findings about migraines in the past few years." He leaned over and pulled out a leather-bound folio from the shelf beside him. "If nothing else, Dr. Merrill can evaluate your medication regimen. Here's her card."

"Thank you."

"Melissa."

She jerked her head up. Julian's brow furrowed as he studied her.

"I don't think your distress meets the criteria for an impaired physician."

Fear and relief sounded a painful chord in her mind.

"But if you miss another appointment or don't follow through with my recommendations, I am honor-bound to report you."

"I know," she whispered. How could she blame him? She would have thought the same if their positions were reversed. As she stood to leave, he called her name again softly. She turned at the door to face him. Julian was still sitting in his chair, his face thoughtful.

"Something to consider. If Borys could travel through a portal, why wouldn't he just have gone home?"

It was a question that had haunted her for years. Her breath hitched in her throat. The past overwhelmed the present and even as she knew she stood frozen in the doorway to Julian's office, she was also seeing Borys's tearstained face as the social worker pulled him away. Then, as if all her pent-up adrenaline released into her bloodstream in a single furious bolus, she grabbed her coat and fled out the door.

δ

Thorne Truthscryer

THORNE WOKE UP TO PRESSURE on his bladder. He blinked into the dim light from the dying fire and stared into Poplar's unblinking eyes. The dog was standing on his torso. ::How are you so heavy?::

::i don't like him::

Still half asleep and shaking off the dreams that continued to plague him, Thorne rolled to his side, dislodging the pup. ::Huh?::

Poplar growled softly and sent an image of a pair of outsized feet flitting through his mind.

The man from the fire barrel. When Harrold had escorted him to a sleeping spot across the room, Thorne had kept himself between the man and Poplar. And listened. For a stranger who ought to be grateful for Martin's charity, he asked a lot of questions. He was especially curious about Reina. ::Can you smell him?::

::you insult me:: Poplar sneezed delicately.

::You know what I meant.:: That dog and her ego. When she didn't reply, he reached out to scratch her behind her silky ears. "Oh, mighty scent hound, please tell me where you sense our quarry."

She made a sound that was very much like a human harrumph, but leaned into his hand. ::still sleeping::

::Good.::

::i could go over and bite him::

::I wish you wouldn't.::

::liar::

::Fine. I wish I could bite him too, but that won't get us any answers.::

The night before, the man had skulked around the room, moving from blanket to blanket asking the other squatters how much they knew about Martin and his sister. Why would he need to know? ::We have to talk to Martin.::

::he doesn't really like me either::

::But Reina does and she is where Martin is.::

Poplar's ears perked up and she wagged her tail hard enough that her whole body wiggled.

Thorne never had to compete with anyone for Poplar's affections before.

::stop being so grumpy:: Panting, Poplar gave him a wide grin.

"I'm not grumpy." But even he heard the anger and hurt in his voice. It wasn't Poplar's fault—and it certainly wasn't Reina's. All of these complicated emotions muddied his senses, but he could feel the danger this man posed. To all of them. Thorne scooted out of the nest of blankets he'd made for the two of them and quietly picked his way across the floor. Most of the people who stayed here last night were already gone. Their beds and gear neatly folded on the shelves lining one wall. He wondered where they spent their days in this cold, harsh city. ::Tell me if the man moves::

Poplar answered with the smallest of rumbles.

They both used the area segregated for the latrine before heading to Martin's room. ::Are they awake?::

::yes!:: Poplar dashed beneath the curtain and yipped happily at Reina.

"Martin? May I come in? I need to talk with you." He wasn't sure what kind of greeting he would get or what Martin was feeling after last night. Thorne wasn't even sure what the others had seen, but he knew what the doctor had done. Knew what her ability to open doorways between worlds would lead to.

"You might as well. It's not like I can keep your damned dog out."

"Martin!" Reina chided.

Thorne parted the curtain and entered. Poplar had hopped up onto the sofa with Reina, wriggling on her back in doggy ecstasy while the girl rubbed her belly. ::Traitor.::

Poplar didn't even bother to answer.

"Say what you need to say and leave." Martin sat on a pile of cushions, staring out the window. Dawn was brightening the sky, though if Thorne's joints were right, they would be getting more snow soon.

As Martin turned to stare at him, Thorne had trouble pulling his incoherent thoughts together. "The stranger from last night…I don't trust him."

"That's funny. You're a stranger, and I don't trust you or your dog."

::told you—doesn't like you::

Thorne sighed. "He was bothering folks. Asking questions about you. And Reina."

Martin turned to glare at him, and Thorne winced. Every time someone said Reina's name, it must have been like losing his sister all over again.

"I told you it was a mistake to let him in," Martin said.

For a moment, Thorne thought Martin was talking about him and Poplar, but he'd been looking across the room at Reina.

Poplar flipped over and stood, shaking her fur back into place. ::likes him less than you::

Reina sighed. "He might have died out there."

It was clear this was not a fresh argument.

"And now what? I'm supposed to be responsible for everyone who shows up at our door?"

A strained silence trapped Martin and Reina. Thorne felt keenly like the interloper he was.

"I'm sorry," Reina finally said. "As soon as your healer friends give their leave, I can go."

A deep red flush spread over Martin's face. "That's not…I didn't mean…"

Thorne shuddered as fragments of last night's visions filled his mind. Reina would reunite with her family, and he would lose

Poplar to some force or event he couldn't yet see. He struggled to keep his fear from his companion, and for once, was glad she was so focused on the girl.

"This is...This is our home. It's not safe out there." Martin turned to stare out the window, so only Thorne saw the tears gathering in her eyes. "Please. Stay. I can get you into a school or a GED program. Anything you need."

"Thank you," Reina whispered. Poplar reached up to nuzzle her face and lick away the tears.

Thorne glanced away. Poplar was an empathetic soul. He wouldn't want her to be any other way. It was just hard to share her.

Martin turned his attention back to the room. "Why are you still here?"

For a moment, Thorne thought he meant here, in the shelter. It surprised him that this old building had already started to feel something like home. Well, home had always been where Poplar was.

::tell him about the bad man::

"Be careful of that newcomer. I think he's looking for something or someone."

"I'm careful of everyone," Martin said, narrowing his eyes at Thorne.

Reina sighed.

Martin softened his expression. "But thank you for the heads-up. I'll keep an eye on him."

::Let's go get you some breakfast.:: Food usually got Poplar's undivided attention, but now, she was sitting bolt upright in Reina's lap, staring out the window, her nose quivering.

::look! snow!::

Reina followed Poplar's pointing snout and clapped her hands. "It's so beautiful! Can I go outside?"

"Daniella, you hate the cold."

Thorne was certain neither Reina nor Poplar heard Martin's quiet comment.

Poplar's eyes glowed as brightly as Reina's.

"It's not safe. I don't want you to be alone," Martin said.

"She won't be," Thorne said. "I can send Poplar with her. If that's okay with you."

Reina held her breath and glanced at Martin. He gave the smallest of nods. The girl's smile warmed up the room.

The small dog bounced from Reina's lap to the nest of blankets beside her to the floor at Thorne's feet. ::really? I can play? with her?:: Poplar's excitement couldn't completely cover Thorne's pain. She leaned against his legs in reassurance. ::but if you need me here—::

Thorne knew if he asked, she would stay. But that wasn't fair. The dog deserved to frolic and run, not be stuck catering to an old man and his sick fear. ::Go with Reina. Protect her.::

"Wait. You need to take your medicine first."

She nodded as Martin fumbled with the little bottles. "And keep your skin covered up. I left Stirling's box full of hats and mittens by the front door."

Reina swallowed the pills before skipping from the room with almost as much energy and excitement as Poplar.

"You're still here," Martin said.

Thorne shrugged and headed for the curtain, but paused before pushing through it. He wanted to tell Martin to do whatever it took to keep Reina safe. But putting that burden on Martin after all the boy had already lost seemed unfair. Cruel. As cruel as the universe taking Poplar away from him. "That man from last night. He's dangerous. I don't know what he wants or why, but he shouldn't be here."

Martin's silence stretched out for a long moment. Just as Thorne was convinced he wouldn't respond, he answered quietly, "None of us should be here, but that doesn't change anything."

The truth of it was a stab in Thorne's heart. What good was seeing potentials if all his choices led to despair?

δ

Reina Vettel

REINA FOLLOWED POPLAR DOWN the unlit stairs. Even the dog complained about the smell. It was rank enough that Reina pressed one arm across her nose and mouth; how much stronger must it be for Poplar?

The dog scrabbled her paws against the metal door at the bottom of the stairwell. ::hurry up::

::Some of us don't see as well in the dark.::

::let's go let's go let's go::

Reina pushed open the heavy door to the lobby area instead of the one that led directly outside.

Poplar whined.

::And some of us don't have fur... :: It was far colder on this level than it was upstairs in the living areas. Martin didn't bother to keep fires going here at night. She was grateful for the warm outerwear that Stirling had left for them.

Rummaging through the box, she found mittens that fit. At least she didn't startle as much at the strangeness of her hands, and she was grateful there weren't any mirrors in Martin's rooms. Reina shied away from what might happen if she did get home. Would her own body be waiting for her? And would Daniella truly be dead, once Reina left?

If she could leave. She didn't want to get comfortable in this body, but she also had to be able to function. For now, she wasn't sure she had any other choice.

Maybe she should go back upstairs and ask Martin how to contact Doctor Melissa. Maybe between the three of them—Melissa, Thorne, and her—they could figure out what to do next. If her parents were on this world, maybe her new friends could help her find them. Surely her parents would know what went wrong.

Poplar's sharp bark interrupted her thoughts. Having that conversation with Martin in the room would be cruel to him. She had to find a way to meet with Thorne and the doctor without him. Maybe Poplar could help. ::Can you tell me where Thorne is right now?::

::hurry! you promised! play!:: She grabbed a long colorful scarf in her mouth and dragged it out of the box.

::Poplar? I really need to... ::

::no. no talk. just play::

::Find Thorne after?::

::after:: Poplar rolled herself up in the multicolored scarf.

Reina couldn't help laughing. She gently untangled the dog from it and looped the scarf around her own neck several times. There was enough length to cover her head like a hood. The ends still dragged almost to the ground. It was made of some soft, thick yarn. The feel of it against her face brought an old memory flooding back.

Snow wasn't common at home—winter meant drenching, chill rain that cut through you no matter how many layers you wore—but Reina remembered one winter morning when their land was covered in powdery drifts of white. She had to have been little. Maybe three. Old enough to walk on her own, but small enough that her father could still carry her.

Her parents had dressed her in her heaviest clothes and wrapped a woolen blanket around her. The blanket and her parents' laughter made her feel warm. Safe. And the three of them had romped in the snow until it was time for lunch.

::come on!:: Poplar bit down on one free end of the scarf and tugged Reina toward the door.

Her memory faded and she yanked the scarf out of Poplar's teeth with more force than she'd intended. ::Sorry!::

The pup leaned against Reina briefly before barking at the door.

::Ready?::

Poplar danced around Reina's feet in answer.

She leaned her weight into the door to open it. A vortex of white powder swirled around them, and Reina gasped at the sharp, bright world outside. Poplar ran into the empty lot next door and jumped up, trying to catch individual snowflakes. The cold was more intense than Reina remembered, but it was the beauty that took her breath away.

A thick coating of snow blanketed the trash, the piles of slush, the broken bricks, softening it all. Even the few scraggly trees seemed graceful, rather than stunted, with their white limbs outstretched. The thick gray clouds sat right on top of the city, smudging the skyline and erasing the tops of all the tall buildings. With very little wind, the snow created a wall of silence that stilled distant traffic noises.

Poplar bounded toward her, snow crowning her head and creating a ridge along her spine. She shook, and it flew off her in a white wave.

Reina smiled, looking up into the softness. "Snow is way better than rain."

A sharp bark signaled Poplar's agreement.

The dog shared an image of her throwing a ball made of snow and stood waiting, her pink tongue lolling from her panting mouth. Reina leaned down and scooped up a handful, pressing it into a dense, round form.

::yes! throw!::

Laughing, Reina tossed the snowball in a low arc. Poplar chased after it, tail streaming out behind her. At the last second, she pounced. The snow crumbled in her mouth. ::again!::

Poplar ran after every snowball Reina threw, huffing in delight each time one would vanish under her bite.

Reina couldn't remember the last time she had laughed like this. Everything had been so serious at home, and not just because of her parents' strained arguments. And then she ended up here. Where Martin's face was a map of pain and loss. She couldn't imagine him ever smiling. Surely he and his sister had laughed together. Sometime. But now, when he looked at Reina, there was only the hurt.

Maybe she should go inside now. Find Thorne. Talk to Melissa.

Poplar barked again, pulling her from her thoughts. Reina bent down to make one last snowball. Her cheeks and the tip of her nose burned a bit with cold, but she felt better than she had since the night of her transit. Her body felt stronger and the shaking and nausea had finally eased.

She threw the ball, but Poplar didn't chase it. Instead the dog stood still, her lips pulled back, a low growl rumbling out of her.

::You cold? Let's head back, okay?::

The growling got louder.

A bundled-up figure emerged from the snow. "Beautiful, isn't it?"

Reina recognized the voice of the man they offered shelter to. The man Martin and Thorne didn't like.

He stopped well out of Poplar's reach. "Thanks for speaking up for me last night."

Shivering, Poplar took a step closer to Reina.

She frowned, glancing between the man and the dog. ::What's wrong?::

::bad man::

He just looked cold and hungry to her. All the people Martin had taken in were as lost as she was, and even if they came from this reality, were just as trapped. She shrugged. "You needed a place to sleep."

"Well, I appreciate it." His eyes gleamed, and he gave her a slight bow. "You're Daniella, right?"

She sighed. "It's complicated. You can call me that." It wasn't worth trying to explain everything to someone who would probably vanish back into the maw of this city's streets as quickly as he had appeared.

::dangerous:: Poplar circled around Reina, as if patrolling a space between her and the man. The dog had stopped growling, but the hackles stood up all down her back.

::I'm just talking with him. I'm perfectly safe. You can go back inside if you want.::

::must protect::

::Fine, but there's nothing to protect me from, silly.:: Reina couldn't figure out what Poplar's problem was. The dog didn't like Martin, either. Maybe it was something about men other than Thorne.

"Well, Daniella, my name is Harnett Wellerman, and I think we might have something in common."

Not likely, she thought. "You mean aside from losing our homes and finding shelter here?"

"I think you must be a very special young lady."

Reina dropped her gaze to the snow-covered ground. Her father used to say that to her. What she wouldn't give to be able to hug him again. Wherever her parents had landed, she hoped they were safe. And together. "There's nothing special about this." She gestured to the building looming behind them.

"What would you say if I told you there was a way for you to escape?"

She might have only been here for a few days, but she wasn't that naive. If Martin had created a refuge out of this abandoned place, there had to be a reason. And there were folks who had lived this way for years. "I'd say you were dreaming." Something Martin had said flitted through her mind. "Or on drugs."

"Fair enough."

The wind rose and snow blew around them like dust devils. Reina shivered and stamped her feet to get some warmth back in them. It was time to find Thorne. "I'm going to—"

Harnett interrupted. "I felt a door opening last night. A special kind of door."

She gasped. Her hand throbbed with the remembered pain of clutching her beach stone. "What?"

He watched her and didn't answer.

"What. Did. You. Say?"

::bad man—smells wrong—go back::

Poplar tried to herd her toward the building's door. Reina stood her ground.

"There are doors—portals between worlds—and I think you have the power to open them." He beamed a smile that somehow didn't fit his face. "I can, too."

"Who are you?" she whispered.

"A friend."

Chapter 16

Harnett Wellerman

HARNETT STOOD SEVERAL ARMS' lengths from the girl as the snow continued to fall. It wouldn't do any good to spook her. Plus that damned dog had parked itself between them, growling. He knew he'd lose any chance of making a connection with her if he tried to get rid of it.

There was something in her fragile expression that felt younger than her years. He leaned forward, keeping his voice soft. "Don't be afraid. What we can do is amazing and rare." It had been years since he'd been a new agent recruiter, but the skills never faded. Create rapport. Connect. The need to be seen and understood was a fundamental weakness to be exploited in people all across the multiverse.

The dog's growl increased in pitch.

"Stop it!" she shouted.

She and the dog seemed to have an unusually strong connection. And it clearly hated him. Harnett needed to find a way to separate her from it. "I've always been a little afraid of dogs. Got bit as a kid." The sympathetic look on her face told him he'd scored a direct hit.

"It's okay. Poplar will behave." She gave the dog an intense look. "Right, Poplar?" It cringed and hid behind her with its tail tucked under its body. The girl turned back to him, her eyes shining. "How did you know about the opening?"

So she understood what she'd done. Good. And he'd set the hook. Even better. Now he had to decide how much of the truth to reveal. So much depended on what she might believe. And if she would leave her brother willingly.

"I have Traveled to many places."

She took a step closer and held her breath.

"And I know what it feels like when someone tears the barriers between realities." The girl was such a surprise. Certainly, she couldn't be the sole reason this world was interdicted. Probably a genetic sport. Individuals with the ability to Travel emerged occasionally from any given gene pool. Like he had. And generally vanished into some random opening they lacked the skill or understanding to control. How this one had managed to stay anchored was a question to answer later. After he'd gotten her to the Network for debriefing and study.

He took another step closer. The dog charged him, its teeth bared. Before Harnett could kick it away, the girl shouted its name.

"Poplar!"

The dog yipped and stopped short as if at the end of an invisible leash. Harnett glanced up at Daniella, impressed at the level of control she had over the animal.

"Bad dog!"

It hung its head and whimpered.

"Go inside. I don't care what Thorne and Martin told you."

The dog slunk away, keening. Daniella turned to watch it retreat, her hands on her hips.

"I'm sorry. I don't know what got into her. She's really a lovely creature."

"I'm sure," Harnett said. Always better to agree with someone you're trying to establish connection with.

"Could you...Could you teach me to Travel? Like you do?"

He kept a tight rein on his triumph and simply nodded. "That's why I came to look for you."

"You came here for me?" She blinked back tears. "I need to find my...find someone. Somewhere else. Away from here. Can you help me?"

The wind whipped snow devils in the space between them, and the girl shivered. Of course Daniella would be desperate to escape from this cold and bleak reality. This would be simpler than he'd thought. Perhaps the bond between brother and sister wasn't as strong as he'd feared. "Of course. I'd be happy to."

δ

Thorne Truthscryer

AFTER LEAVING MARTIN'S ROOM, Thorne went downstairs to take some of the supplies from the stacked crates. A few bottles of water, some bread, and a hunk of bright yellow cheese. At some point, he'd need to find real food for Poplar. He'd survived on far less, but she deserved better.

The past few days had taken more out of him than he wanted to admit. Not to himself and definitely not to Poplar. Bone-deep fatigue and restlessness were a powerful combination that only added to the misery waiting for him in his visions.

He sat with his pile of supplies near the bedroll Martin had assigned to him and stared at his gnarled hands. There was nowhere he could go. Staying here only led to loss.

His link with Poplar brought the echo from outside of her joyful playing—at least Reina could give her that. He knew this wasn't the young girl's fault, and yet, if she hadn't pulled him across the world walls, Thorne wouldn't be here alone, mourning.

He sighed, knowing that wasn't true. He learned a long time ago that lying to himself only made things worse. No, he'd most certainly be dead along with Poplar in the fire that took their cabin. His heart ached. He couldn't separate out the now from all the possible whens fanning out from this moment.

There was nothing he could do.

Facing away from the fire, he tried to sleep. Despite being used to the solitude of his little cabin, being alone in this space felt wrong.

Poplar's wordless cry pierced Thorne's mind. Panic flaring in his chest, he scrambled from the blankets to his feet trying to get a bearing on her location. ::Are you hurt?::

She couldn't or wouldn't answer him.

Thorne raced across the room. He struggled to see through her senses. She was outside. Cold. Alone. ::Poplar, where is Reina?::

Her mind was a tangle of intense emotion, fear paramount.

"Martin!" Thorne shouted. "Martin! She's in trouble!" His voice echoed through the vault of the building as he ran for the stairwell door. He nearly collided with the young man.

"Where is she?"

"I don't know. Poplar…"

"I don't care about your damned dog."

Thorne tamped down a burst of anger. "Outside."

They reached the front doors simultaneously. Martin yanked them open. Wind blew swirls of snow like cold smoke inside. Poplar was huddled under the overhang, shivering.

Thorne bent down to scoop her up and she fought against him in a mindless panic. ::It's me. You're safe. It's okay.::

She scratched him across the cheek. Thorne nearly dropped her. Instead, he tightened his arms around the flailing dog and gathered her into his chest. "What's the matter?" he whispered.

Her mindvoice was hoarse, as if she'd worn it out. ::bad! danger! wrong!:: The words were a jumble. Underneath them, a terrible sense of betrayal. Poplar shuddered once more and gave a long mournful wail, before falling silent.

Thorne quickly looked over her, but could find no injury. The falling snow coated his bare head and he shivered. He held the warm dog against his heart, grateful and afraid.

Beside him, Martin let out a string of curses and ran to the empty lot.

Poplar urged him to follow. Ahead, three indistinct figures stood in a triangle: Martin and Reina, and a stranger with his back toward them. Poplar glared, growling again, and jumped from Thorne's arms.

"Get the hell away from my sister!"

"He wasn't doing anything, Martin. We were just talking," Reina said.

The man raised his hands as if proving his harmlessness. As Thorne closed the distance, he recognized him from last night.

Poplar's wiry fur stood up on end, and her entire body pointed at the man, but she wouldn't leave Thorne's side.

::Did he harm you?:: Thorne was close to growling, too.

The dog pressed against Thorne's legs and she finally spoke to him clearly. ::she sent me away::

Why would Reina do that? Thorne frowned and realized he'd lost track of the argument unfolding in front of him.

"...can help me get back home." Reina shifted toward Martin and was trying to get him to talk to her. He kept his angry gaze focused on the man.

Thorne hadn't really paid him much attention at the fire barrel outside last night, other than to keep Poplar safe and out of his way. Now he studied the man: medium frame, wide shouldered, and well muscled with deep set eyes. His face was free of facial hair. The hair on his head, close cropped, dense, silver. A compact man. A dangerous man. He held himself in a way that suggested he was comfortable using his body as a weapon.

::told you::

How much of his impression was biased by Poplar?

"Your sister has a gift. I can help her understand it. Harness it."

Martin pushed Reina aside and stood between her and the man. "My sister almost died a few days ago. You don't understand shit." Next to him, Martin looked like an underfed child.

Thorne's joints ached in the cold. If this turned violent, he'd be of less help than the boy.

"I don't mean her any harm." The man's smile looked more like a grimace.

"Leave."

"Martin!" Reina's voice was shrill with outrage. "This isn't your choice to make."

"The hell it isn't."

Poplar's hackles were up again.

Thorne's vision clouded. Snowflakes slowed and twirled around him. His breath caught in his throat as potential futures withered and died, strengthening a handful that emanated from this one. Reina's new friend seemed to be the nexus of most of them, and there were none where Poplar remained at his side.

A heaviness settled on his chest. It was getting difficult to breathe. In the haze ahead of him, he could no longer see anyone. And even their rising voices were strangely muffled, as if Thorne were trapped in a private land apart from them.

::Poplar?::

The dog barked. He knew she was at his feet, but the sound came from a long distance away.

He had already lost her.

Chapter 17

Jace Vettel

AFTER THEIR FAILURE, THEY HAD both collapsed into an exhausted sleep. When Jace woke, he was certain he'd gotten no real rest.

"Where do we go from here?" Corinne paced the small room, shivering, a blanket wrapped around her. She looked haggard and haunted.

"I don't know." Jace saw potentialities like dust motes hanging in the air everywhere, but as soon as he focused on one, it faded away. Like his hopes of finding home and Reina.

"We were so close." Corinne was on the verge of tears.

Without her strength to lean on or her anger to push against, Jace felt unmoored. They needed to do something. To move. To choose. But each path seemed hopeless.

Last night the two of them, despite having drifted from one another over the years, seemed to work together in an effortless and familiar synchrony. Even in this desperate situation, there was joy in the process. Surely she had felt it, too. Jace glanced over at Corinne, but she wouldn't meet his gaze.

"You saw our home, didn't you?" It couldn't just have been his distorted hopes.

She nodded. "For a moment. Then silence. Darkness."

Darkness? No. Not darkness. Something got in their way. Something interposed itself between them and their path home. "I think...I think I saw...There was something familiar."

"You should know even better than I do what happens when you let your desire cloud your vision."

He had wanted to find Reina. Not a dilapidated building in this interdicted world. There had to be a reason their attempted transit took them there. "We need to understand what went wrong."

"We need to let it go. Try something else."

A familiar frustration tugged at him. This dance between them had gotten old and tired. It would almost be easier to give up than to fight with her again. But all the reasons he had kept trying in the past were still just as true now: He loved his wife and Reina was in danger. "Corinne, tell me exactly what you saw. I think...I know it's important. I also know you think I'm..." He shook his head. "I know I haven't been the partner you deserve. But please."

She drew breath to speak. Probably to argue.

Jace kept talking. "You have to believe me. I'd do anything for Reina."

"Anything?"

"Of course I would."

She finally stared directly at him. Something in her gaze sent chills down his spine. "If we get out of here—and that's a big if—will you let the Network doctors do a complete evaluation?"

"Corinne..."

Her voice rose in pitch. "If they rule out RDD, we'll know. If you have it, they can help you."

"You don't—"

"Don't you dare tell me I don't understand. This is for our daughter's sake. Will you do it?"

Her voice cut through him. Jace swallowed hard. She couldn't know what she was asking him to do, or she would never ask it of him. An image of his father in the Network's facility, white sheet covering his face, sharpened in his mind. He knew that would be him,

too. But if they survived and escaped this world, and he could send Reina and Corinne to a place of safety, he would sacrifice himself. It wasn't much different from the plan he'd tried to implement by coming here in the first place.

Breaking eye contact, Jace stared at his bare feet against the dull carpet. "Yes. Now tell me what you saw after the way was blocked."

Corinne stopped by the curtained window. "It felt like another portal opening, superimposed on ours, pulling us toward it. I saw a silhouette of a building. Boarded-up windows. Darkness."

Jace drew a startled breath. Something or someone interfered with their transit. Surely they had both Traveled to enough alternatives to know that coincidence meant someone manipulating the multiverse. Usually someone from the Network.

And that building was important. He was sure of it. "Scaffolding up one of the sides. Figures huddled around a fire in a metal barrel."

"Yes." There was a desperate hope in her voice.

"I've seen it before." It was the building from his nightmare at the homeless shelter. The one where Reina had been crushed beneath the weight of its masonry. He shivered as the images shocked through him again.

"Where?"

He hesitated. If he told her he'd dreamed about it, would she believe him? "I'm not sure, but I think it's important for us to find. I think it has something to do with getting home."

"So it's a real place. Here, in this world."

"Yes." Or was this truly his fear creating illusions?

Corinne sighed. "That's not much to go on."

"I know. But it's something." And if they kept moving, it decreased the chances of the Network finding them.

"What's the plan?"

In other circumstances, their best bet to navigate this reality would be the resources in the cache. But even if Corinne was right and no one from the Network could or would track them here, Jace still didn't want to leave a trail to follow. Especially if this place was a weak spot in the Network's control, or if there were native, untrained Travelers here. Either option would be something he and Corinne might be able to exploit after finding Reina.

"Back to the library. Their computers have mapping capabilities."

She nodded.

In wordless partnership, they packed up their scant belongings and left the hotel. In the elevator, Jace reached out to squeeze Corinne's hand. "It's going to be okay." Surprisingly, he actually believed it.

The glance she gave him was full of doubt and pity. She walked beside him, her silence a worry that he shared but couldn't admit. He was grateful for her presence, even as he felt guilty she was trapped here with him. If she had stayed with Reina, at least the two of them would have been free.

A steady snowfall covered their tracks. It quickly accumulated on the sidewalks and the roofs of the city's buildings. In other circumstances, the quiet snow would have been peaceful. Even magical.

Across from the library, they stood in a large open space that was now filling up with people out romping in the fresh snow with their dogs. Children ran around throwing snowballs. It had been far too long since he'd just played with his daughter. Too many times his obsession for finding the truth had isolated him from her and Corinne. "I swear, I will do better," he whispered. If Corinne heard him, she didn't respond.

Jace paused to look up at the imposing building. It felt like the center of the city, or at least its heart. He hoped it would have the critical information they needed.

He stopped short. In front of him lay a metal trashcan, still chained to a streetlight, its snow-coated contents strewn all over the sidewalk. It was identical to the one he'd seen last night near the building.

"Jace?"

He inhaled sharply. Another image superimposed itself on both the memory and the dream imagery. His first night in this reality had been spent struggling to stay warm around a fire in a can like this. Forcing himself back through the haze of fatigue and fear following his transit, he struggled to remember.

"Are you okay?" Corinne's voice was a discordant note.

The building was just down the block from the rough and desperate men who'd let him share their fire that night. "I know where we need to be," he said, even as a chill wriggled beneath his warm clothing and stole all of his body heat. As desperate and as miserable as he'd been that night, his mind had made a map of the route he'd walked from there to the library the next morning.

Jace closed his eyes briefly and leaned into the skills that long hours of training had made automatic. "That way," he said, nodding south from the library.

Corinne drew breath as if to speak and looked deeply into his eyes before nodding silently. The concern and the suspicion were clear in her expression, but so was a spark of hope. He had to hold onto that and believe it for himself, too.

Jace reached for her hand again; this time she let him hold it. He led her south. As they walked, the buildings changed. Closest to the library were quaint brick structures, taller than they were wide, arranged along narrow streets that met at awkward angles. Many of the street-level doors led to storefronts. A steady stream of comfortably dressed people walked by.

The further they traveled, the wider and straighter the streets became. Fewer people were strolling the snowy sidewalks, and the buildings, while still brick, were more generic rectangles. Most had metal shutters in the windows and tall security fencing all around. He felt the pressure of being watched by unseen eyes.

"It feels like a different city," Corinne said.

"It is." Just as there were different instances propagating across the multiverse, there were multiple realities within any given instance. They had just crossed one of those unspoken boundaries into a place where fewer nexus points existed and even fewer potentials branched out from those points.

"Jace, we're walking into a dead end. Are you sure we're going the right way?"

"I know it feels like that. But this is where the opening we felt last night came from. Can't you sense it? We're getting closer." It couldn't just be his desperation to get home to Reina, though that was definitely goading him onward.

"There's so much confusion and overlap. I'm not sure." She pulled her brows together but continued to let him lead.

They paused at a complicated intersection of a jumble of streets. Vehicles whipped past them at ungoverned speeds. He studied all the spokes radiating from the center, feeling like he was choosing which reality to follow. A tree-lined side street looked ethereal, the bare branches coated in white. Even without his skills as a Traveler, Jace would have known that road led to the other city. The one with cafés and galleries and warm homes and bright futures.

Across the intersection was a small tent settlement. Bits of broken and abandoned equipment stuck up from snowbanks. Jace lifted his chin toward the tents. "That way."

He couldn't be completely certain, but he thought he recognized the general shape and feel of his surroundings. After initially arriving here on a cold, damp night and realizing he couldn't find an opening home, he'd wandered the city's streets, alternating between guilt and fury. It was a potent combination that had threatened to disrupt his memories and make it hard to retrace his steps. But it was different now. Corinne was here. They would be able to get home. He had to hold onto that. Despite the hopelessness of their surroundings, he was sure the building was the key.

For the first time since he'd found himself on this bleak world, he let himself believe he'd see his beloved Reina again.

δ

Reina Vettel

REINA GLARED AT MARTIN as he took a step closer to Harnett. "I don't belong here and I'm not your responsibility." As much as she didn't want to hurt him, she also wasn't going to let him get in the way of finding her parents and getting home. Even if it meant that he lost every trace of his Daniella.

Before he could respond, Poplar's howl pierced through the cold. The raw emotion of it chilled Reina to the core. She let go of all her earlier annoyance and opened her mind to the dog. ::Poplar? What's wrong?::

There was no coherent answer, only the animal's pain. She frowned, looking for her in the suddenly swirling snow. And saw Thorne collapse to his knees.

"No!" she cried, racing over to the old man and crouched beside him. Poplar pressed against him, whimpering. Thorne's face was as pale as the snow piling up around them. Was he dying? She could barely let herself think that, lest Poplar hear her. "What's wrong? Are you hurt?"

He lifted his head slowly. His eyes were narrowed with pain. "I...can't...breathe." His voice emerged as a strangled whisper.

"Martin! Help me! We have to get him inside!" There was no way she could move him on her own.

"Here, let me." It was Harnett.

Martin glared up at the larger man. "Fine. But you and I aren't even close to finished."

Poplar's lips peeled back from her teeth as the two moved closer.

"Dani—Rei—" Martin shook his head. "Can you tell her I'm trying to help?"

She nodded and winced. It was the first time Martin had even come close to calling her by her real name. ::It's okay, Poplar. He knows what he's doing. You can trust him.::

The dog didn't answer, but she stopped growling.

As the two hoisted Thorne to his feet, Reina scooped up the vibrating Poplar, half convinced she might bite her. "It's going to be okay," she murmured. The dog gave up and lay limply in her arms.

It seemed like the short walk back inside the shelter took forever, with Martin and Harnett half-carrying, half-dragging Thorne. Reina set Poplar down gently and found the box of blankets Stirling had dropped off the other day. Most of them were still there, folded neatly inside. By the time she dragged the box over, Thorne was lying on the ground and Harnett was nowhere to be seen. He couldn't have gone far. She was sure he would help her. But for now, Thorne needed her. She grabbed a stack of blankets and made a makeshift mat on the floor.

Thorne groaned as Martin rolled him side to side, tucking the blankets beneath him.

"Cover him, too. We need to keep his core temperature up," Martin said, all his anger now channeled into purpose.

Martin glanced at Poplar once more as if asking permission before gently lifting Thorne's head and putting a folded blanket beneath it.

This was a different side of him than Reina had seen. She flushed with shame. Of course he cared about the people living here. Of course he did what he could to keep them safe. Just as he had done with her.

"Okay. I messaged Stirling."

"That's it? We just have to wait?"

"He's breathing and he's got a pulse."

She sat on the floor next to Thorne, slipped off her mittens, and took his hand in hers. It was cold, the skin clammy. Every moment seemed like an eternity. "Where is he?"

"He'll be here."

Reina watched for the slight movement in his chest from Thorne's shallow exhales, feeling useless. She reached out and let her hand rest on Poplar's head.

"There has to be something else we can do!"

Martin cocked his head. "Listen."

In the distance, sirens wailed.

δ

Stirling Hughes

HIS OVERNIGHT SHIFT HAD been busy, but at least none of the calls had been gunshot wounds for a change. Stirling sighed and eased into the booth at the Sunnyside Up. The waitress came over with a fresh pot of coffee.

"Rough night?" Stella asked. Her face was deeply lined by skin that had seen too much sun and too many cigarettes, but her eyes sparkled. Her name tag read Estelle. As far as Stirling knew, no one called her that, not in all the years he'd been coming here after his overnights.

He shrugged. "The usual."

Stella laughed. "Want the usual, too?"

"You know it." The regulars were there along with some new faces—construction workers sat at one of the large tables, one chair piled with their orange vests and safety hats. Stirling wondered what building was slated for demolition this time. And what the cost of the new property would be. Not just in terms of rent, but in the loss of neighborhood places like this one. And the shelter that Martin had created.

What would happen to all the people who lived in that building?

How much longer would it be before Stirling couldn't afford to live in this city anymore?

Stella jolted him out of his thoughts, deftly sliding his food in front of him. "Watch the plate. It's hot!"

There was something comforting in the ritual of her warning and of the hearty breakfast in front of him. Well, dinner as far as his body was concerned. He'd barely dug into the drippy eggs and golden home fries when his phone buzzed.

We need an ambulance. Hurry.

Shit. Martin. He fished through his pockets and threw a bunch of bills on the table. "Stella? Can you wrap this up for me? I'll be back for it." Without waiting for an answer, Stirling shoved his hat on, jammed his arms through his coat's sleeves, grabbed his pack, and ran out into the snow.

Maybe it was something minor. Maybe it wasn't Daniella—Reina—whatever she wanted to be called. But Stirling had learned a long time ago not to put his faith in maybes.

He paused just long enough to notify his dispatcher and text a brief note to the doc before charging toward Martin's shelter.

By the time he got to the hulking brick building, he was out of breath. Sirens wailed in the distance, but either he was hearing another emergency call or he'd just beaten the ambulance here. Where was everyone? The ground had been trampled into a slushy mess. The weather was doing that thing where the sky spit a mix of ice pellets and snow. The kind of cold that cut through you, even inside a warm house.

It would be raw in their shelter, smoky with inadequate fires. The whole building was a health and safety nightmare, but

Stirling had been over that with both Lopez siblings more times than he could count.

He opened the door and stepped into the dim interior of the lobby, waiting for his eyes to adjust. Martin was pacing by the stairwell. His sister was sitting on the ground beside someone nearly swallowed up by blankets. A small dog rested in her lap. The relief that flooded him when he saw her felt a lot like guilt. "What happened?" He whipped out his stethoscope and dropped his pack, coat, and hat to the floor.

"It's Thorne. He collapsed outside. Could be a heart attack," Martin said.

"You moved him?"

"It was either that or let him freeze."

It was the right choice. Martin was steady in an emergency, and he'd certainly seen his share of medical crises. "Keep an eye out for the ambulance," he ordered before turning to the patient. "I'm Stirling Hughes. I'm an EMT. Can I examine you?" The man focused on him and nodded. Stirling moved some of the blankets aside and took a moment to observe. The older man was conscious and breathing, so his airway was clear, though respirations were rapid and shallow. Stirling ran his hands quickly down the man's body. No obvious bleeding. His face was gray and lined with pain. As the EMT leaned in to place the stethoscope on his chest, the man grabbed Stirling's arm with surprising strength and tried to lever himself up.

"Poplar...safe?"

"Just take it easy. Let me take care of you, okay? We'll worry about Poplar later." He looked up at Martin. "Was someone else hurt?"

"Poplar's his dog," Martin said, nodding toward the small terrier-looking animal curled up in his sister's lap.

"Oh, right. She's fine. She's right here." Stirling glanced over to the girl's tearstained face. Daniella's features looked back at him, but the expression was wrong.

He frowned and turned back to his patient. One problem at a time.

Thorne relaxed his grip and let his arm fall to his side.

Stirling listened to the man's galloping heart, wishing for a portable EKG monitor. "Do you have a history of heart problems?"

No answer.

"Are you taking any medicines?"

Thorne frowned.

He took out his penlight and examined the man's pupils. Symmetric, responsive. And he could obviously speak and use both sides of his body, so likely not a stroke. "Lay still. We're going to take you to the hospital." There was little he could do but wonder why it was taking so long for the ambulance to get here.

"Is he going to be okay? You can help him, can't you?"

He'd been watching out for Martin and his sister for a few years now. Ever since his first interaction with them, Daniella had called him Saint Stirling and teased him at every opportunity. The girl who stared at him with such earnest hope in her eyes was a complete stranger.

The chill that gripped him had nothing to do with the weather.

Chapter 18

Jace Vettel

Corinne stopped short and gasped. Jace jerked to a halt.

The building from his dream and from their aborted transit last night loomed across the street.

In the distance, a siren wailed. It sounded like the cry of a wounded animal, and Jace struggled to push away the fear of being hunted. The Network and the threat it posed to him and his family hadn't disappeared. If they managed to escape this interdicted reality, they would still need to run. Convincing Corinne of that would have to wait.

First, they needed to get inside and uncover why their path led them here.

He took a deep breath and studied the run-down facade. Something about the structure filled him with foreboding. There were alternate paths branching off this Moment, but he couldn't see past when he and Corinne stepped inside. His mind had been contending with darkness for so long, maybe he had lost the ability to read the potentials. Maybe that's why he had ended up on this world.

"People live here?"

Jace supposed it was better than the flimsy tents they had passed earlier. "What do you see?"

She gave him a sharp look and then returned to studying the building. "The only strong potentials from here go through it. Everything past that is confusing."

He nodded.

"We don't have much of a choice, do we?"

"I'm sorry. No."

A small part of him had hoped Corinne would say something to ease his guilt, but Jace knew this was his fault. And if he had to do it all over again, would his choices lead them somewhere else? He smiled briefly, remembering the late-night conversations they'd had as young Travelers. The multiverse might be near infinite, but Travelers themselves were still limited by their finite vision.

If by some miracle they did find their way home, Jace would do everything he could to make it up to his wife and child. He owed them that.

"Let's go."

Corinne squeezed his hand.

δ

Harnett Wellerman

HARNETT CHOSE A VANTAGE POINT where he could see the whole room but wouldn't be in anyone's direct line of sight. There were too many people around Daniella: Martin, Thorne, and now the medic. Network protocols demanded the minimum of overt action required for a successful operation, and Harnett was already on shaky ground with Aisa.

The damned dog had complicated things again. He should have taken care of it last night.

It seemed to be surveilling him, even as it attended to its ill owner. He couldn't approach Daniella now without the dog giving a warning. If he got into a confrontation with it, any trust he'd managed to build with the girl would be destroyed. The entire mission would collapse.

He could be patient. If he understood the medic correctly, they would be taking the man somewhere for more extensive care. He could make his move after. The girl was already primed to listen to him.

If Thorne hadn't interfered, she would already be his.

The front door opened.

Harnett drew in a startled breath. Jace and Corinne Vettel stood on the threshold. He stifled the bark of laughter that would have revealed him. How convenient that his quarry had come to him. Corinne was a bonus. But where was their child? If they had all transited here together, he could sweep up the whole family at once and be in a far better bargaining position with Aisa. He could return for Daniella another time when managing her would be simpler. Besides, letting the Network know there were native Travelers here would be another bargaining chip he could use.

As reluctant as he was to leave Daniella behind, she had been an extra anyway. The Vettels were his main mission.

The medic jerked his head up as Corinne and Jace stepped further into the lobby.

Martin intercepted the couple just inside the door. "Who the hell are you?" he demanded.

Daniella gasped and scrambled to her feet, dislodging the dog from her lap.

Poplar barked sharply.

Wellerman gripped the hilt of his knife. Stared at Daniella. Did she know them? How was that possible? She was at least several years older than their child would be. He frowned at the siblings, so clearly from this reality.

Jace glanced at the girl and turned away without any reaction. His focus trained on Martin. Daniella's expression crumpled. Her eyes filled with tears.

What the hell was going on here? Why did Daniella act as if Jace and Corinne should have recognized her? It made no sense. Wellerman quickly reassessed priorities.

Whoever Daniella was, she was going to return with him. He could sort out the particulars at MTN Headquarters.

And once he had Jace and Corinne, it wouldn't be long before he would collect their child, too.

δ

Reina Vettel

TEARS GATHERED IN REINA'S eyes. Her heart soared. Her parents had come for her! She wasn't abandoned after all!

Poplar licked Thorne's hand before dancing around Reina's feet, her tail nearly spinning in circles. ::your people! go greet them!::

Reina hugged Poplar. ::I'm sorry I was mean to you. Everything's going to be okay, now.::

The dog's smug mindvoice made Reina smile.

Thorne groaned softly.

::keep him safe::, she said, before skipping across the lobby.

"This isn't a good time," Martin said. "If you're looking for shelter, there's a place a few blocks away at Mass and Cass."

Reina gasped. If they left, she might never see them again. "Martin, please."

"We've had enough trouble already," he said.

"But they're my—" Her father glanced at her without any reaction and turned back to Martin. She choked back a sob as her mother's measured gaze also flicked to her and away again.

They didn't know her.

A stranger. She was a stranger to them both.

It had been all too easy to forget. There were no mirrors here. As long as Reina didn't stare at her new hands, or down at her legs and feet, there had been little to remind her. Until now.

"You don't understand." Reina could hear the desperate edge to her voice. But now that she paid attention, it was a stranger's voice. More settled in pitch. With a musical lilt to it that emerged when she didn't think about what she was saying. Daniella's voice.

How was she going to prove to her parents who she really was? They would be furious at her for making the transit after they forbade it.

"Look. Whatever your name is, we're not doing this again."

She needed more time. Time to figure out what to tell them. How to tell them. Maybe her new friend Harnett could help her explain. With shaking hands she tried to pull Martin away from the door. "Please. Don't send them away."

δ

Corinne Vettel

WHILE JACE ARGUED WITH the slender young man who blocked their way and the teen girl trying to get his attention, Corinne's gaze quickly swept the room. Large. Rectangular. Round columns scattered throughout. No furniture. Piles of dry leaves and trash strewn across the floor. Cartons of supplies, their contents spilling out. Too many shadowed spaces for someone to hide in.

To her left, a large figure knelt beside someone lying on a pad of blankets. Not a threat. She turned her attention back to the young man and the girl.

He had dark, hooded eyes and a piercing gaze. Despite the sharpness in his voice, Corinne got a sense of terrible sadness. The girl was younger. Maybe late teens. She had the same dark coloring as the man and the same body shape, though she looked fragile where he seemed to have a wiry strength. Siblings, she guessed. Low if any threat potential.

The girl stared at her with some kind of yearning in her gaze. For an instant, she reminded Corinne of Reina, but there was little true resemblance. Just something in the eyes. A vulnerability that her daughter shared.

She pulled at her brother's shoulder and whispered intently as he shook his head. There were tears in her eyes. He turned his back on her to confront Jace.

"You need to go," he said, his arms folded across his chest.

"I can make that happen." The voice was unmistakable. Corinne searched the shadows, ice running through her veins. Harnett Wellerman emerged from behind one of the columns to her right.

Her whole body stiffened.

Jace swore and moved between her and Wellerman, as if he could somehow shield her. Wellerman's gaze was triumphant.

Corinne's face heated. Jace had been right. All this time. Her stomach roiled with shame and guilt. *Oh, Reina,* she thought.

Wellerman took a step toward them. "These people giving you any trouble?"

"And you aren't welcome here, either," the brother said, staring at Wellerman. "Get out."

"No." The girl kept shifting her gaze between her and Jace. "It's okay. They can stay. They can all stay."

"Daniella..." The brother's voice was a low growl of warning.

"Martin, please!"

Corinne didn't want to let Wellerman out of her sight, but something in the girl's voice compelled her. For the briefest of moments, she saw something of her daughter flicker in Daniella's expression.

"Whatever game you're playing, it won't work," Jace said. "Our child is safe and somewhere beyond your reach, Wellerman. Beyond all of us. Your precious Network can't back you up now. It's just us and a reckoning that's long overdue."

What was Jace doing? Antagonizing Wellerman would only put them all in more danger. These innocents had no part in their conflict. There had to be another way to disentangle themselves. To get Wellerman away from any collateral damage he might cause.

"You are sick, Jace. Just like your father was. You should have let us help you. Instead you made things worse for yourself and your family. So much worse."

Was that even true? All this time, Corinne had waited for Jace's disease to manifest, quick to attribute any hint of anger or frustration to RDD. But hadn't she been angry? Frustrated? Why had she been so certain that Jace's hatred of the Network was a sign of paranoia?

Her heartbeat raced. This was her doing. The slow-motion disaster that had begun long before her brief conversation with Wellerman when he'd surprised her during one of her training missions, was now just unfolding.

"You have no power over us anymore, Harnett. And definitely not here," she said.

"Ah, Corinne, I see you've finally chosen sides."

She reached out for Jace's hand.

Chapter 19

Stirling Hughes

"Where's that damn ambulance?" Stirling muttered. There was little more that he could do for Thorne until the EMTs arrived. He was fairly certain the man had had a mild coronary, but a full diagnosis was for the docs at the ER to make. Right now, Stirling would have settled for an IV kit. He had to make do with monitoring vitals and keeping the patient warm and quiet.

"You still with me?"

Thorne's eyes fluttered open, searched around until his gaze found the dog. Then his breathing eased. "Yes."

Angry voices filled the lobby, several he didn't recognize. But Martin's voice rang out clearly. Daniella's, too, though there was a cadence in it that was completely different from the girl he had known for these past few years. He had no frame to understand what had happened to her. Nothing in his medical world or his faith could make sense of walls between worlds and body swapping. But there was no denying she wasn't Daniella anymore.

She and Martin were arguing again. He wished there was something he could do for them, too. But he was as helpless to resolve their conflict as he was to fix the lack of services and support that landed them here in the first place. Not with his ministry. Not with his medical skills.

Beside him, the dog began to growl. The hair on the back of Stirling's neck fanned out. Thorne struggled to sit up.

"Easy there," Stirling said, gently placing a hand on his chest. "It's okay. The ambulance will be here soon." It had better be.

δ

Reina Vettel

REINA FELT A TERRIBLE PRESSURE in her chest. Harnett and her parents. They knew each other. How could that be?

"It's over, Jace. Honestly? I'm impressed you've managed to evade us this long. Come back with me and both your record and Corinne's will be cleared. Assistant Director Oswald has given me her guarantee."

"You and I both know what the Network's guarantee is worth," her father said.

The Network? She covered her mouth with her hands. But that's who her parents had worked for. Before Papa retired. Before she was born.

Harnett reached into his pocket and wrapped his hand around a smooth rope. "The only choice you have now is whether you return willingly or not. That will decide what happens next."

Gone was the kindness in his voice and any shred of his understanding. How could she have been so fooled?

"You've been lied to, Wellerman. Same as us," her father said. "We're all trapped here."

"I'm not sure what game you're playing, but it's over. If you want to help your child, you need to do as I say."

Reina tried to breathe around the bands of tightness in her throat. *Oh, Mama, Papa,* she cried silently. They didn't know who she was. If she could somehow distract Harnett, maybe they could get away. But they would never leave if they guessed the truth. Reina had to make sure they didn't.

She shifted closer to Wellerman, keeping her parents in her peripheral vision. "What about your promise?"

"Stay away from him, Daniella."

Reina couldn't bear to look at Martin and see the pain she knew she was causing him. Poplar's growl echoed in her head from across the room. She had to shut them both out. "You said you could get me anywhere I wanted to go."

Harnett studied her as she stepped between him and her parents, a curious expression on his face. "So I did," he said. "I can take three as easily as I can take one."

He reached out for her hand and before Reina could slip away, he had looped the rope over her wrist.

"What are you doing?" She tried to pull her hand free, but his grip was unshakable.

He yanked her toward him in a single move that spun her around and captured both hands behind her. The restraint coiled over her arms like a cold snake. He shifted his grip to her shoulder.

"You're hurting me!"

"Let her go!" Martin shouted.

"You again?" Wellerman laughed. "This has nothing to do with you. I advise you to stay out of our way."

Martin came at the man, his fists raised. Wellerman easily blocked a punch with one hand and shoved Martin aside.

"Let that poor girl free, Wellerman, it's us you want," her father said, a cold, hard look in his eyes.

Reina felt a sob thicken in her throat. What had she done?

δ

Melissa Klein

MELISSA STARTED THE CAR and sat idling in front of Julian's house, her hands gripping the steering wheel. She stared through the gentle snowfall, seeing instead a formal garden in the rain and the memory of an impossible summer day. Could Borys have gone back home? Then why hadn't he just made a portal and slipped away when her mom had gone to call DSS? He had looked so scared. His eyes had pleaded with her as he was being taken from her house.

Her whole life, she had blamed herself for not saving him, even as she'd tried to bury the memories and believe what her parents believed. She'd been so young. What could she have done? She closed her eyes and rested her forehead on the steering wheel, unsure of what to do next.

For now, maybe it was enough that Julian didn't think she was crazy. Ah, the C word again. Melissa took a deep breath and opened her eyes. Home first. Then fire up her laptop and get coverage for her patients. Then she had a day to figure out how she was going to tell Julian about Reina and about the portals that seemed to open up when she was near the girl. Maybe time and distance would help Melissa make better sense of it all.

She picked up her phone and turned the sound back on. Stirling's message was all it took to evaporate her newfound relief.

Emergency. At Martin's place. Come when you can.

Her rational mind knew that the place and its inhabitants wouldn't hurt her, but the dread that filled her and stopped her breath could not be reasoned with. Returning there would only make things worse. Julian had assured her he didn't consider her an impaired physician. The "yet" was hanging there, unspoken. If she put herself back in the stressful environment that had triggered the memories in the first place, she'd be asking for trouble.

Stirling could handle this. He was probably already handling it. Melissa needed to go home.

Where there wouldn't be any portals for her to tell Julian about. And no reason for him to report her to the Board of Medicine. She wouldn't lose everything she had spent all these years building in her career and in her life.

Whatever was happening at the homeless encampment, the EMTs would handle it. Stirling would handle it. BMC's ER was right there. This wasn't her specialty anyway.

Tossing the phone on the passenger seat, she shifted the car into drive and headed toward Belmont.

There was a surprising lack of traffic and the snowfall made even the city streets magical.

City streets.

City. Streets.

Damn it. She needed to go home.

Her hands tightened on the wheel. She pulled to a stop and parked the car.

The brick building loomed out of the low gray sky.

"Fuck."

Blue and red lights strobed through the snow. Maybe Stirling was one of the EMTs in the ambulance screaming down the street behind her. She could just drive away. She should. Just drive away. He would be a lot more useful in there than she would. Besides, she was under Julian's orders.

It wasn't her responsibility anymore.

The memory of Reina's distress cut through her flimsy excuses. If she walked away now and something happened to the girl, it would be Borys all over again. And no matter what, she was still a doctor. Still responsible for the lives under her care— and in a convoluted way, saving Reina on the night of the count meant Melissa was involved, whether she wanted to be or not.

And as long as she made her appointment with Julian tomorrow, it could still be all right. It would still be all right. It had to be all right.

She grabbed her gloves and her phone and got out of the car, slamming the door shut. Without waiting for the EMTs, Melissa picked her way over slushy puddles and snowbanks until she was standing under the remnants of what had once been an awning over the entry. The large door separated Melissa from her comfortable professional life and a new, uncertain future. She reached out for the handle, knowing it was a mistake. Knowing she was going inside regardless.

"Fuck," she spat out one more time and heaved the door open.

As if it had burst from her memories, a pinprick of brightness opened into a sharp-edged geometric wheel hovering in the air.

δ

Stirling Hughes

THE COMMOTION BY THE DOOR wasn't the EMTs arriving. Stirling turned back to his patient.

"Go. Help her." Thorne's voice was barely a whisper.

"Not going to leave you, sir."

Thorne winced and looked at the dog. Stirling could have sworn that some deep understanding passed between the two of them. The dog looked across the room and then back to Thorne with a whimper. She took a few steps away before returning to press her small body against his.

"Please. He'll hurt her."

"Martin would never hurt her." Stirling had witnessed, time after time, Martin's patience and kindness with the folks under his care, even as he pushed away any hint of outsider interference.

"No. Harnett." Thorne's words ended in a hoarse cough.

Stirling didn't know who Thorne was talking about. He bent down to listen to the man's heart and lungs. Thorne waved his arms and pushed the stethoscope away. "Not me. Help Reina."

Torn, Stirling glanced across the room. Five people stood in a close knot by the door. He couldn't tell what was going on, but the tension in their bodies was clear. He stared down at the dog, who seemed to look back at him with an ancient and weary understanding. "Fine. Stay with him. He needs to keep warm." He slung his medical kit over his shoulder and stood. The dog whimpered again. "I mean it. Stay." He hoped the dog would listen.

The middle-aged man and woman by the door weren't familiar. Certainly Stirling didn't know all of Martin's regulars, but he'd spent enough time checking in here that he should have at least recognized their faces. The wide-shouldered man standing behind Reina wasn't one of the residents, either. How did she know him?

"Leave my sister alone," Martin said.

He bristled with fury, and Stirling was frozen by a moment of terrible realization: If this was the drug dealer, things would get ugly. Quickly.

"I'm warning you." Martin's voice was quiet and deeply serious. Anyone who didn't know him wouldn't hear the menace in it. Stirling had seen him take on neighborhood gangs and Social Services agency representatives with the same controlled fury. But something about the man he faced made Stirling afraid for Martin. For all of them.

Reina glanced over her shoulder and he saw the terror in her wide eyes. The disparate pieces of Thorne's warning clicked into place. The stranger was holding her trapped against his body.

A surge of adrenaline pushed him to action before his brain could fully process what he was seeing.

Reina cried out, a wordless fear that unlocked battlefield flashbacks Stirling had worked for years to banish.

A door slammed. Voices rose in anger. A bright haze turned everything sharp-edged and blurry at the same time.

He had to get to Reina. The distortion in the air thickened, turning into an impossible headwind.

Chapter 20

Jace Vettel

A SHUDDER RAN DOWN Jace's spine as he saw the look of fear in the strange girl's eyes. He didn't understand why Wellerman had shackled her, but it didn't matter. He was done with being afraid. Done with running. Done with the Network. Most of all, done with Harnett Wellerman and the shadow he had cast across Jace's entire life.

He moved to Wellerman's right, making himself a tempting target. Jace met Corinne's gaze and nodded slightly toward Wellerman's left. She moved smoothly and quickly until they flanked him. The girl's eyes widened and she shook her head frantically. Jace had spent far too much of the past thirteen years letting others deal with the consequences of his actions. No more.

Right now, his focus was on separating Wellerman from anyone else he could harm. That meant the girl and her brother. She was squirming against the pressure of Wellerman's hand on her shoulder, her hands tied behind her. The brother was strung wire-tight and ready to spring.

Ideally, he and Corinne could free the girl and isolate Wellerman before anyone got hurt. After that? He didn't really have a plan.

"You're even more damaged than I realized," Wellerman said. "I can't imagine you'd be any value to the Network anymore, but for some reason, they still want you brought in. And one way or another, I'm happy to comply."

"These people aren't part of this. We can end this now." Jace measured the distance between them. One more step and he would be close enough.

Jace took a breath. It was now or never. He charged at Wellerman, forcing him to choose between keeping control of the girl or confronting him. If Corinne had taken his cue, she would be able to help clear everyone else out of the way.

The girl cried out as Wellerman flung her to the floor at his feet. She went down hard, unable to use her hands to control the fall. He turned his back to her and stared at Jace.

He'd been right. "Run," he said to her, hoping she had enough sense to stay out of the way.

"Papa! He has a knife!" she whispered urgently.

It wasn't Reina's voice, but impossibly, he also knew it was. Time crawled. He felt his heart pound in a staccato rhythm. The girl. This young woman with haunted eyes and hollowed out cheeks. How could she be his Reina?

There was no time to make sense of it. He could only react and trust Corinne to do her part as he slammed into Wellerman, taking him down. They grappled for control. Wellerman bashed his head into Jace's nose. Warm blood flowed down his face. The back of his skull hit the hard floor with a sickening thud. Despite the pain and the surge of dizziness, he kept his hold on Wellerman's muscular arms. Jace struggled to focus his fuzzy vision on the blade gripped in the man's right hand. Something even shinier than the knife glittered in Jace's periphery. A geometric silver shape turned like a wagon wheel, pulled at his senses. Hope fueled his lagging strength. Corinne had done it. Somehow. After all their failures. Good. She could escape this place. Save Reina. Protect her.

The girl's features swam in his mind.

With an effort, he kept his gaze locked on Wellerman and the knife.

Someone was shouting, but it sounded so far away.

Grunting with effort, Jace managed to roll them closer to the portal. Blood dripped from his nose, splattering both men, smearing red across the floor.

The opening was just behind them now. Only a little farther and they would be through. Jace growled his fury at Wellerman. Had to keep him focused on their fight. On him. Until it was too late.

He had no idea where it opened to. It didn't matter. If he could just get Wellerman across the threshold. But Jace would have to hold him there until the portal sealed itself. With the two of them somewhere else.

So be it. So be it.

δ

Thorne Truthscryer

Thorne didn't need to watch the scene unfolding in the center of the room. It was one of the futures he had already lived through. Seeing it move forward instant by instant increased the ache in his chest a hundredfold. Poplar licked his hand, her concern a wordless warmth that washed over him.

In a way, she was already gone. Lost to some other reality without him. One he couldn't see how to reach. Some part of him was mired in grief. All that remained was to see which path of the hundreds that splintered from this moment would be the one that separated her from him.

That pruning had started when he urged Stirling to help Reina. The many potentials collapsed into a few. They would soon become just one terrible inevitability.

Thorne closed his eyes. Maybe this was where and when he died. That was the one thing his gift withheld from him.

Poplar nudged his side.

He was being so careful to keep his thoughts from her, but she could read his emotions far too easily. She was such an empathic creature, and right now her emotions were a roil of worry for him and for Reina.

::Go to her. I'll be okay.::

Poplar whimpered, pawing at his hand.

::I know what the medic said, but Reina will need you more than I do.:: It hurt him to say that. No matter that it was true. But as the moments passed, Thorne felt the realities narrowing even further. He foresaw all the separate events in the room unspool in a single moment. Felt the opening between worlds. Saw the light glint off the sharp edge of Wellerman's knife. Understood the menace of Martin's hidden, dull gray weapon. Heard Stirling's shout and Poplar's growl as she ran toward the conflict in front of the portal. Heard Reina cry out for her father.

Thorne closed his eyes, as if that would prevent him from seeing the chaos happen in real time, each tiny tragedy ripping a large gash in his soul. Despite the blankets, an icy wind stole all his warmth. He called out for Poplar, even as he knew he was powerless to prevent what was to come. Unable to keep himself from poking at the fresh wound of the impending loss.

Maybe this was for the best. She would have a life without him, and he could finally let go.

Everything around him felt dim, faded, dulled. Poplar had always teased him about his limited senses. Thorne didn't realize until now how much of her awareness she had shared with him.

"Can you hear me? Can you open your eyes?" A stranger's voice intruded on his pain, forcing him to think about his survival instead.

He looked up, unsure whether what he was seeing was happening now or yet to be.

"Just lie still. We're going to start an IV and get you to a hospital. It's going to be okay."

It wasn't, but it was nice of the earnest young woman to say so. Thorne nodded. It was never going to be okay again.

δ

Reina Vettel

Reina pulled at the bonds, but couldn't release her arms. She could barely take her eyes off the sharp blade glittering in Harnett's right hand, willing her father to get control as they fought. There was blood everywhere.

"Come with me."

Her mother grabbed her by the shoulder and tried to lead her to the door. She jerked loose, working to keep an eye on her father.

"I'm not going to hurt you."

There was a softness in her mother's voice that Reina hadn't heard in a long time. She longed to say something, anything. Fear kept her silent.

"I'm going to free you. Then I want you and your brother to run. Understand?"

Her mother loosened the bindings with a gentle hand. Reina's gaze darted around the room. Harnett and her father were both grasping for the knife, rolling across the floor in a pile of arms and legs. Martin stood staring at the men, his expression cold, distant. It chilled her.

"You have to go. This isn't your fight."

Reina shook her head, knowing there was nothing she could do, but helpless to look away.

A shimmer of a portal caught her attention.

The men were rolling closer to it. Harnett didn't notice, but her father did. The breath caught in Reina's throat.

They were directly in front of the opening now. Its light illuminated their flushed faces and the ruin of her father's broken nose.

All he had to do was push one more time and Harnett would fall through the portal.

And then they'd all be free.

Reina's heart raced. She reached out for her mother's hand. Papa was going to save them all!

They rolled to the portal's threshold, grappling for control. Time slowed. A smear of distortion oiled the air. Her mother's hand slid from her grasp.

Her father shifted his grip, letting go of Harnett's arm. In the pulsing crystalline light, the knife glittered. Sharp-edged reflections turned the room into a kaleidoscope. She couldn't blink away the chaos.

Her mother screamed. "Jace!"

And then for a heartbeat, everything was still and silent.

Harnett staggered to his feet and stared down at the floor in triumph.

Reina's gasp rang the room.

The hilt of Harnett's knife stuck out from her father's throat.

"No!" She ran toward Papa, tears blurring her vision. She nearly stumbled and fell as Harnett grabbed her again. He smelled of blood and sweat.

"I guess I don't have to return empty-handed after all." The satisfied purr of Harnett's voice terrified her. "Now, where is Corinne hiding?"

She twisted and struggled against the man's strength with all the wild power of her grief, but she couldn't free herself.

A low growl filled her mind and then she heard it with her ears, growing louder and louder. Poplar's snarl sent shivers down Reina's spine. The dog's rage was primal and wordless, and it amplified her own.

Linked with the dog's fury, Reina felt Poplar launch herself at her captor, barely dodging the kick he aimed at her. Gagged on the taste of blood as Poplar's jaw latched onto Harnett's lower leg, piercing the flesh. As he stumbled, Reina gave one more mighty heave. Harnett's hold on her eased. She spun away, panting hard.

The still-open portal spun and shimmered behind him.

::Poplar! Let go! Now!::

A cold wind swirled around them.

The sound of sirens wailed through the room.

Chapter 21

Stirling Hughes

"MARTIN, NO!" THE MEDIC SHOUTED.

The young man was smiling tightly. His right hand held a gun, his left steadying it in a stance that looked practiced. Deadly.

The far too familiar sound of a sharp crack of thunder drowned out every other sound in the room. Stirling's ears rang. A circle of blood bloomed across Harnett's shoulder. He stumbled, swore, and pressed his other hand against the wound.

The doppler of sirens pierced the air. Good. Finally. They could take care of the GSW. The damage even a small handgun did to human flesh was something Stirling seen too much of, both on a personal and a professional level.

Martin dropped the gun and kicked it away.

Not that it would do him any good when the cops came. Ballistics didn't lie.

The man Martin shot was still standing. Which meant he probably wouldn't die in the next few minutes, but the man on the floor wasn't moving. He was Stirling's first priority.

Before he could reach the man with the knife wound, the gunshot victim staggered into him and they both stumbled. Stirling hit the ground, sandwiched between the lumpy medical bag and the solid victim. As he worked to free himself, pixelated shadows and light played across his face. With the light came a pressured silence, cutting him off from the sirens and the scene in the room. It was like the aftermath of an IED, only without the shrapnel.

He sat up, blinking furiously, but the dusky haze now obscured his vision. His ears popped painfully and some distant observer part of his mind wondered if he'd somehow ruptured an eardrum. He was sure he'd sustained a concussion. It wouldn't be his first.

Then he lost all sense of his body, except for the pressure of the bag's handle grasped in his right hand.

He couldn't move. He couldn't feel. He couldn't speak. His lungs felt stiff and he was having trouble bringing in enough air.

He was having a stroke.

His mind splintered. Part of him felt like a fish flopping around in the bottom of a boat. He needed cool, fresh air. An oxygen mask would be good. An IV as well. The observer part of his brain coolly noted that his EMT colleagues were going to be busy.

Talk about bad timing.

Surely, the first responders were doing everything they could to stabilize him for transport. But Stirling couldn't tell what was happening. He was somewhere far distant, desperate to connect to his body again.

With a brutal jolt, he felt himself slam into something hard.

What the hell?

Brightness seared his gaze, and he furiously blinked away afterimages from his watering eyes.

His arms and legs tingled, and his head throbbed with an incipient headache.

His medical kit was still beneath him, all hard angles and rigid canvas.

Stirling sat up carefully, doing a silent inventory. He could move his fingers and toes. His vision was perfectly normal. No field-cuts or blurring. It couldn't have been a stroke, then. Maybe a TIA? He could feel a symphony of aches and pains everywhere. What had happened to him?

It took him a long minute to get his bearings. He was still in the building's ground floor, but it was empty. Not just empty, but scoured. Clean. There were no signs of Martin's settlement. His head began to throb.

A weak groan sounded from nearby.

He swiveled around and saw the GSW victim lying on the floor a few feet away.

No one else was with them. Not Thorne. Not Martin. Not Reina. Not the EMTs. And where was the man who'd gotten stabbed?

Seriously. What the hell?

The man groaned again. Stirling compartmentalized his confusion and pain, the way he had shut away the chaos of the battlefield when he needed to attend to a wounded soldier. As he dragged his medical kit over to his patient, Stirling could have sworn he heard a dog barking from somewhere behind him.

He stripped off the gloves he'd been wearing to assess Thorne (Where had the man gone? Where had everyone gone?) and grabbed a fresh pair.

"Are you still with me, sir?" he asked. There was a good chance that this man had just killed another. Stirling let that go as well. He had a patient in front of him. One that needed his help. What came after wasn't up to him.

Another groan. The man's uninjured hand grabbed his forearm with surprising strength. It was all Stirling could do not to react with violence. That life was in the past. "I'm an EMT. You've been shot. I need to examine you."

The man held on for a moment longer and Stirling thought he was going to have to pry himself loose.

δ

Corinne Vettel

EARS STILL RINGING FROM the weapon's discharge, Corinne felt cut off from everything around her except Jace's still body. She had to get to him, but her muscles didn't seem to be under her control. All she could do was stare at the metallic glitter of the knife handle as sound and movement surged around her.

Jace was gone. She'd known it the moment Wellerman had stood, his knife buried to the hilt in her husband's throat. If there were any justice in the multiplicity of worlds, Wellerman would die of his wounds. But that was a child's fantasy of parity.

Finally Corinne was able to move and crouched beside Jace's body, whispering an incoherent apology. There would be time for mourning. Time to reconcile her grief and her guilt. But she needed to find a place of safety before she could let herself truly feel.

A group of people swarmed in from outside, all dressed in identical tan slacks and jackets, carrying emergency gear. Local medics. She gathered herself to stand, to leave them to their hopeless task, when the glint of Jace's ring caught her eye. Twin to the one on her thumb, she vividly remembered the day they had exchanged them along with all the promises young lovers made to one another.

So many of those promises, long broken. She slipped the ring from his hand and grasped it tightly as the medics surrounded them.

The young girl Corinne had tried to free threw herself over Jace's body, screaming for them all to stay away. Who was she? What was she doing?

"We're here to help. Please, let us do our jobs."

The girl sobbed, ignoring the man who spoke.

He nodded to a woman standing nearby who leaned over the girl and pulled her away from Jace.

"Papa! Don't leave me again!" she cried.

Corinne gasped. Her hands shook. The voice wasn't her daughter's voice, but still, she could hear Reina's pain in it. The face, the body, too, belonged to a stranger. And yet, there was something almost familiar. Their eyes met and for an instant, Reina's expression rewrote the girl's features—and then it was gone. Corinne couldn't stop staring.

"It's all my fault. I'm sorry. I'm sorry." The girl crumpled to the ground, hugging her arms around her lanky body.

Corinne knelt close to the girl, afraid to reach out, afraid to speak. They crouched together in silence as the medics lifted Jace's body to a gurney and covered it with a sheet.

"Reina?" she whispered. "Is it really you?" How was it possible? Corinne gripped Jace's ring tighter until her hand cramped.

The girl lifted her head. Stared at her with unfamiliar glistening brown eyes and a narrow, tear-streaked face. "I should have listened to you. I should have stayed home. You left me and I was so afraid."

The voice was different. And yet it had Reina's cadence and rhythm. The way she held her head and moved her hands when she talked, familiar. Why hadn't she recognized her sooner? Would it have changed anything? "Oh, Reina," she whispered. "You were supposed to be safe." This wasn't the time or place to interrogate her. Corinne could only hope that something in her long training would help her get her daughter back. In her own body. As quickly as possible.

"It's my fault Papa is dead."

Corinne lifted Reina's chin. "No. It's not."

She shook her head. "He said he could help me get home. He said he was my friend."

"Who?"

"Harnett."

Wellerman. She had lost track of him after his injury. A surge of adrenaline coursed through her as she scanned the room and couldn't find him. All around them emergency personnel moved with practiced efficiency, but Wellerman wasn't being ministered to. He was nowhere in sight. He could be hiding anywhere. Waiting for his chance at her and Reina. She had to be ready.

The girl pulled at her coat. "Mama, please don't be mad at me."

The tears Corinne had been holding back filled her eyes and blurred the girl's features. In her mind's eye, she struggled to see her daughter's delicate face and bright, clear eyes. She slipped Jace's ring onto her other thumb and pulled Reina into her arms, ignoring the awkward feel of the larger body with its more mature curves. Nothing made sense. What had happened to her daughter?

Reina gripped her with a desperate strength. "Mama, I'm so sorry."

"It's going to be all right," Corinne said, hoping Reina would believe her. "It's not your fault," she insisted. If only she could believe that for herself. If only she deserved forgiveness. But if she could keep Reina safe, maybe that would be enough.

Reina wiped her face and looked up. "Where are they taking Papa?"

Corinne followed her gaze. The medics were wheeling the gurney out the door. Wellerman still hadn't shown himself. "I'm not sure."

δ

Martin Lopez

MARTIN STAGGERED BACK AGAINST a support column, still not sure what had just happened. His ears still rang from the gunshot. He'd never shot anyone before.

His mind replayed the scene over and over as if he could somehow make it make sense.

His finger squeezing the trigger.

Blink.

Blood blooming across the man's shoulder.
Blink.
The dull thud of the gun dropping to the floor.
Blink.
The glint of metal spinning away from his kick.
Blink.
The rasp of his hands wiping across his jeans.
Blink.
The bleeding man staggering into Stirling.
Blink.

Stirling. Maybe Stirling could help him. Or at least keep Daniella out of the mess he'd just created. He shook her head. Reina. She insisted her name was Reina. Martin hated asking anyone for help, especially Stirling, but this was all too much. He'd tried to handle everything, and this is where it ended. He lost his sister and messed up the community they'd started. He could so easily be thrown in jail. Or shot by the cops. Just because.

He looked up and squinted hard, trying to focus. But a wave of distortion that made his eyes water filled the middle of the lobby. Martin had seen a smaller version of it in his room the day the doctor came, but thought it was just a trick of the light. Like the way oil made rainbows in street puddles. It shimmered as it expanded, and no one else seemed to pay it much attention.

It popped like a soap bubble and left no evidence of its existence behind. The air cleared and he could see the whole lobby again. The big-hearted EMT and the man Martin had shot were nowhere in sight.

"What the fuck?" he whispered. Too much weird shit. Too much added to all that he couldn't fix.

Then sirens pierced the strange bubble of silence he'd been trapped in. A swirl of cold and a dusting of snow came in with the emergency people through the open door. The cops would find the gun. His fingerprints were all over it. It was the end of everything he and Daniella had built here.

Until now, the cops had mostly let them stay with the minimum of hassle. Martin kept the place clean of drugs, gangs, and weapons. He guessed the cops figured anything that made their job easier was simple to ignore.

But Daniella was sick, and nothing made sense anymore.

He'd just shot a man.

The gun wasn't even his—one of the regulars who'd sheltered here for almost a year had left it with him when he found a more permanent place. He'd apologized for breaking Martin's rules, but admitted he never even kept it loaded.

Martin had stashed the weapon under his bed and kept the bullets in an old cigar case on the shelves in their room. Until Daniella's first OD. Then he'd always kept it on him. Loaded. Just in case.

If he could hide the gun again, maybe he'd be able to get out of this. While the EMTs came to deal with Thorne and the stabbed man, Martin scrambled to find the weapon. But it was missing, just like Stirling and the man who'd threatened his sister. No gun and no gunshot victim meant no police interrogation. Maybe it would be okay after all.

He scanned the room for his sister, suddenly guilty that he hadn't done that first. She was sobbing near the body. Even from here, Martin could tell the stabbed man was dead. You didn't come back from a wound like that. He watched the EMTs gently pull her away and started to go to her, but the woman got there first. She was the one to comfort her.

It should have been him. But that wasn't Daniella anymore. He had known for a while now, but until Martin saw the grief transforming his sister's face into a total stranger's, he hadn't let himself accept it.

He shivered, tucked his hands under his folded arms, and turned away from the last link to his childhood. To family. To his life's purpose. There was nothing left for him here.

Martin followed the EMTs wheeling Thorne's gurney out the front door. No one noticed him.

Chapter 22

Melissa Klein

TIME SLOWED AS MELISSA leaned against one of the concrete columns for support. Her legs trembled. The pulse thudded in her ears. The smear of colors from the portal captivated and terrified her in equal measures.

There was the sense of movement around her, but Melissa couldn't focus on anything except the visual distortions. It was the day in El Alhambra all over again. But this time, she knew what she was seeing. A weak spot between the worlds. A doorway from here to there. A clear demarcation from the life she clung to and the impossible unknown.

The sound of sobbing pierced her heart and cleared the distortion in her senses as if it had never been. Melissa was left with the ghost of a headache she knew she would have to deal with soon.

Now that she was freed from her stasis, she saw a group of EMTs swarm around a body that lay on the ground. Reina was collapsed nearby, crying. A woman held her close and both of their faces were etched with pain. Their low voices penetrated Melissa's confusion.

"Where are they taking Papa?"

"I don't know."

Papa? That's what she had always called her father. Melissa took a deep breath as the EMTs covered the man with a drape. She could almost feel the thin white material sliding between her own fingers. For a moment, she was back in the small ER cubicle, just days after her mother had died, pulling the sheet up over her father's face this time. It had been her choice to silence the life support machines. She had waited, alone, as he took his final breaths and the room rang with his absence.

Melissa shook off the memories. That was the past. It had nothing to do with the here and now. "The hospital morgue. Until they identify the body." She winced at how clinical she sounded. But that was the person she needed to be right now. Especially here, with the echo of a portal still in her head.

The woman glanced up at her and pulled Reina closer.

Was this Reina's mother? But that would mean the girl's story was true. All of it. That she and her parents had come from another world. That Reina was only inhabiting Martin's sister's body. Was that how this "traveling" worked? Had Borys traveled like that? For an instant, she wondered how she could explain any of this to Julian. But as understanding and supportive as he was, his warning was also very clear. There would be a price to pay for her choices.

She took a deep breath. "Reina, are you okay? What happened?"

"Harnett…He killed Papa." Her eyes were red-rimmed, her face blotchy.

Who was Harnett? Did she even want to know? She glanced around, but didn't see anyone who could pose a threat. Just

EMTs milling around and the young man, Martin, skulking at the far side of the room.

"My parents. They came for me. But then Harnett..." She paused, sniffled, and wiped the back of her hand across her face. Her mother wrapped an arm around Reina's shoulders.

For a moment Reina's grief was Melissa's as well. But she had been an adult when her father died. Not a young child already dealing with too much trauma. The line between empathy and transference was thin and razor-sharp, and Melissa knew she had been teetering on its edge for far too long. "I'm so sorry, Reina." Julian had recommended she not work with patients. But this was different. Wasn't it? Where was Stirling? He had known these people for far longer than she had. Surely he could help give her context and support.

He wasn't with the group of responders transporting Reina's father. Nor was he with the others attending to Thorne. That was odd. Where had he gone? She turned to the woman with Reina. "Can you tell me what happened here?"

She gave Melissa a rueful smile. "I think you would neither understand or believe anything I told you."

The last person who had said that to her was Thorne, and it didn't sit any better coming from this woman. "I think you'll find that I understand a lot more than you realize."

More sirens wailed in the distance. This was now a crime scene. The police would come. They would clear out Martin's shelter and everyone in it. Everyone not taken in for questioning would scatter. She couldn't let all these people be lost to follow-up. Even if only for Stirling's sake.

Melissa took a deep breath, knowing she was about to make another dangerously questionable decision. One that she would have a hard time justifying to Julian and the medical board, should he report her. The blue and red emergency lights cast strange moving shadows through the lobby. Borys had vanished under lights like these. She wasn't going to let that happen to anyone else. Not again. Not ever.

"You have no reason to trust me, but if you and your daughter stay here, the authorities will insist on interrogating you." And if they started talking about portals to other worlds, they would be sent for psych observation. Under the supervision of someone like her. Or a version of her that didn't believe in impossible holes in reality. It would not end well. "I live not far from here. At the very least, I can promise you a hot meal and a warm place to sleep."

The woman shared a questioning look with Reina.

"She was the one who found me, Mama. If it wasn't for the doctor, I would have died."

"Then we should go. Now." With a resolve that nearly gave Melissa whiplash, the woman scrambled to her feet, pulling Reina up after her.

Melissa glanced back toward the EMTs who were now placing Thorne on a gurney. Stirling was still nowhere to be seen. Well, he knew how to contact her.

"This way." She led Reina and her mother to the stairwell and the exit door she knew had to be at the bottom of the stairs. Technically she wasn't doing anything illegal, but walking out among the first responders and a contingent of law enforcement would bring more attention than she wanted.

Another unprofessional choice she would have to disclose to Julian.

They emerged from the building into a gray and gloomy late morning. The snow had stopped, but the wind still whipped snow across the sidewalk. She was grateful that her two charges both had warm coats. Her car was right where she'd parked it, and an unexpected flood of relief washed over Melissa at seeing it there, sitting alone on the block. Three police cars and two ambulances were clustered near the building's front door.

As she bundled the two into the car, the EMTs were loading Thorne's gurney into one of the ambulances. The other held Reina's father's body. Melissa looked back at the girl, but she either didn't know the significance of the emergency vehicles, or was still in shock. Probably some of both.

"I'm sorry. I know this is all strange and overwhelming..."

"Just go," Reina's mother said. "Explanations can wait until we're someplace secure."

That wasn't the reaction she had expected. The woman seemed as cool and as competent as Melissa strived to be. She drove past the strobe lights grasping the wheel tightly to keep her hand from shaking. Nothing to see here, she told herself. We're just Boston gawkers. No reason to stop us.

She repeated that mantra until they were halfway to Belmont and still she kept glancing in her rearview mirror until the car was safely parked in the garage.

δ

Corinne Vettel

CORINNE CLUTCHED REINA'S UNFAMILIAR hand as they followed the doctor into her dwelling. She still wasn't sure they had done the right thing in leaving the scene, but at the very least, it would confuse Wellerman's search. Besides, she also knew she was in no condition to talk to this world's authorities. And now that the cache no longer felt like a safe option, this was at least a strategic choice.

She choked back a flood of tears. Who was she fooling? Jace was dead, and Reina, somehow transformed. There were no safe options. This wasn't some random mission gone wrong.

The doctor glanced back in the corridor and paused. Corinne took a deep breath and closed the distance between them. This wasn't the time or place to start talking. Maybe after she got Reina settled. If this doctor could truly be trusted.

The woman unlocked the door and ushered them into a colorless collection of rooms. It was as if no one lived there. Or perhaps the person who did felt the need to be invisible. Reina stumbled to a stop when Corinne did, but didn't look up or speak. Corinne knew her child was in there, somewhere, hidden in someone else's body and reeling with shock and loss. She squeezed her hand, trying not to react to its unfamiliar feel.

"Please, sit down." The doctor indicated a white sofa next to a glass and metal table.

Corinne glanced at Reina again. The girl's face was tearstained and dirt-streaked. Her clothes, grimy. Corinne knew she couldn't be much cleaner. "Is there somewhere we can wash up?" And then maybe there would be a place Reina could rest.

"Oh. I'm sorry. Yes." The doctor shook her head as if castigating herself and showed her a washroom.

Everything was gleaming white and silver surfaces. Corinne caught sight of their reflections in the array of mirrors and winced. Somehow seeing a stranger in her daughter's image made this more real and far worse.

Reina washed her hands and splashed cool water on her face. Corinne handed her a white towel. It was gray when she returned it. The soap smelled like lavender and mint, and it reminded Corinne of the garden they'd had in the first home she and Jace had shared. She gripped the towel. There would be time to grieve later, she promised herself, even as she felt the weight of the lie pressing against her heart.

The doctor stood waiting for them in the hallway beside the washroom. "Can I get you something to drink? Coffee? Tea?" She paused and wrung her hands. "Do you know what those are?"

Corinne gave her a wry smile. So the woman believed they were from another reality. That gave her a place to start, at least. "Yes. Tea for both of us, if it's not too much of an inconvenience." It was a comfort to find some semblance of a culture of hospitality here, but Corinne knew to stay wary. Reina may have trusted this woman, but that didn't mean she couldn't pose a threat. Even inadvertently.

"Please, make yourself comfortable. I'll be right there."

Corinne reached out for Reina's hand again and her fingers brushed the girl's palm. She gasped as she traced a familiar scar. How was this possible? Her Reina had that exact same mark on her hand from the day she'd nearly drowned at the beach as a toddler. Corinne could almost feel the sharpness of the stone, creating it in her mind from the imprint.

"Nothing will ever be the same again, will it, Mama?" Reina's soft voice, exhausted, thick with emotion pulled Corinne back to the present.

She knew what her daughter was desperate to hear. Corinne was desperate to believe it for herself. But comforting lies wouldn't help either of them. Not now. Not ever. "No, my love."

Reina nodded.

She led her to the colorless sofa and sat. Reina sat stiffly beside her for a moment before curling up on the too-soft cushions and resting her head in Corinne's lap. Her hand went to her daughter's hair in an automatic motion. If Corinne closed her eyes, she could believe they had rolled back time and were home. The hair was slightly coarser and longer than Reina's had been, but similar enough to let her hold onto a moment of fantasy. But that was all she'd allow herself.

What had happened to her daughter was supposed to be impossible. Something senior trainees told to unsuspecting and impressionable novices. But this was no late-night hazing.

The doctor walked in with a tray and three steaming cups. She glanced at Reina and quickly looked away before setting down their refreshments.

Corinne followed the doctor's gaze and noticed Reina's dirty boots shedding slushy muck on the pristine sofa. Not quite what the woman had bargained for. Then again, none of this would fit into her neat and tidy world view. No one with a house this empty, this colorless, had room for a reality that didn't easily slot into smartly defined categories.

"I wish I could give her something for the shock, but she's not technically my patient and I've already made too many questionable decisions this morning."

So it wasn't the mess the doctor had been reacting to. That was a bit unexpected. And interesting. "There's nothing your technology can provide to fix this, but thank you for caring."

The doctor lowered her head but not before Corinne could see the flush warming her face.

"I didn't know what you liked in your tea. There's milk and sugar. Help yourself." The doctor handed her a white mug.

"It's just fine as it is. Thank you." Corinne looked down at Reina. Her eyes had closed and her breathing had slowed. Good.

She needed the rest. Her own fatigue gnawed at her, but she had to make sure they were secure before she could risk sleep. The tea was hot and aromatic, full of spices that were almost familiar, comforting despite their strangeness. As the doctor seemed to be. "What will happen to my husband's body?"

The doctor winced, but to her credit, answered as bluntly as the question demanded. "Because a crime was involved, they'll likely hold it for autopsy and attempt to identify it."

"And when they can't?"

"There's an island off the city that's used to inter the unhoused."

Corinne nodded. It wasn't as if she could take Jace home to be buried. This would truly be an interdicted world for him. Her hand paused in stroking Reina's hair. What if her daughter couldn't get home in her borrowed body? Was there even a body for her to return home to?

"I'm sorry if I distressed you."

"You didn't. Thank you for being so straightforward, Doctor."

The woman sighed. "Please, call me Melissa."

"Corinne."

"What will you do now, Corinne?"

"Go home. If we can."

"If?"

Corinne took another deep swallow. The warmth traveled down her throat and spread through her chest. "It would help if I knew how much you understood about my daughter's arrival here. About Traveling between worlds in general." It wasn't as if she was protecting the Network anymore, but still, this had been classified information her whole career. Talking about it so openly and with an outsider felt wrong.

Melissa paused and Corinne wondered if she was preparing some kind of cover story. *Oh, Jace, I'm getting as paranoid as you were,* she thought.

"This is hard for me."

Corinne raised an eyebrow, but waited for Melissa to continue.

"The last person I told nearly reported me to the Board of Medicine." She smiled wryly. "You probably don't have any idea what that means."

"We have regulatory bodies in the Network. Truly, bureaucracy crosses all realities."

Their quiet laughter cleared the tension between them. Maybe Corinne could trust this woman after all.

"I have a guest bedroom if you think Reina would be more comfortable there."

Reina hadn't stirred. She was still petite enough to be carried, but suddenly Corinne didn't want to be separated from her. The fear was irrational, but what if Reina vanished again? "She's fine here. Anyway, anything we discuss also concerns her."

Melissa took a deep breath, opened her mouth as if to speak, then laughed and shook her head. "Well, it's not as if you'll think I'm crazy."

Corinne waited.

"I saw my first portal when I was six. I didn't know what it was at the time, but it was a door into a sunny summer day from a raw and rainy one. There was a little boy on the other side, and I wanted to go and play with him."

That wasn't supposed to be possible. The ability to see the folds and creases of spacetime showed up much later in development, and even then, opening a way took training. Perhaps the doctor had just been in the right place at the right time when someone else had come through. Still, if it had been a Traveler, they should have known how to avoid notice. And was this before or after this world had been interdicted? "What happened then?"

"Someone on the other side pulled the boy back and the opening slammed shut."

There was more, but it was clear Melissa didn't want to talk about it. Interesting.

"We were traveling." The doctor gave a short bark of a laugh. "Not the kind you mean. Just a family holiday. When we got home, I kept thinking about the little boy and how lonely I was. And there he was, at the end of a tunnel of sparkling light." She shrugged. "We were children. We played together. Somehow we both got good at knowing when a grownup was coming, and he would run to his side of the open doorway before we got caught."

There was a long pause. Melissa broke eye contact and stared down at her tea as if all the answers to her confusion lived there.

How did an untrained child open a portal and keep it open? Even seasoned agents couldn't accomplish that. "And?" Corinne pushed. Could this unassuming woman have the answers she needed?

"And then one time, we didn't notice. My mother found a strange boy in our house." Another pause. Her voice sank into a hoarse whisper. "The authorities took him away. I never saw him again." She paused. "But this probably isn't so unusual for you."

Could the doctor be a genetic anomaly? Was this world, itself, the anomaly? "Truly, it is. More than unusual." Corinne tried to keep herself calm. "Young children can sometimes see a portal a seasoned Traveler opens, but to force an opening by themselves? One stable enough for someone to Travel through? That takes training and practice." She vividly remembered the agent who recruited her. Corinne was sixteen, absolutely vulnerable to being told how special she was. How needed. That her gift gave her purpose and an escape from a tedious and unpleasant life where her talents were being wasted.

And she had believed it all.

Corinne glanced down at her sleeping child. What other lies had the Network taught her and generations of Travelers? And to what end? Oh, Jace, she thought. What have I done? If she'd just believed him, he'd still be alive. Reina would still be Reina.

The doctor sighed and Corinne pulled herself out of her self-pity. Maybe she could make use of this woman. "It's not how it's supposed to happen. But somehow, you did open a way."

Melissa slammed down her cup and stood, her hands on her hips. "I was just a child. It wasn't my fault!"

"No. No. Of course not," Corinne said. It would not do to alienate her one potential ally in this place. How she figured out how to pierce the world walls was less important than the fact that she could, anyway. Did that mean they weren't lost here? "I'm sorry you've carried this alone all these years."

The doctor's anger softened and she sat again, slumping in the chair.

"Did you continue to see them after that?"

She winced. "No. I mean yes. But I convinced myself it was part of a kind of headache. A visual distortion. It was easier to cope."

Corinne nodded. In another set of circumstances, this was the kind of person Corinne might well have recruited for the Network. "And you were there when Reina came through?"

A look of horror transformed her face. "Oh, God. Did I do that?"

Reina stirred. Corinne smoothed her hair and she stilled again. Could this woman have created the portal Reina had followed? Or did Reina already have the talent to Travel on her own? Her hand trembled on Reina's head. This was also supposed to be impossible. Was her child's body still waiting for her back home? Could it have remained alive without the spirit that animated it? "I don't think so. Can you tell me exactly what you saw that night?"

Melissa leaned forward, her head resting on her hands, her elbows on her legs. "I followed Stirling Hughes—my medic partner—into the building. We were there as part of a city census of the unhoused. I didn't want to go inside. I knew something was wrong. The air was thick, distorted. I couldn't make my eyes focus. And then something fell into what looked like a pile of old clothing at my feet.

"The next thing I knew, it was morning and I was sitting in my car with no memory of anything that happened after. Stirling was the one who told me I had saved Reina. Except it wasn't Reina—Stirling had known her before. Her name was Daniella, and she had a history of abusing drugs." She paused and sat up. Her eyes were red-rimmed. "I'm sorry. Does any of this make sense to you?"

"I don't know. Some of it. Maybe." This wasn't how Traveling was supposed to work, but here they were. She slipped Jace's too-large ring from her thumb and turned it over and over in her hand before setting it down next to her teacup. "Okay. I'm going to try to give you an overview of what I know. But there are elements at play that will complicate things and my ability to explain some of the technicalities is limited. Bear with me."

The doctor nodded. "It's too bad I don't have anything stronger than tea."

There was raw, untapped talent here. And Corinne was still enough of an agent to use any advantage that presented itself.

δ

Reina Vettel

AS REINA CURLED AGAINST her mother, her mind replayed the terrible fight over and over, always ending with her father's still body and the red strobes of emergency lights washing out the portal's distortion.

He was gone. Across a threshold there was no coming back from.

A dull pain throbbed in her chest and she had to force herself not to cry out. Her mother's hand paused on the top of her head.

It had been a few years since she'd accepted her comfort like this. Despite her father's frequent silences, he was the one she had always turned to when she had been sad or hurt or ill. Now, it was just the two of them. Reina was afraid if her mother knew she was awake, the gentle hand would go away.

Her mother and the doctor were talking about Traveling. At home, her parents wouldn't talk about the important things when she was in earshot. Reina kept herself still and silent.

"I don't know the state of your world's knowledge of physics," her mother said, "but are you familiar with the term multiverse?"

"My last physics course was in college—that was forty years ago—and I'm sure we didn't learn about it there. But I read a lot of science fiction, if that helps."

"There are stories about the multiverse?"

"It's a common trope. Stories, comic books, movies."

"So what do your movies and such say about it?"

"That there are infinite worlds, each hinging on a choice made or not made. Those choices lead to new timelines. Sort of like a tree in the way things branch out. Or that there are cracks between worlds and some people fall through them, ending up in some kind of mirror universe with another version of themselves."

"We avoid such close instances," Corinne said. "Odd things happen when the potentials are that similar. But there are also dangers in jumping too far afield. The disconnect can break a mind."

They fell silent. Is that what happened to her? Reina felt the heat of the doctor's gaze.

"Huh. I just remembered. There was a TV show called 'Quantum Leap' about a scientist who lost his physical body in some botched experiment. He ended up wandering through the timeline jumping into other people's bodies. He could only jump out again when he fixed some choice the person had made."

Reina sucked in her breath. Was there something she was supposed to fix? So far all she had done was break Martin and lead Wellerman to her father.

"I don't think your world's fictions hold the answers to Reina's situation," her mother said. "I still don't know what happened to my daughter. There are stories—we used to scare one another with them in our training days, but no. When we Travel, we physically shift from one reality to another."

If her mother couldn't fix this, could anyone? Would she be trapped in Daniella's body forever?

"What Reina experienced shouldn't even be possible. But this is an interdicted world, and we have next to no data on it."

"Interdicted?" the doctor echoed the unfamiliar word.

"A world sealed off from the rest of the Multiverse. I don't know the reason. I just know that even working together, Jace and I couldn't open a way home once we got here."

Reina drew her breath in sharply and covered up the sound, mumbling as if she were talking in her sleep.

Her mother fell silent for a moment.

"Is that common?" Doctor Melissa asked.

Her mother hesitated briefly, sighed. "No. Not really. But some worlds have more inertia than others, if that makes sense. They take more work to reach and permanent changes are much harder to make. We say such worlds are very sticky. Then there are realities where changes are simple to make, but don't have much of an external impact. We were always most active on worlds with moderate stakes and moderate stickiness."

"So we would be more of a high-stakes world?"

"I'm sorry. I don't know. The files on this place listed the first Travelers who came here as missing in action. Other than that, your guess is as good as mine."

"So you open a doorway and then what? How do you know where to go? How long does the doorway stay open?"

Her mother was silent.

"I guess you could tell me but then you'd have to kill me, right?" the doctor said. "Sorry—a joke in bad taste."

"It's complicated. And I can't tell you everything. For starters, Traveler training takes years."

Years? Her parents had made it sound a lot simpler than that. Why hadn't they taught her more?

"The way we told Reina about it when she was a child was using the analogy of pages in a book where each page is a unique story, a completely separate reality."

As her mother explained to Melissa, Reina remembered bedtimes when she was a young child, cozy and safe in her mother's lap. *"In the beginning, the infinite worlds pressed against one another like the pages of a tightly bound and closed book."*

"Huh. So the worlds in the multiverse are more distinct than the comic books would have you believe."

"Yes and no. Remember, this is an analogy. Don't strain it too far."

"Okay. So if you could turn the page, you could read a different story, right?"

"Possibly. There are some people who have the ability to see through the pages and read from more than one story at a time."

That made Reina think of Thorne. She hoped he was going to be okay. And who was taking care of Poplar? Maybe they could go back for her.

"And still others who can influence the story being written."

The memory was so strong, Reina could almost feel her mother's arms around her, a quilt wrapped around them both. *"As time passed, every once in a while letters from one page bled through onto another. Most of the changes were gibberish—not even words really—or if they were words, made no sense to the story they ended up in. And so, they were easily ignored. But sometimes, it was enough to change both stories forever."*

That was the part Reina had always loved the most. The bits and pieces of conversations she'd gleaned had made her parents feel like heroes to her. Going into the broken places and fixing them. Kind of like in the doctor's entertainment show. She had wanted to be a part of what her parents did from as far back as she could remember. But this wasn't some fantasy story. She had erased someone's life. There was no fixing that.

There was a long silence.

"I'm sorry. It's a lot to take in," her mother said.

"Honestly? This doesn't sound all that far-fetched. In the medical world, we're just getting control over our body's genetic code. It's like the words in the world's stories. Except with DNA, combinations of four nucleotides write all the processes for life. If you know the right code to change, you can cure disease. But it's been a challenge to figure out what's important and what is just junk carried through from changes made over eons of evolution."

"And if your doctors write the wrong code?"

"Well, we try not to. There were early experiments where people died. We're more careful now. Is that what you do when you Travel? Rewrite things?"

Her mother sighed. "It's what we thought we were doing. Acting to make things better. But now?"

Reina forced herself not to stiffen.

"The man who stabbed Jace..." Her mother paused to take a ragged breath and Reina's heart broke for her. "A long time ago he was Jace's handler at the Network."

Tears gathered in Reina's eyes. Everything Harnett told her was a lie. It was her fault her father was dead.

"You've used that word before. What kind of network?" the doctor said.

Her mother sighed. "This goes against all of my training." A long pause. Reina wasn't sure her mother was going to continue. "Jace and I, we were part of an organization. The MTN—Multiverse Travel Network."

The doctor's laugh surprised her.

"I'm sorry," she said, "It's just... .Why is it that these things always have three-letter acronyms?"

"I don't understand."

"MTN. CIA. FBI. KGB. We have all sorts of covert agencies. So you're a multiverse spy. Or some kind of law enforcement."

"I don't know all that much about this world, but I'm guessing we'd be a little of both in your terms. I'm not proud of my part in it, but we thought we were doing the right thing. At least at the start. At least I did."

Her parents were supposed to be the good guys. How could her mother think that?

"Jace tried to tell me. But it was easier to blame his paranoia on RDD."

"RDD?"

"Reality Disintegration Disorder. It's a kind of illness Travelers are susceptible to. I don't think there's any analogue in your world."

Melissa smiled tightly. "I am a physician. Try me."

"We were always told there was a limit to the number of times an agent could Travel without experiencing side effects. But it wasn't an absolute number. More like a combination of how often someone forced open the world walls and how far from their own time and reality they Traveled."

"Goldilocks."

"I'm sorry?"

"Just a children's story from my world. So you can't Travel too close, but you can't Travel too far. Okay. So, what kind of side effects?"

"Confusion. Paranoia. Memory gaps. Too many timelines coexist in the mind at one time to make sense of them."

"What causes it?"

"Our scientists don't know why it happens or who is susceptible. Every agent undergoes mandatory evaluation after a certain number of years and trips. Jace told me his father died from it. And when Jace started showing the same symptoms..." She shrugged. "But now, I'm not so sure."

Her mother's hand lifted off Reina's shoulders and she shivered with a sudden rush of cold. No one had ever told her about her grandfather. Only that he had died before she was born. Oh, Papa, she thought, struggling to keep from crying again.

"Could it have been something familial? There are genetic factors in expression of some kinds of diseases."

Corinne laughed, but Reina heard no humor in it. "Apparently one of the other peculiarities of Traveling is that those of us who have the ability are also usually infertile. Jace was convinced that Reina is the only third-generation Traveler in the history of the Network."

Reina stiffened. That had to mean something.

"None of that matters anymore. The truth is, I betrayed my family. Jace is dead because of me."

Chapter 23

Martin Lopez

AFTER MARTIN WATCHED THE EMTs load Thorne into the ambulance and pull away, sirens blaring, he started walking aimlessly.

Several more inches of snow had fallen while they were inside, blanketing the area of Mass and Cass, covering the trash, coating the tops of the tent city, and giving the long-ignored blocks a kind of otherworldly and silent beauty.

He knew it wasn't real. Good things rarely were.

Coatless and shivering, Martin kicked over a trash can and kept going. When he looked up, he was at the ER entrance of Boston Medical Center. Where it had all started just a few days ago.

Martin started to turn away when he heard the sharp bark of a dog in the distance. It reminded him of Thorne's mutt, Poplar. He didn't remember seeing it back at their place; they wouldn't have taken it to the hospital. He shook his head. It would find a way to survive in the streets or it wouldn't. Thorne and his dog weren't his concern. The man wasn't one of his regulars. It would be best for all concerned if Martin just went on with his business.

But Daniella's voice wouldn't stop haunting him. *"We're here for everyone and we're no better than anyone, so don't you dare turn them away."*

"Fuck," Martin muttered, before walking through the automatic doors into the ER.

"Another one of yours here?" the receptionist asked.

He never remembered their names, but this one was the lady with the long red fingernails and braided hair extensions down past her waist.

"Old man. Named Thorne."

She turned to consult her computer.

"Admitted. Seventh floor. 726."

It probably wasn't exactly legal for them to tell him, but he was the only person in the city who gave a shit about the folks he and Daniella took in. And anyway, who was Martin going to snitch to?

"Thanks."

"Thank you. God bless."

Martin turned so she wouldn't see him rolling his eyes. Another one like Stirling. He paused, holding a breath. Stirling. Then his mind shied away from the haze that swallowed the big EMT along with the man Martin had shot. He had to focus. All he needed to do was check in to see if Thorne was still alive. Maybe warn him not to talk to the cops. Then go.

Not that he had any idea where.

Another thing he didn't want to think about just yet.

The elevator came and Martin stood in the far corner as it filled up with white coats and other visitors. No one looked at him and he didn't make eye contact with anyone. He got out on the seventh floor like he belonged there, walked swiftly past the nurse's station, and found Thorne's room. Martin paused just outside. Why was he here? He shook his head again. Swore softly. Whatever. It was better than figuring out what to do next. Without knocking, he pushed his way inside.

A steady beeping came from the far side of the room where Thorne lay in bed, facing the window. The bed closest to the door was stripped and empty.

"Hey, you alive?" Martin asked.

The old man rolled over with a groan. An oxygen tube snaked along his side into his nose. Through the gaps in the hospital gown, Martin saw sensors attached to the man's chest.

"It seems so."

Martin nodded, unsure of what else to say. The monitors' strange percussion made the silence that much heavier.

"How is Reina?"

"I don't know. She's gone." It hurt Martin to say that. He wondered what the monitors would hear if they were listening to his heart instead. It would almost be easier to believe he'd been the one on drugs instead of his sister. That this was all some chemical hallucination and he'd wake up strung out and half dead in some anonymous alley. It would be worth it, though, if Daniella could be Daniella again.

"I'm sorry."

Tears shone in the man's eyes. No one had ever cried for Martin before. He turned away, his chest heavy. "I don't know where your dog went. I'll try to find it."

"She's gone somewhere I don't think I can follow."

Martin sucked in a sharp breath. He didn't want to share anyone's pain. It was just a fucking dog. Not the same as his sister. But he knew it was the same. Pain. Loss. All the same. Thorne had no place in this world. No home. No money. No family. He didn't even have his dog anymore. Martin wanted to hold on to his anger, but he was so damned tired. "I'm sorry about Poplar."

"Thank you."

Martin crossed to the window and gripped the sill until his knuckles went white. "Are you really from"—Martin gestured vaguely past the glass—"somewhere else?"

"I know you won't believe me, but there are futures where you survive this pain."

The man's quiet insistence reminded him of Stirling. "I don't need your charity or your hope."

"I'm sorry."

He couldn't cope with Thorne's pity, either. When Martin was little, he thought if he could just keep his sister with him, everything would be okay. It had been the story he'd clung to long after he'd stopped believing in anything else. And like the rest, it was also a lie. "Don't be. Some things you can't change."

"I know."

There was nothing else to say. Martin owed him nothing. Thorne had lost a dog. Martin had lost everything. Why should he even care?

A flutter of color outside caught his gaze. A woman walking by the hospital wore her hair wrapped in a brightly patterned scarf. It reminded him of the hair wraps the women at Stirling's church had given his sister. Thinking of their kindness was more than he could bear. He leaned against the wall for support and closed his eyes. "What about your future?"

"I'm not sure I have one."

Martin turned sharply and glared at Thorne. "What the hell does that mean?"

The man's face was grim with pain. "I think I'm not supposed to be here. I think Poplar and I died the night we slid through into your world. Maybe that's why she's gone. At least she'll have a life now."

"That's bullshit. You're here. You were both here. That's got to mean something."

"I thought you didn't do hope."

"I thought you saw possibilities."

Thorne laughed bitterly. "I guess we were both wrong."

"This is all fucked. Fine. You're welcome to stay with me. When they let you out of here," Martin said in a rush. "It's not much, but it's better than the shelters or the street."

"None of this was your fault."

"You don't know me. You don't know what I've done."

"I know you love your sister. You let me and Poplar in when we needed help. What else do I need to know?"

I shot a man, Martin thought. *I shot a man.* And he would do it again if it meant saving his sister. He turned to leave, fatigue making his body heavy and slow.

"Did you mean what you said?" Thorne asked.

"What?"

"About staying. In your shelter."

Martin sighed. "Yes."

"Thank you." Thorne sat up and pulled off the sticky monitors. Alarms filled the room.

"What the hell are you doing?"

"I don't belong here."

A red-faced nurse charged in and glared at Martin. Thorne was already sitting up in bed. His oxygen tubing hissed quietly by his side.

"What do you think you're doing, sir?" she demanded.

Thorne looked at Martin and nodded. "Going home."

δ

Reina Vettel

WATCHING HER MOTHER'S SHOULDERS heave as she sobbed was more than Reina could take. She sat up and took her mother's hand. Circling Corinne's thumb was her familiar silver ring. Her father's glinted on the coffee table.

"No, Mama. I was the one who brought Wellerman to the shelter. Papa would still be alive if it wasn't for me." She could barely force the words out.

Her mother shook her head. "Wellerman and the Network have been searching for us for a long time. Your father tried to make me understand, but I..." She took a shaky breath. "I thought I was being so careful. Doing the right thing. But he must have been following me the whole time."

"Please, Mama, stop crying."

Doctor Melissa interrupted. "Are we in danger? Will Wellerman come after us?"

Reina gasped and rubbed her wrists where he had bound her. Everything had happened so fast and by the time her mother pulled her from her father's body, Wellerman was gone. So was the haze of the portal. In a just universe, he would have been sucked in and trapped on the other side. Forever. But her father was dead, and the universe didn't care.

Her mother blinked her eyes clear and glanced around the doctor's colorless home. Reina had never seen her face so filled with pain and fear. "I don't know," she said and wrapped her arms around her chest.

"Mama, what should we do?"

She shook her head. "I don't know," she repeated.

A surge of anger burned through Reina's sympathy. "You have to know! You're supposed to make it right! Papa's gone, and you're all I have left." Her throat thickened and unwelcome tears smeared her vision.

"If I had listened. If I had believed, we would be safe. You would be okay. I'm so sorry, Reina. For everything."

"You have to fix it!" She wanted to scream. To break something. To run until she couldn't push her legs any more.

"Not everything broken can be repaired," her mother whispered.

"Someone I respect once told me it's our job to try anyway," the doctor said, gently.

"You don't understand." Her mother stared into the distance, refusing to meet either the doctor's gaze or Reina's. "I lied to Jace. I went back to the Network. In secret. Believed I could do the work I loved and keep my family together."

Reina gripped a couch pillow so tightly, she was afraid she'd tear it apart.

"I was wrong."

"Mama, how could you?"

Her mother closed her eyes and shook her head.

How could Reina feel so many things jumbled together? She could barely breathe past the pressure in her chest.

"Corinne," Melissa said. "Look at me."

The doctor's voice was so compelling, Reina turned to her as well.

"I know you're hurting. I know you're afraid. But your daughter needs you now."

Mama was supposed to know what to do. She was supposed to make everything okay. But that was as much a fairy tale as any story her parents had ever told her. Reina looked down at her hands. At the familiar scar traced on a stranger's palm. What if there was no way to return? No way for Reina to find her own body?

"Oh, Mama," she whispered, but no one seemed to notice.

If her mother hadn't left her to go after Papa, would things have been different? It would be so easy to blame her mother for everything. And maybe the Reina of a few days ago might have. But she had also made choices that led to heartache and loss. Far more than her outward self had changed, and she was still reeling from it all.

Her father was gone. Her old self was gone. She had no idea if they would ever get home. And if her mother didn't have the power to fix any of it, how could Reina hope to?

It would be so easy to give up.

But Reina knew one thing for certain: In this reality, there was a small creature who was all alone, and she was the one person who could care for her until Thorne returned from wherever the medics had taken him.

That, at least, she could do.

That small part of a broken world she could fix.

Everything else could wait.

Reina sat up and dried her eyes.

"We need to go back."

"I don't think that's a good idea," Melissa said.

"I have to. Poplar needs me." How could the doctor not understand?

"Poplar will be fine. She's warm and safe and there are plenty of people at the shelter to care for her. It's you I'm worried about. You need space and time to process. To begin to grieve."

No matter how many times Reina went over her memories, her father would still be dead. She would still be trapped in a stranger's body. What was left to process? "If you want to help me, let me help Poplar."

Melissa sighed, as if she were disappointed in her. "Corinne, I can't make decisions for you, but in my professional opinion, Reina should stay here."

Her mother frowned, but didn't answer.

"But you said it yourself. What if he—if Wellerman followed us? We're not safe."

"It was just a question, Reina. Honestly, it's far more likely he's still at the shelter." Melissa again looked to Corinne.

"He's a trained agent. He'll have found another hideout," her mother said. "We need to find out where he went. Our safety depends on it." She rested her warm hand on Reina's arm and fixed her attention on the doctor. "There are ways to track a Traveler, but your world is too chaotic for me to read the potentials without getting closer to his last known position."

Reina held her breath.

"My daughter is right. We must go back."

Her mother excused herself to use the washroom and Melissa retreated to the kitchen insisting they needed something to eat. Reina bit her lip, worrying that going back was absolutely the worst thing to do. What if Harnett returned? How could she face seeing where her father had died? Fear left an acrid taste in her mouth; Reina reached for the tea Melissa had set out. Her father's ring lay next to her mother's empty cup, and Reina curled her hand around it. The metal chilled her palm. The breath hitched in her throat, but she had no tears left. She slipped the ring into her pocket.

When her mother returned to sit next to her, she said nothing.

They picked at some crackers and dried fruit in silence. The food was tasteless, but Reina forced herself to eat anyway. Her body was still healing from its hurts, and she was going to need her strength.

Melissa drove them back to Martin's shelter without argument. She circled the block slowly several times before parking her car nearby. The weather had cleared, and the sun and traffic had turned most of the snow to dingy slush. All of the emergency vehicles had gone.

Reina paused at the door to the building, thinking about Martin. She'd left without thanking him for everything he'd done for her. That was wrong. She looked down at her hands, still unfamiliar. She owed him more than she could ever repay.

"Are you sure we should be here?" the doctor asked. "It's still a crime scene." She pointed at some yellow tape sagging across the doorway.

"I'm not sure there's any better option. Remember, Wellerman is still a threat—to your world as much as to me and Reina. This is the only way to find out where he went."

"And make sure Poplar is safe," Reina reminded them.

"The dog. Right," her mother said.

Reina frowned. Poplar was not just some dog.

They slipped under the tape and stepped inside. As the door shut, Reina blinked in the sudden darkness. And then she was falling again. Reliving the moment when everything went wrong and she lost all connection to her family and her senses during the transit. She didn't realize she had cried out until she felt the weight of a hand on her shoulder, grounding her, bringing her back to the room and her physical self.

"Are you okay?"

It was the doctor. And for a brief moment, Reina burned with a surge of anger. It should have been her mother comforting her, supporting her, telling her it was going to be all right. She took a shaky breath, working to get her emotions under control. "I will be."

"It's normal to be afraid. Or overwhelmed. You've experienced a lot of trauma in a short amount of time all tied to this building."

She glanced toward her mother, who was striding through the lobby with a purpose that didn't seem to include Reina.

"And you need time."

She shook off the doctor's hand. First she needed to find Poplar. Then she had to figure out what to say to Martin. The lobby was unnaturally silent. Where were all the people who made this place their home? Martin would be furious if the police had emptied out the building. And where was Poplar hiding? Reina focused on her memory of the scrappy little animal and called out for her in her mind.

No answer.

::Poplar? I'm sorry. I should have listened to you.::

No answer.

::You were right. Harnett was a bad man.::

She turned her head from side to side, listening intently for any hint of a response.

::Please. Let me make it up to you.::

No answer.

"Poplar?" she finally called aloud. What if she had gotten hurt in the skirmish? Reina gasped. She couldn't bear one more loss. It wasn't fair. It wasn't fair. Tears spilled down her face and she swiped them away.

"Reina?" her mother called.

She fought for control and steadied her voice. "I can't find Poplar."

"I'm sure the animal is fine. Can you come here a moment? I need you to tell me what you feel."

Her mother was pacing near where her father had fallen. Reina struggled against the urge to run. Somewhere. Anywhere. She couldn't look away from the dark stain of her father's blood on the cold floor. How could her mother be so focused? She forced herself to walk across the room, skirting the taped outline of his body.

Her mother took Reina's hand in a tight grip. "Here. What do you sense."

Reina wanted to pull away, but this was important. They needed all the information on Wellerman they could gather, in case he returned for them. She closed her eyes and reached out with her awareness. Small pinpricks of energy pierced her skin. It wasn't like the Moment she had experienced at home before that first transit, but it did have the same shape and sense. It was as if something was waiting for the right trigger to sweep down over them, opening a way again. "There's a weak spot here."

"Yes! I feel it, too. And it's where I lose track of Wellerman."

The excitement in her mother's voice felt wrong. Shouldn't she be worried? Should they run?

"Do you think he went through?" It was what Reina had hoped for. If Wellerman was trapped somewhere else, then they were safe. Right?"

"Yes."

"So he's gone?"

Her mother paused. "Yes."

"So we can go home?" Hope and fear shot through her. Could she return to her own self? But what would happen to the body she inhabited?

Her mother shook her head. "I'm sorry. I'm not sure I can open that way again. But this feels different. Easier, somehow. It shouldn't take much to slip through." She took a deep breath and turned to Reina. "This may be my only chance."

Reina frowned and slipped her hand free. "Mama?" Her mother had always been the steady one. The balance to her father's unpredictable mood swings.

"You mean to go after him," the doctor said, quietly, without judgment. Just a fact, like a statement about the weather or the time of day.

Reina shivered. Him. Wellerman. She never wanted to see Harnett Wellerman again.

"Will you help us, Doctor? You clearly have some talent."

"I may not have your skills, but even I can recognize a bad plan when I see it."

Follow Wellerman? How could her mother even consider such a thing?

"Dr. Klein, you have no idea how dangerous this man is. With him free to Travel, we are all at risk. You and your world, included."

"So you said," the doctor agreed.

"Mama, I'm so afraid," Reina whispered.

"Your daughter almost died..."

"And I appreciate more than I can express that you were here to help her." She raised her hands as the doctor tried to speak again. "Understand this is my call. Unless you're willing to follow my lead, step aside. I doubt your meager talent would contribute much anyway."

The doctor's face paled and then reddened before she got herself back under control. "Hasn't Reina been through enough?"

"How dare you!"

Reina had never seen her mother so enraged.

"I'm doing this for her. To keep her safe."

The doctor nodded and stood her ground. "I see. By going after a man who's already shown his capacity for deadly violence. And what will happen to your daughter if he kills you as well?"

Reina stiffened. The air tightened in her throat.

Even as her mother got right up into the doctor's face, the woman held her own, head tilted in curiosity, expression soft, hands quietly at her sides. Reina shifted foot to foot, her body flooded with the urgency to do something, anything.

Her mother flinched in the face of the doctor's focused calmness and took a step back. Reina let out her breath in a long exhale.

"I thought you would understand, if anyone in this broken reality could. But obviously I was wrong." She turned to focus on where the portal had been earlier this morning.

The doctor nodded as if in agreement. "You'd be surprised at what I understand."

Reina's heart raced. She swallowed hard against a lump in her throat. "Mama? Don't leave me, again, Mama. Please."

"Never." She reached for Reina's hand again. "Besides, I don't think I can do this alone."

"I'm scared." What if Wellerman was waiting for them? What if she lost herself again?

"Just do what I say. It won't be like before. I'll be right beside you. I promise."

Her mother was lying. All Travelers journeyed alone. It was one of her earliest lessons, learned long before her sensitivity to the world's weak places blossomed. All Travelers journeyed alone. Reina's borrowed body stiffened. Her hand, slick with sweat, slipped from her mother's grip. She crossed her arms, hands tucked in tightly. Her mother was lying. Reina could hardly bear to look at her, but she forced herself to meet her mother's gaze. It was defiant. Harsh. Her mother was lying, and worse, so much worse than just the lie: She knew it.

Blinking back tears, Reina broke eye contact. Nodded to herself. Took a breath. What choice did she have? "Tell me what I need to do."

"Reina? Are you certain?"

She didn't want to look at the doctor. The kindness in the woman's voice was nearly enough to break her. Reina slowly unfolded her arms and reached for her mother's hand again.

"If we work together, we can force the Moment. Wellerman's transit left a fracture that hasn't yet healed. If we hit it just right, it should reopen."

Reina stared at her feet. Of all the parts of her strange body, they felt the most familiar. What if it happened again? She imagined Daniella's body falling back to the floor, empty, finally, left to die. She knew it would destroy Martin. And would whatever was Reina just drift away, like fog burning off in the sunshine? At least the pain would stop. She needed the pain to stop.

"It's now or never. I won't be able to hold the opening for long."

"Yes, Mama." It was hard to force the words from her tight throat. Reina glanced back at the building's lobby. Had it been only three days since she'd found herself here? She tried once more to call out to Poplar, but the dog wasn't there, or wasn't answering. ::I'm sorry.::

Reina turned to her mother. "I'm ready." She nearly choked on the lie.

Chapter 24

Corinne Vettel

IF THE BOUNDARIES BETWEEN universes were tapestries, what Corinne sensed in this place of violence and death was a threadbare patch. Reality was thinning in a way she hadn't experienced before. She glanced at Reina. Maybe that's why her daughter had ended up here. Why her physical self hadn't transited with her was a question Corinne had no answer to. It was something to figure out later. When they were somewhere safe. When Wellerman was taken care of.

She shied away from what exactly that meant. For now, Corinne needed to see where he'd retreated and find a way to keep him there. Then, they would be free of him forever. And even if they couldn't return home, she and Reina could lay a false trail for the Network to follow. Oh, Jace, she thought. It had been his plan. The irony was a bitter chaser to the grief.

Holding tightly to Reina, she studied the threads separating this world from the one Wellerman punched through. "The weakest area is right here." She nodded toward the wall in front of them. "Can you see it?"

"Yes," Reina whispered.

Good. "I'm going to need your strength. When I say so, imagine you are parting the strands so we can slip through." It had to work. She shook off the memory of her and Jace's failures. With a transit so recent and the boundary so frayed, it should be easy to follow. She could do this. Her ring felt heavy on her thumb. She frowned. Where was Jace's? Had she left it at the doctor's home? There was no time to retrieve it. Corinne shook off her uneasiness and took Reina's hand, hoping to ground herself and find reassurance.

As Reina squeezed back, Corinne inhaled sharply. "Do you have something you can use as a focus?"

Reina flinched but then held up her free hand. "I have this."

An imprint of the sharp stone that Corinne had noticed earlier made a kind of star shape on Reina's palm. How it had come to scar this stranger's hand was another mystery for another time. She only hoped it would be a strong enough anchor.

Corinne felt a cold breeze stir both the air inside the building and the fabric of reality. In her mind's eye, she saw the cloth ripple. "Can you feel it?" It was like a tailwind and it should help them get through. Beside her, Reina stiffened. "Steady. Steady."

A haze coated the air around them. The doctor gasped. She must have seen it, too. Corinne pulled her concentration back to the nascent opening. Nothing else mattered. Then brightness exploded from a pinprick, tearing a jagged rent between this world and another. She only hoped it was where Wellerman had gone. It was foolhardy to walk blindly into an unknown, but staying posed too many dangers. Reina would never be safe while Wellerman was looking for them. "Now. Let's go."

She stepped forward, Reina stumbling behind her. Through the portal, Corinne saw into that other place. A large, empty lobby with a gray concrete floor. Columns mirrored each other on opposite sides of the opening. It was a reality nearly identical to this one. A close cousin, then. But since this doctor's world wasn't Corinne's own home reality, it shouldn't matter. It shouldn't matter.

The key was that Wellerman Traveled there. And they could follow. She took another step. A golden shimmer hovered just in front of her. All they had to do was cross the threshold.

Then make sure Wellerman would never threaten them again.

And everything would be all right.

δ

Martin Lopez

THORNE HAD BEEN SILENT as they walked away from the hospital. At least Martin had been able to navigate the paperwork the old man had to sign to leave against medical advice. They really hated when you did that. He hoped Thorne would be warm enough. The sun had come out, but it was still raw. And their shoes were wet. "You'd better not keel over on me."

"Everything dies, Martin. But I don't think I'll die today."

He sounded disappointed. Martin understood more than Thorne would ever know. If it hadn't been for Daniella, there had been so many times when he might have walked in front of a train or taken the product the dealers hawked with such brutal efficiency in the neighborhood. Now Daniella was gone. And even Reina—who he would have taken care of—had gone, too. If no one needed him, then what was the point?

Something Thorne had said to him seared through his mind like the pulsing of emergency lights. *"There are futures where you survive this pain."* How could he know that? Why did he even care?

When they got to the building and there were no police cars parked outside, Martin exhaled heavily. Then he noticed the yellow tape fluttering in the breeze. He swore and yanked it from the door. There would be no one left inside. The cops would have chased them all out. At best. Martin hated having to suck up to the precinct. They should be grateful. If it weren't for him and this place, all the people who sheltered here would be in the growing tent city near Mass and Cass. Martin didn't think all the developers and speculators buying up the nearby vacant lots and shuttered businesses really wanted that.

If he was lucky, they didn't also trash the place or throw out everyone's stuff. The cops liked to do that. Probably because they could.

He opened the door and pushed Thorne inside. A series of short, sharp barks rang out from somewhere ahead, distorted and distant, but recognizable. "Hey, it's your dog."

Thorne shook his head, his eyes sad. He looked like hell.

"Go sit down. Give me a minute and I'll get you settled... Shit!"

The air inside the building was charged like before a thunderstorm. Martin tried to blink his vision clear, struggling to adapt from the brightness outside. And then he blinked again. Shit. It was happening again. A shimmering curtain of light cut the room in half. It was the same weirdness that swallowed up Stirling and the man he had shot.

"Don't move!" he told Thorne.

He squinted and made out three standing figures eclipsed by the brightness.

"Reina," a woman's voice urgently whispered, "Now. Let's go."

"No!" he shouted and leaped toward her. The doctor and the other woman could fend for themselves. But Martin wasn't going to lose his sister again. Even if she wasn't his sister, not really. He grabbed the girl's free arm and pulled. Daniella, Reina—he didn't care what she called herself—stumbled toward him. He reached out to catch her and she slammed against his chest. Martin instinctively hugged her the way he'd held his baby sister through the bad dreams and the long nights of her detox last year.

She stiffened and broke away. "What are you doing?"

He let anger swamp the anguish. "Keeping you from disappearing like those other guys. You're welcome."

Reina turned back to the middle of the room. "Mama?"

The air was clear. Dust motes hung in the indirect light streaming in through the broken and unboarded windows. The strange woman was gone.

"What other guys?" the doctor asked.

"The man I...the man who was threatening Reina. And Stirling." And his gun, which had skittered away to wherever they went.

"Mama!" Reina shouted again. Her distress cut through him.

"What do you mean disappeared? What the hell did you do to Stirling?" the doctor demanded.

"Me? Nothing! This place isn't safe. What if that light comes back and swallows us all up? We have to get out of here." It wouldn't be the first time Martin had to abandon a squat, and it probably wouldn't be the last. But fuck it all, this one was supposed to have been home for a while.

"It won't come back," Reina said softly. She was staring across the room, her eyes glassy, her shoulders slumped.

"How do you know?"

"It shut behind Mama. And I can't open it alone."

"It's not your fault." Thorne picked his way carefully through the lobby. His face looked gray and drawn. Pain clouded his eyes. His hands shook. Maybe springing him from the hospital hadn't been such a good idea.

"I'm sorry. I can't find Poplar. She won't answer me."

Thorne took her into his arms. Martin suppressed a flare of jealousy when she melted against him.

"It's not your fault," he said again. "This future was set in motion long before you met her."

"I heard her barking. When Mama opened the way."

"Yes," Thorne said softly. "I know."

Martin turned to confront the doctor. "The only reason I let you in was because Stirling vouched for you. Now he's gone. Who the hell are you? Are you one of them?"

The doctor winced. "I don't know who I am anymore."

Thorne pulled away from Reina and doubled over in a coughing fit.

"But I'm still a physician, and that man needs to rest."

"Fine," Martin said through clenched teeth. "If the cops didn't toss my room, he can have the bed. And you and me? We need to talk." He led them to the stairwell. Reina and Melissa flanked Thorne, supporting him up the stairs. On the main floor of the shelter, blankets and folks' personal stuff were scattered around, but nothing looked destroyed. Martin let himself relax just a little bit. Maybe the cops had left his people alone and they'd be back come nightfall.

Reina and the doctor fussed over Thorne while Martin stood in the corner of the room, his fingers gripping the edge of the curtain that separated it from the rest of the floor. He felt like a ghost in his own place. The two of them got Thorne propped up on pillows, and his breathing got easier. His face was a healthier color, too.

"Okay. You wanted to talk. Let's talk," the doctor said.

Martin glanced up. They were sitting in the same places they had chosen the day before, when he and Stirling were arguing about Reina. Only Stirling and the dog were missing. Down the rabbit hole. A brief image of the big man as Alice—complete in the blue and white dress—just about got him choking before he forced himself back under control. He pointed at the doctor. "You. You started this. Everything was fine before you got here. You walked in my place and everything went sideways."

She nodded. "I know. That's how it felt to me, too."

That wasn't how it was supposed to go. She should have argued with him. He needed her to fight back so he had someplace to put all the jangled emotions surging through him.

"She saved my life, Martin."

Somehow, hearing his name in Daniella's voice, just the way she used to say it and in the rooms they lived in was what did it. He turned away to hide the tears he couldn't stop. "But you're dead. I know you died that night." His throat felt raw, as if the words had razors in them.

"I'm sorry I can't be her."

Martin let go of the curtain he was strangling. He couldn't bear to look at the girl who wore his sister's body like a set of secondhand clothes. "So now what?" Thorne's words floated back to the surface of his mind once more. *"There are futures where you survive this pain."* He turned to old man. "You're the one who swears he sees the future. So, tell us. What happens next?"

He smiled sadly. "It doesn't work that way. Besides, once Poplar followed Stirling through the portal, everything I see is muddled."

"So open another one and get your damned dog back."

"I don't have that gift."

"You came here through some gateway, right? Just do what you did then."

Thorne shook his head. "Poplar and I followed Reina's pain from our world to this one. That's all I know."

"I'm sorry. I can't get you back," Reina said. "My parents are…" She choked back a sob. "…were the Travelers. If my mother doesn't come for me, I don't know what to do."

He wanted to argue with her. To tell her he'd be there for her. Just like always. But this wasn't his sister. No more comforting lies.

The doctor's hand on his shoulder startled him. He nearly slugged her.

"I'm sorry for your loss. If there's anything I can do…"

Martin shook off her hand and her sympathy. "You have done enough already." More than enough. Every time the doctor was around, fucking doors to nowhere opened. He turned to face her. "Maybe try undoing everything for a change?"

She swallowed hard. The shame and guilt that flickered across her face felt familiar, but Martin couldn't stop until he vomited up all his pain.

"You were here the night Daniella died. The night she—Reina —came through. Then when you came back—right here, in this room, the air got weird and there was a hole to somewhere else.

And this morning. You walked in and that's when everything went to hell again."

The woman's pale face went even paler.

"So fucking do it again. Turn everything back to the way it was. Make it right. You owe me."

δ

Melissa Klein

IT COULDN'T HAVE BEEN HER. After Borys had been taken away, she'd tried to find a way to his world, hoping he'd somehow made it home and she would see him again. But nothing she did opened the doorway back into the summer garden where he'd come from. All it got her were migraines and lost time and visits to doctors who were sure they had the right meds or the right therapy to fix her. And more guilt. She couldn't forget the guilt. It had been a goad for her entire life. It's what drove her into medicine and then psychiatry.

If she couldn't understand herself, she figured she might as well try to understand others. And if she helped enough people, it might make up for what she had done to Borys.

But she'd been caught in a trap of denial and repression for far too long. She could see it now, as clearly as if she were reading a progress note she'd written on herself:

Patient is persistent in her belief that she can see doors to alternate worlds. While this delusion goes back to a childhood traumatic event, it has been triggered by the recent deaths of both of her elderly parents and her prolonged and complex grief. Even so, she seems well compensated and is not an active danger to herself or anyone else. As her delusion is long standing, it may not be amenable to direct challenge. Treatment options include supportive psychotherapy for prolonged grief disorder and medication for the migraine presentation, as it seems like the aura is what reinforces her delusion. While patient has been treated for migraine in the past, there are new approaches that may also impact her rigid belief system.

She could just as easily see Julian writing such an assessment. Julian. Melissa tugged her fingers through her tangled hair and slumped against the back of the lumpy, folded-up futon. She had a follow-up appointment with him first thing tomorrow morning. What the hell was she going to say to him? What could she say that wouldn't have her deemed an incompetent physician and cause her to lose everything she'd built the last thirty years? Melissa knew she had to tell him something.

"Tell me you don't see the pattern," Martin said. "I dare you."

Melissa stood, her restless energy needing some kind of outlet, but there was barely room to pace. Could it have been her? Because if it was, then it was also her fault that Borys was lost.

Reina came up beside her. "It's not a terrible thing to be a Traveler."

She frowned, thinking of what Corinne had and hadn't revealed about the people who trained her, stalked her family, and murdered her husband. Despite the more mature body Reina was wrapped in, she was still a child with a child's perceptions. "I think it's a complicated thing." And not something any child should have to feel responsible for. Not her younger self then and certainly not Reina now.

Melissa could use Stirling's steadiness and faith right about now. And then she felt guilty for not thinking about him sooner. What kind of reality had he landed in? There were far too many alternate histories in which being a Black man would make him even more of a target than in this one. She owed him. She'd dragged him into this mess. If she hadn't been having a midcareer crisis, if she had really dealt with her parents' decline and deaths, if Ellie hadn't challenged her to move outside of her comfort zone, she never would have volunteered for the Boston Homeless Count. And they would never have assigned her to Stirling. He would have continued with his somewhat-off-the-books ministry at Martin's shelter without ever seeing a portal to another world, much less falling through one.

It was like what happened to Borys in reverse. And Melissa couldn't bear the responsibility for another life derailed.

She turned to face Martin. "I'm trying to understand. And I need you to go over everything you saw this morning. Every detail. Even from before I got here, okay? Even if you don't think it's important."

He looked startled. His face flushed and he wouldn't meet her gaze. She cocked her head and waited. The silence lengthened.

"What good will that do?"

"Honestly? I don't know." She let the silence stretch out between them.

"Fine. But you don't get to judge me if there are parts you don't like."

The irony nearly choked her. "I'm just here to understand, Martin." She glanced around the room, briefly nodding at Thorne and Reina. The old man looked as weary as she felt. Reina just seemed lost. Melissa wished she could offer any kind of comfort to either of them. "I think that's all any of us want."

"Fine," Martin repeated and sat on a stack of folded blankets by the window. "Thorne and the dog came in this morning."

"Her name is Poplar," Reina said.

Martin winced. "Thorne warned me about Wellerman. He didn't trust him. Reina and I argued. She and Poplar went outside to play in the snow. After a little while, Poplar came tearing back in, barking up a storm. Thorne got me and we went outside."

His reporting was terse, expressionless. Melissa wondered how much all this was costing him.

"She was talking to Wellerman. Poplar went after him. Thorne collapsed. It looked like he was having a heart attack. Wellerman helped me bring him inside." He paused for a long minute. "I guess he didn't care about helping me. Just about staying close to...Reina."

"And then?" Melissa prompted.

"I texted Stirling. He said he'd come. I figure he was the one who called 9-1-1."

"And he texted me."

Martin nodded. "And then it got weird."

"My parents came for me," Reina said, her voice thick with tears. "I didn't know Harnett was a threat. He said he'd help me. But then he grabbed me and everything happened at once."

She hated putting the girl through this, but it was the only way. "Where was Stirling?"

"He was taking care of me," Thorne said. His face was still lined with pain, but his breathing was less labored. "Reina's father and Wellerman were fighting. I sent him to help Reina. I knew...I saw...She was in trouble. I'm sorry. I couldn't stop it from happening. I never can."

That's when Melissa had walked into the maelstrom. Disjointed images played through her mind: Reina's father, dead, the knife protruding from his throat. The jagged wheel of light that turned the center of the room into bright chaos. The echo of a gunshot. Martin staring at the gun in his hand. She frowned. "You shot someone."

Martin's face flushed, but he didn't turn away, didn't deny it.

"He saved me from Wellerman," Reina said. "And Poplar, too. She bit him."

Thorne made a sound that was part laughter, part misery.

"What happened to Stirling and Wellerman?"

"Your portal thing opened and they got swallowed up."

My portal, Melissa thought. But that didn't feel right. She hadn't done anything. Not the first night she was here, or the other day, or this morning. The bright shape of what she'd rationalized as a scintillating scotoma was simply there. It could just as well have been something about this building. But no. That wouldn't explain her childhood. And El Alhambra. Until the night of the count, it had been over fifty years since she last let herself see a portal.

Except that wasn't exactly true. She'd seen plenty of auras, but taking the migraine meds made them melt away. Funny, though, they never actually prevented the headaches afterward. She was a psychiatrist. Helping patients face their truths was the breakthrough that led to healing. In this case? Her carefully constructed world would break apart.

The memory of her college friend's voice broke through all the confusion in Melissa's mind. *"It's when the world feels the most broken that we must heed the call to repair."*

Oh, Ellie, she thought. *It's not that easy.*

But she knew what Eleanor would say: Of course it wasn't easy. She would say that the work was valuable and necessary nonetheless. That each of us had the power and the obligation to just do the work.

Ellie and Stirling were so damned much alike. It was probably why Melissa had instinctively trusted him. He chose that work—his ministry in every sense—every single day, no matter what the cost. How could she do any less?

"Tikkun fucking olam," Melissa muttered.

She took a deep breath. Jullian would do what he had to do. And so would she.

δ

Thorne Truthscryer

Suddenly the terrible pressure in Thorne's chest that had begun when he saw Wellerman standing with Reina outside in the snow eased. The pain behind it remained: the ache of Poplar's absence. But everything else had changed. A blossoming of futures branched out from this Moment.

Some brought more loss, death stalked others, but there were a few shining strands where he and Poplar survived. Together. He could breathe again. There was a path forward for him. He looked around the room, searching for what had changed, and met the doctor's steady gaze. "You. You've done something," he said.

Her face flushed as if she were embarrassed or ashamed. "No matter what it costs, I can't abandon Stirling somewhere over the rainbow." She cocked her head and gave a half smile, though her eyes remained sad. "But there better not be any flying monkeys waiting for me."

He raised an eyebrow. The words were nonsensical, but her intent was clear.

Martin snorted. "You've got to be kidding me. So who's the fucking wicked witch? Wellerman?"

"I'm sorry. I know this isn't a joke," the doctor said. "It's how I deal with my fear." She turned to Reina. "So how do I do this? What did your mother say?"

Thorne frowned. She was intending to go after Stirling on her own. That choice pruned the possibilities down to a few, and they all led to failure. Loss. Death. He struggled to sit up. "No."

The doctor threw her hands in the air in exasperation. "What do you mean, 'no'?"

"If you go alone, you won't survive."

"You can't know that."

Thorne smiled sadly. "Actually I can. And I do." He could see her weighing the alternatives.

"I'm sorry. I won't put anyone else in harm's way. I can't. It's bad enough..."

He understood the doctor's pain more than she would know. "But that's not your decision to make. There is more at stake here." Even more than his beloved Poplar. He got out of bed slowly, not fully trusting his legs.

"What are you doing?"

"I'm going with you."

"You're going right back to the hospital."

He shook his head and smiled. "I don't think so. Young Martin already taught me how to assert my own choices in your medical world."

"I could compel you. I have that power."

Other possibilities glinted in his periphery. They would all end poorly, especially for the doctor. "But you won't."

She lowered her gaze, but not before he saw her face blaze red again. "No."

"You can't go without me," Reina said.

"Definitely not. It's too dangerous," the doctor said.

Thorne opened his mouth to concur, but his relentless vision wouldn't let him spare the girl. There were no paths he wanted to travel if they didn't make this journey together.

Martin paced the room, his hands tightly curled into fists. "This is crazy. You just had a heart attack, and she almost died!"

"I'm sorry, Martin," Thorne whispered, wishing he had the power to roll back the timeline to before it all began.

"Well, fuck," Martin said. "Where she goes, I go."

Something squeezed around Thorne's heart. He had promised Martin a future where he survived his pain. It wasn't much, but it was the best he could see. And even that would be a terrible lie if the boy tried to follow them. Thorne had seen how determined he was. How he had loved his sister. Losing even the echo of her again would be brutal. He didn't know what to say that wouldn't just make everything worse.

"Martin," Reina said softly.

The boy's head jerked up. His eyes were red.

"I don't belong here."

He opened his mouth as if to argue.

Reina took his hand and eased open his fist. "You have done so much for me. I owe you everything. More than I can ever repay."

They looked so much alike, even down to the shine of tears in warm brown eyes. It wasn't fair. The boy had lost too much. He was far too young to have lived through this much grief.

"Who will take care of all the people who shelter here if you're gone?"

"That's not fucking fair!"

"But it's true. And you know it." Reina paused, as if considering her next words. "And it's what Daniella would want."

Thorne saw the pain strike Martin like an arrow to the heart.

"Please. I know you loved her. I never had a sibling, but if I did, I'd want it to be you."

Martin pulled away from her, slid to the floor, rocking, his hands pressed to his eyes.

The doctor knelt beside him. "Give me and Stirling an anchor to find our way back home. We're both connected to this place. To you."

He didn't answer.

"Can you do that for us?"

Thorne could feel the instant Martin understood. He hadn't said a word, but the matrix of potentials shifted again—toward hope.

Chapter 25

Reina Vettel

"MAMA SAID THE BOUNDARY was weakest downstairs," Reina said. She didn't really know what to do, but acting like she did made the fear a little easier to bear. They were relying on her. Even if they didn't realize it yet. She only hoped she'd gleaned enough knowledge from snatches of overheard conversations and the little training her father had given her to be the guide they all needed.

Reina was not truly a Traveler, but maybe with Melissa's sensitivity and Thorne's ability to see potential futures, together they could find a way through.

"I'm not going to watch you vanish," Martin said.

Reina could hear the hurt behind the anger and ached for him.

"Thank you for everything you've done for us," she said. "For me." Nothing she could say to him would ever be enough.

He wouldn't meet her gaze. She blinked back tears.

Thorne cleared his throat gently. "When you took me from the hospital, you offered me a home. If..." He paused. "When we return, Poplar and I would be honored to be part of your community."

"This?" Martin gestured around him. "Some home. Well, you're welcome to it."

Reina exhaled. At least he wouldn't be alone.

She looked back from the curtain at Martin. He stared somewhere past her, struggling to accept a future she was no longer a part of. Something in her mourned the loss. She turned and followed Melissa and Thorne back downstairs.

"Now what?" Melissa asked, standing in the center of the large room, empty of everything except discarded gloves and a few rumpled blankets.

It was colder down here than in Martin's room, but that's not what made Reina shiver. What if it happened again? If transiting with her parents' support went so terribly wrong, what did she risk now?

For a moment she couldn't breathe. The memory of falling into nothingness made the room spin. Her stomach lurched. She swallowed hard. Curled her hands tightly. The two of them waited, watching her. She had to focus. Focus. Took one deep breath and then another. Opened her hands and dried them on her clothes. Pulled out the ring. "You're supposed to have a focus. Something part of you that connects you to you, if that makes sense. This was my father's." She returned it to her pocket. Her tiny stone was long gone, but the imprint of it lived on in this body. It and his ring would have to do.

The doctor looked around, her eyes distant. "I'm not sure I know who I am anymore."

Reina didn't know what to tell her. Would she even be able to make the transit without a strong enough focus? This wasn't going to work. They were trapped here.

Thorne took the doctor's hand in his. "You haven't changed. It's reality that has shifted around you. In the core of your soul, you are a healer. Hold onto that."

The doctor nodded, though her face was still lined with worry. "Thank you."

"As for me? Poplar is part of me. That will suffice."

And who was Reina connected to? Her mother had chosen vengeance over their safety. Over family. Over her. Still, Reina yearned for her. For home. Somewhere on the other side of this reality, her mother was waiting. Regardless of her choice, she had come for Reina. Had tried to protect her. That had to count for something.

The doctor reached for Reina's hand. "You are not alone."

They had all lost so much. Reina felt a sense of connection to them as deep and as secure as what she'd once had with her parents.

She would risk the transit, even if it meant losing herself again. Or facing Wellerman.

Thorne nodded and took her other hand, then linked to the doctor as well. She hadn't been abandoned. Doctor Melissa, Thorne, Martin, Poplar, Stirling, and even her mother were all a part of her. She was held at the center of a six-pointed star, secure. As safe as she could ever be.

And in this moment, it was enough.

δ

Martin Lopez

HE HAD LIED TO HER. She wasn't his sister and still, he hated that he'd lied to her. Martin folded up the ragged blanket Daniella had carted around from one foster home to another and finally to their room here and carefully left it on the couch.

She wasn't coming back.

And he couldn't just hole up while she disappeared from his life again.

His footsteps echoed in the empty space where he and Daniella had tried to make a home for themselves and anyone else unlucky enough to be out on the streets. Maybe they would be back. It was hard to care one way or the other right now.

Martin eased open the door to the stairs, wincing at the metallic screech. Then he crept down to the lobby and paused at the fire door, terrified that he was too late. Terrified that he wasn't.

But he had to witness. Even if he didn't understand what was happening or why. If he let her vanish like this, it would be too easy to make it a story of her abandoning him. The way everyone always did.

She wanted him to keep Daniella's dream alive. Part of him wanted to just walk away and keep walking, but he didn't need to have Thorne's sight to know how that would end.

Martin eased into the lobby. They were standing in the center of the room, holding hands. Near where the man had been stabbed. Where Harnett and Stirling had been swallowed up.

Slipping behind a support column, Martin forced himself to watch the girl in his sister's body. Gone was the awkwardness and the uncertainty. It was so painfully clear she wasn't Daniella.

He hadn't been willing to admit it, but he'd known she had never really stopped using. That morning at the hospital, he was just grateful she was still alive. Forced himself to believe in a miracle. No matter how impossible. Maybe he wasn't so different from Stirling after all.

The doctor's voice murmured something he couldn't make out, but he didn't dare move any closer. Reina nodded. Thorne looked somewhere over her shoulder as if he were staring out an invisible window.

Muted colors thickened the air. It was starting. Again.

Martin gripped the column. Would the doorway swallow him up too?

The haze brightened. Sharpened. A breeze circled through the lobby, picking up trash and creating a dirt whirlwind that began and ended at the distortion. The air plucked at his hair and clothes, but Thorne, the doctor, and Reina seemed unaffected.

Martin remembered one winter when the city gave out free passes to the ice rink on the Frog Pond and he and his friends played crack the whip. He was spinning at the outside edge. Waiting for the jolt that would send him flying out of control.

Everything was out of control.

He bit his lip to keep from crying out.

Then between one breath and the next, all the flying debris dropped to the floor. The pressure against Martin's body eased. He blinked and the three of them were there and not there at the same time. Or rather, they were like the painful afterimages from when a cop would shine a flashlight directly in his eyes.

When he could focus again, he was alone.

The air had cleared.

They were gone.

A metallic bang came from behind him. Martin jumped and reached for the gun he no longer had.

"Safe to come back?" Harrold stood just inside the doorway, a blanket wrapped around his threadbare coat.

Martin took a deep breath and relaxed his hands. "Will you help me get the fires going?"

"Sure thing, boss."

He tossed the old man a lighter and they walked up the stairs together. They stood and took stock of the chaos. Fire barrels were overturned. People's belongings were scattered across the floor. A few pillows had been slashed open, foam padding strewn everywhere.

"Cops made a mess of the place."

Harrold smiled, showing the gaps in his teeth. "Coulda been worse."

"Doubt it," Martin said.

"We're still here, ain't we?"

Before Martin could answer, the sound of voices filled the stairwell. About a dozen or so of his regulars spread out around him. It was probably something in his face, but when they saw him, they all fell silent. Then without a word from him, while Harrold lit the barrels, they started picking up trash and organizing the bedding.

One by one, each of them passed by him. Some with a nod. Others with a smile or a quick thank you.

None of them was his sister.

He took a bedroll and found an empty space by the edge of the room.

They were still his responsibility. And this was still their home.

Epilogue

Stirling Hughes

HE CAREFULLY CUT AWAY the cloth around the man's wound. "Can you tell me your name?"

"Wellerman. Harnett Wellerman."

"Mr. Wellerman, you've lost a lot of blood. It looks like the bullet is a through and through, which is good news." He kept up a patter of conversation while his hands probed the edges of the wound. "This may hurt. I'm sorry. I don't have anything for the pain." It looked like the bullet missed all of the major arteries running through the upper arm. That was also a lucky break. He pulled out a large piece of sterile gauze. "I need you to hold this against your shoulder."

"Why are you helping me?" The man winced as he pressed the gauze over the wound.

"You're hurt. I'm a medic. It's my job." He glanced around the room again, puzzled. Where were his colleagues? "You doing okay? I'm going to call for an ambulance." Stirling pulled out his phone and stared at it. The display was lit, but there was no signal. None of the icons he was expecting were showing. That was odd. He pressed 9-1-1 anyway. Nothing happened.

"Do you know where you are?" Wellerman asked.

"That's what I'm supposed to ask you," he said, smiling.

"You have no idea what just happened, do you?" The man's barking laugh turned into a groan as his shoulder shifted.

It was a strange response, but shock affected different people differently. Stirling tucked the phone away. He'd just have to stabilize the man and go outside. Funny, he'd always had signal here before. "I'm going to wrap your arm in a sling so you don't jostle your shoulder. We don't want it to start bleeding again."

A low growl from across the room snagged Stirling's attention. A small terrier-type dog was walking toward them, hackles raised from neck to tail. Stirling had had encounters with feral dogs before, none of them pleasant. He stood, grateful for his leather boots and thick work pants. The dog stopped abruptly in front of him and sat down by his feet, whimpering.

"Wait. You're that old man's dog. Did they leave you behind? Poor thing."

Stirling turned at the sound of the door opening. What the hell? His patient was limping outside. He grabbed his medical kit and jogged across the lobby to follow.

The man disappeared into a crowd of people. Stirling's mouth fell open. Instead of empty lots and chain link fences, all around him rose shining buildings and bustling storefronts. He whirled around to look at the door to Martin's shelter. A banner stretched over the bright, striped awning announcing luxury apartments coming soon.

He fell back against the door, his knees wobbly. He breathed slowly through his mouth fighting a wave of vertigo and nausea. What the actual fuck?

The dog stood up on its hind legs and licked his hand.

Stirling backed away from the impossible city and returned to the too-sterile lobby. By the stairwell was a stack of packing crates. He made his way there to sit down, the dog padding beside him like a shadow. He hadn't remembered hitting his head, but that would explain everything. Reaching up, he palpated gently around his forehead and skull. Nothing hurt. "Do you know what's going on? 'Cause I sure as hell don't."

The dog cocked its head as if it understood every word he said. Which wasn't crazier than anything else right now. And at least Stirling could honestly say he wasn't talking to himself. He pulled out his phone again and turned it over and over in his hands as if the blank screen could give him the answers he was looking for.

"Okay. I know who I am. Stirling Hughes. I'm a Boston EMT. It's January tenth, and I got off shift a few hours ago. That all seem right?"

The dog sneezed.

"I'll take that as a yes." Now what? He couldn't hide here forever. What would happen when the work crews came in? He could go home. But what if his apartment was also somehow wrong, the way this building and the city beyond was? He needed to find the doc. If anyone could help make sense of this, she could.

"What do you think? Should I try to find Dr. Klein?"

This time the dog jumped up into his lap and licked his face.

"I guess that means we're a team." Okay. The dog didn't have a collar. Stirling looked around for something he could use as a leash and found a length of rope next to the stacked cartons. "You okay with this, dog?" he asked as he made a loop and slipped it over the animal's head.

It barked once.

"Maybe we can find your person, too." But that would mean tracking down which hospital they took him to. "What did Thorne call you?" He frowned, trying to remember. "Oh, right. You're Poplar."

Poplar barked again, tail wagging.

"Okay. Ready?" He stood, and Poplar waited by his side. "This may get weird, but we really can't stay here."

Stirling took a deep breath before walking back to the door. The dog trotted easily with him, keeping the leash slack. He hoped Thorne was going to be all right.

"Let's try this again."

He pushed the door open. The far-too-pristine neighborhood that absolutely couldn't have been there still waited. As he stared, a kind of double vision nearly made him stagger. He saw two cities superimposed on each other: his Boston and the abandoned building with its empty lot, and this gleaming new construction.

Stirling remembered them both.

He remembered Martin and Daniella. He had never met the siblings.

There had never been a homeless encampment here. All the services were in a permanent facility on Long Island. Emergency and transitional housing. Medical treatment. Addiction counseling.

The night of the count was just last week. It also didn't happen.

The image of the tents around Mass and Cass flitted through his mind. They weren't real. They were all too real.

Something was so very wrong.

He must have made some noise because Poplar pressed against his legs and looked up at him, concern in bright brown eyes.

"Toto, I really don't think we're in Kansas anymore."

Stirling couldn't control the surge of nausea rising from his gut. His mouth filled with saliva and his head began to throb. He turned and vomited on the street.

No one even noticed.

Acknowledgments

This story began as a series of what felt like disconnected ideas: Features on NPR about the medical staff that work with the unhoused population in Boston. The growing homeless encampments around Massachusetts Avenue and Melnea Cass Boulevard after the removal of the bridge to the treatment facilities on Long Island. A memory of seeing ghosts as a six year old child visiting El Alhambra. My first fieldwork experience as a physical therapy student providing home care in the South Bronx. The concept of Tikkun Olam and feeling lost in a world that didn't seem to make any sense.

Slowly, over the course of six years, these elements coalesced into *Litany for a Broken World*.

Along the way, I doubted myself, my ability to write, and the story itself more than any other time in my creative life. And as often as I decided to quit (the novel, my writing), the characters and their journeys kept dragging me back to the computer.

If I have succeeded, it is in good part to the support I was given along the way.

My family and their belief in me makes the hard work possible. You keep me honest. You make me a better human.

I am a part of several incredible writing communities, some formal, some informal. Thank you to the folks at Writer Unboxed and Broad Universe for surrounding me with inspiration, commiseration, and camaraderie.

To my Monday night craft group: Elaine Isaak, Jill Shultz, Brent Smith, Linda Kepner, and Christine Row. Thank you for keeping me connected throughout the pandemic and beyond.

A special shout-out to Jill Shultz for her incisive and brilliant developmental edit when I thought I was getting a general beta read. You rock.

Thank you to Jo Weston and Sarah Tuttle for the struggling writers support group.

Without the weekly write-ins with Marianna Martin, I don't think I would have ever finished drafting this novel. If you're lucky enough, you will find a writing partner like her who is both your biggest cheerleader and best accountability buddy. Not to mention a kick-ass writer in her own right.

I was also fortunate to be named a STAR artist in residence at the Eagle Hill School in Hardwick, MA. The space, time, encouragement, and financial support I received there allowed me to complete revisions on this novel over an intense Fall semester in 2023.

Over the six years this book needed to come to fruition, many readers have lent their time and suggestions, including Jo Weston, Nicole Hamm, Patrick Horgan, Tom Gaskill, Maureen Czabaj, Nightwing Whitehead, and Diane Heimer. I am endebted to them for their help with early drafts of the manuscript.

Working with an editor as skilled and knowledgeable as Karen Conlin is a joy—even when I'm cursing the red ink. Thank you for making me a better writer.

And finally, my eternal gratitude for Chris Howard, friend, writer, artist, who created the gorgeous art that is this novel's cover.

With thanks,
LJ

(February 2025)

About the Author

LJ Cohen writes novels across the science fiction and fantasy genres and was among the first wave of indie writers to qualify for SFWA membership. DERELICT, the first book in her Halcyone Space series, was named a Library Journal self-e select title and book of the year in 2014. LITANY FOR A BROKEN WORLD is her ninth novel.

A retired physical therapist, LJ now uses her clinical knowledge and skills to injure characters. She serves on the board of Broad Universe as well as several local non-profits in her community. In addition to her creative work as a writer and role as a community organizer, she is also a potter and fiber artist. She lives on a homestead farm in central MA and is extremely proud of her tractor riding and tree pruning skills.

lisa@ljcohen.net
www.ljcohen.net

Sign up for Blue Musings, an occasional email newsletter complete with book release notifications, reading recommendations, and free, original, short fiction offered in a variety of drm-free formats. (www.ljcohen.net/contact.html)

9 781942 851080